Hunters

Out of the Box, Book 15

Robert J. Crane

Hunters
Out of the Box #15
Robert J. Crane
Copyright © 2017 Ostiagard Press
All Rights Reserved.

1st Edition

This book is a work of fiction. Names, characters, places and incidents are products of the author's imagination or are used fictitiously. Any resemblance to actual events or locales or persons, living or dead, is entirely coincidental.

1.

"There are hunters and there are prey in life, see," Charlie Cooper told the clerk behind the counter of the shop, nestled in a corner of East London, "and I don't figure you for a hunter." Cooper held his hand up at the clerk; it didn't shake at all. It hadn't shaken when he'd fired a blast of red laser beam out of his palm a second earlier, past the clerk's ear and into the display behind him, and it didn't shake now, pointed at the fellow's heart.

This wasn't Charlie Cooper's first robbery. It wasn't even his tenth. He'd lost count after twenty. London was all in a tizzy, wondering where he was going to strike next. He didn't care about the stir he was causing. Hell, he reveled in it. Maybe they'd make him a folk hero, like Robin Hood, except he wasn't sharing any of the loot with the villagers.

"Hurry up and get the money from the till, Charlie," Billy Fischer said behind him. Billy was all swelled up, muscles stacked on muscles. When his metahuman power had shown up, it had taken this form, growing three sizes too large, like a bodybuilder who'd gone overboard. Charlie's was to shoot laser beams out of his hand, lethal blasts that could take the heart right out of this poor, sweating shopkeeper, who actually was shaking, who had his hands behind his head, the poor bastard, a pitiable sort that Charlie Cooper didn't have an ounce of actual pity for.

"Just you shut it," Charlie tossed back at Billy. Why would he want to rush this? It was another fine opportunity to show off a little, give another resident of this east London neighborhood a glimpse at his magnanimity. He stared down the clerk, then pinched his nose at the stench of the man's body odor, especially keen in his metahuman sense of smell. "You stink, mate. How long's it been since you left this smelly shop?"

"This is my shop," the man said, his eyes registering hurt. "Sometimes I sleep here, as I did last night."

That only amused Charlie more. "You slept in this smelly place?" Charlie cackled and waved a hand at one of the displays. He let loose a blast of red beam that sheared the shelf in half. A burnt smell, steel mingled with other aromas, food and wrappings, filled his nose. Charlie glanced over to find a whole display of Terry's Chocolate Oranges seared into a puddle and he smiled. He could faintly smell the orange and chocolate aroma mixed in with the other burning scents. "There you go," he said, "now it smells…well, nicer." He swiped a Mars bar from the counter and lasered off the top, causing the shopkeeper to duck to avoid having his eyebrow singed. "Now empty the till like the man said." Charlied nodded back at Billy, then took a bite of his candy.

The shopkeeper did as he was told, but slow and surely, like he was counting every pound and penny as he did so. When he was done, there wasn't much on the counter, but Charlie didn't care. Half the reason he did this was fun anyway, not profit.

Charlie shoved the rest of the Mars bar in his mouth and grinned, showing his chocolatey teeth, then swiped it up, smearing Queen Elizabeth's serene face with a smudge of brown. He blasted the shopkeeper in the shoulder, said, "You should take some time off, mate. It'd be good for your health," and laughed as the man fell. Charlie brought his hand around and liberally doused the shop with his red beam. Refrigerated displays popped and hissed as the energy ripped through them, and Billy was forced to duck behind him as Charlie swung around fast. That only tickled Charlie more, and he said, "Come on, you git, let's go," as he made for the door and out onto the London street.

"Stop right there!" The voice was stern, authoritative,

breaking the quiet London night and drowning out the sound of cars in the distance. Hearing it, Charlie did pause for a second, a rippling chill running down his back. He looked left; it was a copper, of course. One of the Met's finest, standing there with a baton, hand raised like Charlie's if he was about to fire off a beam.

Charlie grinned. This was going to be a bit of fun. Stupid copper, not even with an armed response team. Charlie pretended to raise his hands like he was going to surrender—

And lasered the dumb bastard right in the shoulder. The cop screeched, his piggy squeal carrying over the midday street, echoing down the canyon of four-level apartments and shops, a car buzzing by not even drowning it out when the owner stepped on the gas and sped up.

The copper hit the ground and continued to cry in agony, grasping at his arm, which was hanging loose, a good solid burn running across his armpit. Charlie surveyed the damage he'd caused, quite content in what he'd accomplished. Yeah, it was a good one, might even kill the poor sod if the ambulance didn't get here quick. "Stupid shit," Charlie laughed, and yielded to the tug of Billy upon his arm. He hadn't even felt it when Billy had started to pull him, trying to get him back to the getaway car just on the street.

"Oh, all right then," Charlie said, slipping into the passenger seat as Billy got in the driver's. "I guess that's enough fun for one day."

Billy slammed the door and started up the car. It belched a cloud of smoke behind them. An old Vauxhall, it probably wouldn't pass an emissions test. Charlie grinned again. Who'd dare try and enforce that on them, anyway? "No one," Charlie whispered, the thought breaking loose and speaking itself aloud.

"Whassat?" Billy asked, looking at him as he shifted the car into gear, pulling away from the curb and down the street. He wore a worried look, and that made Charlie laugh again. "What?" Billy asked.

"You, you barmy old bag," Charlie said, still laughing. "You're looking like you're about to piss your pants. Every time we rob a shop you get all worried." He held his hands

3

up and pulled a face, mocking Billy with his expression. "'Oh no! The big bad coppers are after us! They'll get us for sure this time!'" Charlie dissolved into laughter once more. "Every time. When are you going to realize—" Charlie grabbed his arm, diverting Billy's attention from the calm, quiet, London night "—not a sodding person in London— not the cops, not Scotland Yard, not the bloody Queen herself—has got the stones or the power to stop us—"

The car's roof collapsed in and the Vauxhall squealed, the tires exploding from the force of whatever had landed on them. Charlie was thrown forward into the dashboard, thumping his head against it hard, while Billy next to him made a rich thump hitting the steering wheel. Charlie's head whipsawed back into the headrest and bounced a couple times, jarring his brain, shaking it like it was in a cocktail shaker.

When he opened his eyes again a second later, he found Billy clutching his forehead gingerly, a stream of blood rolling down his furrowed brow. Charlie blinked; his neck hurt, his chest hurt from where the seatbelt had caught him—good job he was wearing it this time—and the whole car smelled like sweat and burnt metal, like the inside of that shop—

It took Charlie a second to realize the roof of the car was ripping off, something searing its way through the metal. It pulled free and suddenly the sky was black above them, the innards of the car exposed to the cloudy London night, and…something else.

Someone else.

She leered down at them, hovering above what was left of the front windshield, her face obvious and familiar from a million times Charlie had seen it on TV. Her hair was just the same, and—holy hell, there she was, and Charlie wondered, *Is someone taking the piss outta me…? I just asked…and… she's…she's…*

…she's…

"Sienna Nealon," he muttered under his breath.

She looked down at them, hovering in the air, dark hair hanging around her shoulders and her eyes glistening, bright

blue like they were sparkling from amusement.
And she smiled.
"Hi."

2.

I couldn't resist landing on those robbing sons of bitches the moment I heard one of them spout off about how there was no one in London powerful enough to stop them. I mean, really, why would anyone invite the ruin of spouting such hubris into the heavens when they're nothing but a stickup artist with delusions of grandeur? Man, these metas got arrogant fast. In America, this guy would have been lucky not to have his brains exposed to air by a local cop with a Glock.

Ahh, the kinder, gentler Brits, and their lack of guns on every corner. What the hell did the metahuman criminal class have to fear over here?

Oh, right.

Me.

"I bet you're wondering why I pulled your roof off," I said in a conversational tone as the two guys gawked up at me, jaws practically in their laps. "It was for irony. A little bit because I hate thieves and people who prey on those weaker than themselves...but mostly the irony. Now..." I looked down at them, still staring up at me like I was going to turn into a dragon and burn them out of the vehicle (which I totally could have). "Are you coming quietly, to jail? Or loudly for a brief few moments, and then really quietly, to the morgue?"

They looked at each other, an almost comedic gesture in the face of what they were up against. I mean, I'd just ripped the roof off their car, after all, and they clearly knew my face, my name.

The question was, would they take my appearance as an opportunity to retire from this life of crime? Or would they feel that my mere appearance was a challenge to their—I dunno, manhood, or something similarly small and stupid?

They're going to view it as a challenge to their manhood, Gerry Harmon said within my head. *Here, listen:*

OHGODOHGODOHGODOHGOD—I can't let this bitch show me up in front of Billy—

I blinked. *That's really what he's thinking? But it's so stupid! What about the other one?*

Not much better, I'm afraid:

I shouldn't have come here, I should not have—why did I come here? Why did I let Charlie talk me into this? Into any of this? Mum was right: I am coming to a bad end. I should have married Penny when I had a chance and settled down, become a plumber. Now I'm gonna die on the streets of London under the fist of Sienna Nealon because dumbass Charlie—

Wait, why is that not better? I asked Harmon. *He's clearly terrified of me.*

Because I abhor whining, Harmon said.

"Billy, Charlie," I said, plucking their names out of their respective internal dialogues and causing them both to look up at me as though I'd just goosed them both unexpected, "I'm gonna need an answer on whether or not you're ready to die. Sharpish, as you Brits say." I thought about it a sec. "Actually, I think maybe I've only ever heard a Guy Ritchie character say that, so I'm not so sure you Brits actually do say that on the regular—"

"I give up!" Billy threw his hands in the air. "I don't want to die. This weren't even my idea!" He looked about two seconds away from collapsing into a sobbing pile.

"Cool. We're understood, then," I said and yanked him out of the car by his collar. My Wolfe-enhanced speed and strength made it an easy thing, sending him flying with but a cry, and I hit him with one of Eve Kappler's light nets, binding him to a nearby light post. He didn't really resist, and within a second he was just hanging there, whimpering a little in the night.

I never took my eyes off Charlie as I was tossing Billy away, and it was a good thing I didn't. I could still hear his thoughts in my head, and they took an ugly turn:

This bitch thinks she's going to take me in, she's got another think com—

"Lemme stop you right there, Charlie," I said, and blasted him with three nets that bound him to the back of his car's seat, like spiderwebs of glowing light. They wrapped him tightly around the chest before he could do anything immensely dumb, like attack me with his powers, whatever they might be. The strands of light that wrapped him around the face cranked his neck back, and now he was unnaturally mated to the seat, stuck there in a very uncomfortable position until the cops arrived. "See, my job is to try and avoid killing you. Not that you deserve that mercy, but the idea of me being here in London is low profile. Or medium profile, maybe. But not 'bodies everywhere in the streets,' see? That's kind of a condition of my asylum here, to not make a massive mess, or else they'll have to try extradite me to the US and I'll have to deal with the inconvenience of making your law enforcement officials look like idiots—it's all a huge bother, and I'd rather avoid it than kill you, frankly, Charlie, because—although you don't seem like a nice guy, you're not quite bad enough for me to put you down like a rabid dog, so…" I waved, and dismounted the hood of the car, stepping off lightly as I killed my hover capability with but a thought. "Enjoy your time in HMP Belmarsh, Sir Douchenozzle. May it make you a better person, or at least last until you've got no more starch left in your shorts." I waved at him, already putting thoughts of this ass clown out of my mind, my business with him done—

This isn't over, Harmon said.

"I just bound his ass to the car seat," I said. "I'm pretty sure ol' Charlie here is clocked out."

Never turn your back on a foe, Little D…Sienna, Wolfe whispered in his gravelly, guttural voice.

I rolled my eyes. "Have I mentioned how happy I am to have shed that particular nickname?"

His power, Harmon said, voice rising in urgency, *it's*—

The car exploded before he could even finish his warning.

3.

The car exploded, and I hit the curb and caught myself on both hands. My wrists decried the pain I'd just put them through, and a woman's laughter echoed in my head while shards of glass rained on the curb all around me, ending that whole quiet London night thing I'd been sort of enjoying up to now. "Laugh it up, Eve," I said, dusting myself off as I rose. "This is clearly cause for it."

You were so stupid and arrogant, Eve said, still cackling. *Did it not occur to you he might use his energy projection abilities to cut his way out of his bindings through the car?*

"No," I muttered, "it did not occur to me." I looked over my shoulder. Charlie had, indeed, cut the car in half. What I'd perceived as an explosion was actually just the car sheared into pieces by his powers, the metal smoking where he'd ripped through the seat, the frame, and everything else in the way to secure his freedom. Now he stood there, the car neatly sawed in half, pulling himself free from the last strands of my light web and looking around for me, half-blind in his panic. He saw me at the same time I saw him, and we both raised our hands—

QUICKDRAW! Roberto Bastian shouted with apparent glee as I released a blast of compact fire, like a bullet of flame, at the same time Charlie sent a sizzling beam of a laser at me. I dodged, my shot already fired, my aim already certain.

My arm hairs singed as the laser caught the faint, blondish

9

hairs on my upper arm and sent the smell of them burning up to my metahuman-enhanced nose. They stunk, and the feeling of the laser passing was like a sunburn, as close as it got to me. I staggered, bumbling my way back up onto the curb and off the street.

The flaming shot I'd sent at Charlie hit home, dead center in his chest, as he cranked his laser beam, a continuous scarlet stream of hissing energy, back at me. When the fire shot impacted, the laser just sort of…fizzled out, and Charlie jerked once, then twice, keeping his feet.

That wouldn't last.

"I'm sorry," I said, watching him, genuinely contrite. I would have liked to have left him be, to have bound him and had him stay bound for the London police to take him away to serve his lawful sentence. Maybe things would have gone badly for him in prison; maybe he would have continued to make stupid, arrogant, bullheaded choices that would take him out the doors of prison someday and into a worse situation, one where he actually killed someone.

But now he wasn't going to get the chance.

Charlie's chest smoked, steam pouring out of the rapidly-expanding crater of a wound where my shot had hit him. He opened his mouth to scream and smoke poured out instead. The fire shot had been something like 5,000 degrees Fahrenheit; the human body couldn't deal with that, not even in a musket-ball-sized dose, especially when it wormed its way inside the soft tissue in his chest and stopped there, forward momentum spent.

I could have snuffed the shot right then, but that would have been cruel. Charlie's body had suffered fatal damage already; what others might have perceived to be mercy would actually be unbelievably harsh and prolong his agony by another few crucial seconds. His blood was boiling in his veins, his metahuman body trying its level best to repair the damage surging through it even now, carried in his veins by blood evaporating to a superheated gas and a scorched residue—right to his brain and other tissues.

He bucked a couple more times and his legs finally collapsed, keeling straight over, face-first, into the ruin of the car. He was still smoking, but dead, and I snuffed the fire out from within him. "Sorry, mate," I said, in the inimitable British style. Which I imitated. So I suppose it's actually imitable. "I tried to warn you."

"You bloody well killed him!" This from a cop who had padded up at a run, baton in hand. His shock was clearly overcoming his faculties, because usually these guys were trained to try and de-escalate a situation before it got really hostile. Accusing me of murder? Not going to de-escalate things. He spoke with a thick accent.

"Where are you from?" I asked, keeping my hands firmly at my sides. I wasn't going to escalate things any further.

He just blinked at me, like he was surprised I was engaging instead of beating him or something. "Scotland."

"Ahh," I said. "Sometimes my American ear can't tell the difference between Scottish and Irish."

He glared at me, and apparently my vow not to escalate things had failed just as thoroughly as had my desire to not kill Charlie.

"I left the other one alive," I said, raising my hands in front of me in a posture of surrender. "This one, though—he tried to kill me. It was self-defense. These guys have been robbing a lot of shops. You know this. They've hurt quite a few people in the process."

"I bloody well know that, don't I?" He was still steaming at me, that baton clutched tight. But he wasn't making a move. "But you—ye've the power of a goddess of the old tales— and ye didn't have to kill him, did ye?" God, he hit the, "ye's," really hard, the Scottish coming out.

"If I'd knocked him out right away? Dealt with him way harsher on the upfront? Not provided him a choice on surrendering?" I asked, engaging in a rare moment of candor. "No, maybe I wouldn't have. But I'm not death, officer, swift and sure. He made his choice, and his choice was—"

Death, Wolfe whispered in the back of my head.

"Death," I finished, regretting that I was speaking the exact word Wolfe had just spouted, because coming to the same conclusion as his crazy, serial-killing ass, even after all these years and all we'd been through, was still appalling to me.

The Scottish cop just stared at me. "I dinnae believe that. You could have stopped him. You had the power."

"He wasn't exactly powerless, officer," I said, and lifted into the air a few feet. "You know that by the trail of bodies he'd left behind him."

"Aye, his killing days are done," the cop said, and he just seemed…sad. "What about yours?" That accent bled through again.

"God, I hope so," I said, lifting off into the air. "But every time I think I'm done…someone provides me another compelling reason to end their ass." I shot into the sky, not waiting for what was, I was sure, bound to be another scourging reply that would fill me with yet more self-doubt.

4.

I flew over the City of London, watching the lights sparkle below. The city was all aglow, as it tended to be at night, and the cool night air was a marked contrast to the alternating heat and rain that had marked the summer days since I'd arrived in this place. I'd mostly avoided trouble since coming to the UK, but this…

He needed a good killing, Bjorn, son of Odin, said in the back of my head. *He challenged you, he lost. A natural course of events.*

You could have been tactically smarter about how you handled that, Bastian said, clearly trying to replenish my confidence. Not that it was utterly shaken, but my conversation with the Scotsman hadn't exactly left me doubt-free. Then again, Charlie had been heading down a bad road.

"Now he's heading down the morgue road," I said.

But he won't hurt anyone ever again, Eve said. *Some people are just too bad to let live—*

"At what point does that include me, I wonder?" I spoke the words aloud, the night air blowing in my face and giving me a little chill. I was a little too tired, a little too jaded, not to say it aloud because it was there, on my mind. I'd been hunted out of my homeland, the USA, after months of constant attacks that had finally escalated to a, "Shoot first, ask questions after she's dead," confrontation in Montana that had damned near ended in my death.

Fortunately, an old acquaintance from the UK, Alistair Wexford, the Foreign Secretary, had offered me a nice olive branch, or perhaps a lifeline—come to jolly England, do a little metahuman policing for them over here, and they'd ignore my presence and any requests from the US government to turn me—or my not-so-lively corpse—over to them.

Talk about an offer you couldn't refuse. Remain a hunted party hiding out in your own country or go somewhere that you won't be constantly shot at. Gee, I wonder which I picked.

I dipped over the skyline, avoiding smashing into the giant, stretched Fabergé egg of 30 St. Mary Axe on my way to my hotel, which was a charming American brand settled in central London. I liked the Brits overall, but their hotels were kind of ass. Tiny rooms, hot and cold water on independent taps, and a dozen other little differences that only served to highlight the fact that not only was I far from home, but unwelcome in my own home any longer.

You're not that bad, Wolfe said, which was probably the most encouraging thing he had ever said to anyone. It was also, probably, from his perspective very truthful.

"Sweet talker," I said aloud, as I often did while flying. Or standing still, without people around. Or with people around. I was weird like that, talking to the voices of trapped souls in my head. I started my descent, which would include a quick stop-off to pick up a wig and overcoat to help me hide my identity. No one needed to know that Sienna Nealon was staying in London, or at the least they didn't need to know where I was staying. Let them think I just popped in every now and again and vamoosed off to the continent. I'd done overflights to Paris, Rome and Berlin to help muddle the trail a little, keep people guessing.

I came down low over the rooftops, swerving to avoid a pronounced turret, then landed lightly on one that had a nice, castle-like battlement around it. I kinda doubted it was ever an actual castle, but it bordered an alley, had no roof access, and there was a nice, clean approach to it where I could go low and avoid being seen from nearby streets, allowing me to effectively disappear, so I'd dropped off my wig and costume here on my way to answer the call of duty and settle the hash of these serial robbers.

The roof squeaked beneath my feet as I settled on it. I'd bundled my wig up inside the heavy coat that I was habitually wearing as a shield against the London weather (read: rain, rain, and more effing RAIN). I even carried an umbrella and sunglasses, because they helped me blend in a little more.

I spent a few minutes affixing my wig, applying a little makeup, putting on my glasses, and re-dressing before I leaned over the bulwark on the alley side of the rooftop, staring down to the silent pavement below. It was getting close to eleven o'clock at night in London, and unsurprisingly, this alley was abandoned.

Climbing over the side like I was going to dip my feet into a swimming pool, I waited there, legs hanging over the edge, to see if anybody said anything. Nobody shouted from the shadows, so after a few seconds, I dropped onto a fire escape below. I used my power of flight to catch myself just before impact, eliminating any sound but the billow of my coat in the ten-foot fall.

I scoured the alley again, waiting to see if anyone had made any sound, any sign. I tended not to use the same landing location twice, fearing a pattern might give someone an opening to ambush me. Even absent the US government, I was not short on enemies, and not desirous of giving any of them a free shot at me.

Once I was sure no one had reacted, I dropped to the alley floor, avoiding the puddles that littered the uneven pavement. I looked both ways just to see if somehow I'd missed someone lurking, some poor soul huddling in the alley, or maybe doing something illicit that I'd interrupted.

Paranoid. I was probably being paranoid.

Good way to stay alive, came the voice of Aleksandr Gavrikov.

"But not such a great way to live," I said under my breath as I headed off down to the main avenue at the end of the alleyway.

I emerged onto a brightly lit London street that was still quite alive, even at this time of night. I wasn't too far from Piccadilly Circus, a choice I'd made for the ease with which I could get lost in the crowds. The theater shows had already let out for the evening, and I could see the people streaming out of the West End as I headed that way. The scent of an Italian restaurant I passed on the right caused my nostrils to flare almost involuntarily; pasta with cream sauce almost beckoned to me, summoning me in for a dose of carbs and luxuriant fat.

"Not tonight," I muttered. I'd done my daily exercises, worked my body exhaustingly enough to feel like, yes, I could have a reward, but I wasn't going to indulge, not even after this evening's efforts in battle.

It is just as well, Eve said, *to stay focused upon your goal to the exclusion of all else.*

"Because tight shoulders don't come without effort and sacrifice, right?" I said half-jokingly, but Eve didn't take the bait. Maybe because she knew she was being baited. She'd probably meant it sincerely; I couldn't always tell with the voices in my head. It wasn't like I could read their minds, after all.

Nothing good comes without sacrifice, Harmon said. *File that one under TNSTAAFL.*

"Tin-what?" I asked. "Did you just quote me a B-52's lyric?"

It's an acronym. It means, Zack Davis said, quietly, *'There's No Such Thing As A Free Lunch.'*

Zack had been quiet all night, which was usually a bad sign. I could have asked him what was on his mind, but given the recent, heady topic of conversation, I was pretty sure that was not going to be a route I would particularly enjoy coming to the end of. Because it was unlikely to be a favorable insight.

I took a turn onto a side street, my hotel sticking out from where it had been neatly sandwiched into the existing street architecture, complete with a mostly matching facade that somehow didn't stick out like the expansive, American sore thumb that it kinda was.

"Oh," I said, pretty willing to leave it at that.

Because there's always a trade-off, Harmon said. *Always a string attached. No one does anything for no reason. They have a motive, and if they give you something—*

"Yes, I am aware of the mediums of exchange in our society," I said, "which is why I'm currently policing metas in the United Kingdom in exchange for a country in which to hang my metaphorical hat." I touched my wig, lightly. "Maybe I should get a literal hat too, though, y'think? Might be a good disguise, something to change up the shape of my head a little. Plus, I mean, as a woman, wearing a hat just says something different about you. Like a baseball cap says, 'I'm down to earth and fun,' while one of those larger hats with a big brim says, 'I'm fashionable and bold.'"

What does a bonnet say? Bastian asked for the benefit of the rest of the male audience.

"'I'm old and didn't feel like doing my hair,' probably," I said as I headed toward the entrance to my hotel. Out front a kid in a t-shirt and with long shorts that hung past his knees was skating in the street, his board making a low rattling, scratching noise as he took advantage of the lack of traffic presently down this side road. The sound caused me to blanch, because it hit the register of noises which annoy the hell out of me without any effort on the part of the annoyer at all. "That's gonna get old fast," I said as I ignored the youth, his ballcap backward on his head. He looked about fourteen, and I had to wonder why his parents were cool with him just skateboarding on a London street at this time of night.

I ducked into the lobby of my hotel, all lit up like it was daytime and the bar humming with a dozen guests drinking their night away. No one took notice of me as the front desk clerk did double duty as a bartender and refilled a tall guy's glass with something clear that didn't look like it had been cut with anything other than liquor. He was laughing as the patron dashed it back, and the bartender went right back to work refilling it.

The air smelled of alcohol—beer, whiskey, even vodka, my sensitive nose detecting the notes of all those, plus some other flavors. Mint, because someone was deep in their mojitos, and a dizzying amount of lime from a couple ladies on business downing margaritas like they were about to dry up forever.

I pushed past the front desk and pulled out my card as I headed to the elevator bank. It dinged, I stepped inside, and after scanning my card, I rode the elevator up to the third floor. I walked down a beige hallway to the last room and unlocked it, stepping inside and waiting a beat to see if someone would make a noise in the darkness.

No one did, so I plugged my room key into the socket just inside the door, and the room's lights sprung on. It wasn't a big room; a bed, dresser, couch, a desk, a couple of end tables, and a bathroom. They were all the very generic, mass-produced furniture that big chains tended to gravitate toward, lacking the personality of individual furniture pieces by necessity. This wasn't a boutique hotel, after all. The comfort was in the sameness of the experience, whether you were in London, UK or London, Kentucky. It was why I picked the place, after all—I knew what to expect. A little bit of home, far from home.

And I missed home.

Except for the bullets. I didn't miss having those fly at me.

I didn't bother to take off my wig, though I did throw my coat onto the couch rather than hang it up. I tended toward keeping things squared away, but I did my cleaning in the morning, and didn't feel like dealing with the mess that had accumulated during the day, at least not right now.

It was eleven o'clock in London, which meant it was only five in the evening back home in Minneapolis.

But I was still ready for bed. Ready to scratch another day off the calendar, just as I'd ticked the box next to the task that had presented itself—deal with the meta crooks tearing up London and hurting shopkeepers. Another goal accomplished, another bad guy group out of circulation, however mild their criminality might have seemed to this point to outside observers.

The rattling of those damned skateboard wheels outside my window signaled that the unsupervised skater boy was still doing his thing just outside, and I sprang up, eyes narrowed and a sigh of deep displeasure making its way out between my lips. "That's not going to work for me," I said, and waited a few minutes in silence, trying to muster up the control not to do something that I'd regret.

But the longer I sat there, the more the scratching and skidding of the wheels against the pavement, the rattle of him trying to jump the curb and failing, followed by laughter, drove me nuts. It was eleven o'clock at night, and the Brits around here might have been too polite to point out his rudeness, but I damned sure was not suffering from that problem.

Don't do something you'll wish you hadn't later, Sienna, Zack said quietly.

"I won't," I said, "on any level."

I made my way to the window and opened it just a titch, hiding behind the blackout curtains. Sure enough, there he was, skater boy, attempting another ollie off the curb. He did his jump and failed, massively, but managed to land safely on his feet, though his board went in the other direction. He guffawed as he stood back up.

While his back was turned to his board, I slid a finger out the window, pointed it at the board, and in a perfect imitation of how I'd burned Charlie to death just a few minutes earlier, sent a blast of miniature fire right at that damned skateboard.

It lit off immediately, flames spreading along the length of it as the wood caught. The skater boy turned at the sudden blaze of bright light and it took him a minute to realize it was his board that had gone up. I could see him get it over the course of a few seconds, leaning forward, trying to get his perception of what happened to align with the fact that— hey, his board hadn't been on fire a moment ago, and yet now…

"Oh shit, oh shit!" he screamed and went for it, stopping when he got close enough to really feel the flames. I didn't know if maybe he thought he'd done it himself with his hot skating (har har) but he sort of danced around the board, ineffectually torn between stomping it and fanning it. It was a little like the chicken dance, and after the annoyance he'd caused me, it didn't pain me at all to see him flop about like a fish in a boat.

"Whoa!" someone shouted from below, and a guy came

charging out, a little stagger to his step, with a martini glass sloshing, and dumped it on the burning skateboard. I snuffed the flames immediately, before the drunken moron could accidentally light up the whole neighborhood, and he stood there, next to skater boy, admiring their respective handiwork—skater boy for his too-hot skating skills, drunken master for idiotically charging in and doing the absolutely wrong thing at the wrong time.

And there I sat, watching from behind the curtains. I reached out and closed the window with a soft click, then pulled the curtains back together, before I could hear whatever exchange of non-wisdom was about to take place. I crawled back to the bed, shed my wig, and started to lie down again.

Was that really necessary? Zack asked.

"Good question," I said, wondering about it myself. "Are we talking about me immolating the board or Charlie the robber?"

Both, Zack said. *Just because you're here, just because you're…I dunno, isolated, alone—*

"Let me stop you there before you go digging for more adjectives," I said, "because either way…I don't have an answer for you. I do what I do. I give it some thought, but when it gets past a certain point…I just act. Charlie lasers me, I respond lethally. Some kid pisses me off with his rudeness, I don't call the front desk and whine about it, I fix the problem—"

Permanently.

"But not lethally, in skater boy's case," I said. "And hopefully he won't get another board until he's safely back in the US and not on a major urban thoroughfare in the middle of the night, skating where people are trying to sleep." I rubbed my face against the rough surface of the bedspread. "I dunno. I gravitate toward order, and where it falls apart…"

You're a hunter, Wolfe said. *Others are prey. If they cross your path—*

"You can stop, too," I said, turning my attention to the door. Right in front of the exit lay a shadowy piece of paper on the faux wood floor. I stood, an effort unto itself, and went to examine it. It had my name on it—my real name, not the assumed one I'd checked in under—and I opened the envelope to find a small note waiting.

Alistair Wexford requests the pleasure of your company at eleven o'clock tomorrow morning.

An address followed for a place that seemed to be outside London. I looked back at the door and realized I must have stepped over the invitation while I was standing at the door, waiting to see if someone was going to ambush me. "Looks like I've got a meeting tomorrow."

Feel the delicate tug of your string? Harmon asked, and I could almost hear him crowing. *No free lunch.*

"I pay for my lunches, thanks," I said. And pay and pay and pay, I didn't say, and tried not to think it, as I climbed into bed. I wanted the hours to pass so I could get to the meeting, but I ended up staying awake until nearly dawn locally…

…Which was roughly the time I would have gone to bed had I been back home.

5.

"So good of you to join us, Sienna," Alistair Wexford said, extending a hand as I walked, guided, into what looked like a laboratory. The address in question had been on the outskirts of London, and I'd taken the Underground in an effort not to wear out my cover by constantly flying everywhere. It was slow and boring and the carriage smelled a little funny, but it got me within walking distance and I didn't murder anyone, so it was kind of a win.

I shook his hand quickly, not daring to hold on for very long. Wexford, a telepath, caught the meaning behind my short gesture just as I suspected the symbolism behind his willingness to shake with me, a soul-stealing succubus—he was trying to reassure me that he wasn't scared shitless of being vacuumed up into my head like a loose hair. Or that he respected my control. Or maybe that he was just so set in his gentlemanly ways that he couldn't pass up a good handshake. Any way I sliced it, I took it as him being willing to continue our mutually beneficial partnership, and replied accordingly.

"Well, my social calendar was clear, so I appreciate you boys inviting me down and giving me something to do," I said, taking in the second man in the room. "A girl can only eat lunch so many times by herself before she starts to wonder if her sparkling personality is actually broken glass and not diamonds."

Wexford gave me the courtesy of a good-natured chortle. "I appreciate your discretion in handling that little matter of the robbers. It threatened to spiral out of control, as these sort of meta matters tend to, so your intervention was well-timed. I'm afraid that Charlie lad was quite headed into trouble from what I can gather. The shopkeeper is going to be in the hospital for quite some time, sorry to say."

He didn't even call me out on slaughtering poor Charlie. Not that he needed to, but sometimes I felt like I'd lost all perspective. What most people might have called justifiable homicide (because Charlie's blazing laser could have killed me if he'd hit me in the head with it) was no longer a black and white thing for me. I questioned myself constantly about this sort of thing now, probably the result of my own government having cast a few suspicions on me for other conduct.

And, uh…some genuinely bad things I'd done in the past.

"Will he be all right?" I asked.

"He will," Wexford said, guiding me farther into the sterile lab room and toward the other man, who I'd taken some notice of already in my usual threat-assessment sort of way. "As will the police constable that Charlie assaulted on the way out the door, though the man is still in some danger of losing that arm." Wexford went a bit solemn for a moment, then changed gears quite naturally. "But enough of past business—Sienna, I'd very much like to introduce you to Dr. Marc Logan."

Dr. Logan was a middle-aged fellow in a lab coat, wore glasses and had brown hair that went neatly to the back of his neck. It was unfettered, but styled, and his eyes were brown, with a very dulled look to them, as though he were taking in everything through a filter of British manners. His hands were clamped safely behind his back and he did not proffer them as he said in a quintessentially British way and with a great deal of reserve, "How do you do, Ms. Nealon?"

"Usually, I use fire," I said, and he stared at me for a moment until I elaborated. "Sometimes, my bare hands. Weapons, occasionally."

Dr. Logan bore the look of a man who'd missed something. "I'm sorry…?"

"You asked her how she did," Wexford said with only the

thinnest trace of amusement. For him, it was a lot. "She's providing a basic accounting of how she does…what she does."

"Technically, I was going through the methods I use most often to kill," I said, wondering why I'd gone that dark with my joke. I was probably just in a mood. "Sorry. Black humor, I guess."

"Oh, yes, I see," Dr. Logan said, nodding. "Very droll."

"You're too kind. It wasn't one of my better jokes," I said, matching his posture by putting my hands unthreateningly behind my own back. I looked at the doctor, then at Wexford. "Well, gentlemen…I assume you didn't summon me here for my somewhat flagging comedy skills."

"Quite right," Logan said, then seemed to realize that his words might give offense. He flashed a look of contrition and then moved on, which was probably a better move than getting caught in a very British cycle of apologizing. He waved us deeper into the lab and I followed, past a few rows of highly specialized equipment that probably had purposes well beyond my understanding. It was just that sort of place. "I suppose you recall making the acquaintance of a Dr. Ronald Sessions."

That got me to raise an eyebrow. "There's a name I haven't heard in a few years. Yeah, I know Dr. Sessions—or knew him, before he died." Wexford looked at me curiously, presumably because he wasn't able to read my mind anymore, thanks to the presence of Harmon. "He was the research doctor at the Directorate, the place I worked when I first…entered the world of metahumans." That was an oversimplification, but I went with it. "He studied metas at the Directorate, including me."

"Indeed," Dr. Logan said. "A few years ago, some relations of Dr. Sessions found a backup of a great many of his notes, his research into you, your powers, as well as those of other metahumans." He kept walking, taking me into the very back of the lab, where a display screen was set up.

"I think I might have heard about that at the time," I said. "He'd kept another outside of work just in case of catastrophe, proving once again that you should always back up the hard drive, especially when you're working for an extragovernmental agency that's in danger of being blown up." They both stared at me, probably trying to figure out if they should politely laugh or just smile in pain. "This is not my best joke day ever. Guys, let's just move on."

"In any case," Logan said, acceding to my wishes, "I've delved quite deeply into his archive, which contains quite a few gems, including his preliminary autopsy of the subject known as Wolfe—" Wolfe growled in my head "—as well as your physical examinations from when he first met you as well as those conducted later…"

I was trying to keep my eyes from glazing over. "Anything interesting in there?"

"Quite," Dr. Logan said, with the subtle hint of a smile. "In the autopsy for the subject Wolfe, there was a peculiar trace along the skin—signs of—I don't know how to say this in layman's terms without making it sound immensely complicated, but…there was an aftereffect of the cell death, a sort of…abnormality we hadn't seen before."

I shrugged. "Wolfe was abnormal." Wolfe growled again. *You were, dumbass. And that could be a compliment, if you were willing to take it as one. You were nearly invulnerable, FFS.*

"Based on the record, I have no doubt of that," Dr. Logan said, "and without the actual tissue samples from said autopsy, which was apparently interrupted for some reason—"

"I believe the corpse was destroyed in the explosion of the science building," I said, and waited a second. "Uh, the first explosion of the science building, not the one that killed Dr. Sessions." They both just looked at me quietly. "Like I said, things exploded there a lot."

"I would have been prepared to accept that this… signature, if you will…was a unique abnormality of Wolfe's powers," Dr. Logan said. He was kinda getting into it now, brushing his hair back from his ear. "However…in propagating this research out to colleagues of mine here in the UK, we've…run across it several times since."

That caused my eyes to go wide like unbroken egg yolks on the hard fried eggs Brits eat for breakfast. "Wait, what?

You're telling me you've found more Wolfe-types out there? Or their corpses, at least?" That was cause for worry. The number of metahumans was definitely increasing right now, due to unnatural means, but the thought of more Wolfe-types—extremely tough, resistant to killing, stab them and they heal in ten seconds, skin adapting to absorb bullets—was unsettling to me to say the least. "Because their kind was basically wiped out. Or it was supposed to be."

"No," Dr. Logan said with something like triumph in his eyes. "I don't believe that what we've found are Wolfe-types at all. I believe we have found subjects that have died in the exact same manner as Wolfe."

"But Wolfe died of a succubus—of me—draining his soul," I said, my mouth speaking faster than my brain could process the implications of this.

"Exactly," Dr. Logan said with a flourish. "I believe we have located a sort of cellular signature for victims of succubi and possibly incubi, your male counterparts."

I frowned, the full implications of what he was saying washing over me. "Wait. You said there were more victims? But…" I put a hand on my forehead, which felt like it was swelling. "There are no more incubi or succubi. I was the last…" I didn't need to finish my sentence.

I was the last succubus, just like Wolfe was the last of his kind, and a dozen other kinds of metas that had vanished off the face of the planet now had a second chance at existence.

Because someone was making new metas with the help of modern chemistry.

"Shit," I muttered. "There's a new one out there? Killing people?"

"Indeed," Wexford said, speaking up at last. "And this is why I've summoned you, because obviously this is a problem that you are uniquely suited to deal with—one of your very own, making the rounds, killing people."

"Where?" I asked, my head spinning. "When?"

"Edinburgh," Dr. Logan said, flipping a switch and turning on a projector screen. "Scotland. And as for when…well…" He looked sideways at the screen, and my eyes were drawn to the photo. "There have been a few. This one is the latest."

There was a body in a graveyard, laid out. It could have been a man sleeping, but it wasn't. I stared at him; the photo wasn't of particularly good quality, but the open eyes and shocked look made it obvious he was dead.

"And as for the when," Wexford said, "this one was found this very morning. I hadn't anticipated having a new one to show you, but…alas, here it is: a fresh body."

"Sonofa," I muttered. "There…were more?"

"Oh, yes," Dr. Logan said. "Dozens. Mysterious deaths, no cause obvious. They've been showing up in the Edinburgh morgue for months."

"It would seem," Wexford said, putting himself in front of the screen, the grisly footage of the dead body projecting over him as he adopted a serious look, "that we have ourselves a metahuman serial killer."

6.

"What the hell?" I asked as I sat forward, trying to make sense out of what I was seeing and hearing. Bodies showing up all over the place in Scotland? An incubus or succubus on the loose? My mouth felt dry at contemplating that.

A meta serial killer with the powers I called my own. Well, some of them anyway, I thought as Wolfe growled in my head.

"It's hard to say how long this has been going on," Wexford said in that uptight, under control British manner of his. I doubted he'd have been so damned buttoned up about it if it had been one of his distant relations going out there and ripping the souls out of people, but there it was. The old metahumans being somewhat closely related (like my Uncle, Guy Friday the clown) adding an additional, darker cast on it. What if this wasn't a new meta at all, but one of my second cousins or something, killing people? Or first cousin, once removed?

Whatever. It would be in my best interests to be once-removing them from the damned planet as soon as I could get to it.

"Well, okay then," I said, and stood up straighter. Now I had a job, and it wasn't just busting some assclown committing an ever-escalating series of petty crimes. This was serious stuff, an incubus or succubus absorbing the souls of victims who didn't have any defense. My aunt Charlie had been this type of person, cold and crazy and addicted to the high of absorbing

28

people. I didn't have much stomach for it myself, as evidenced by the fact only seven souls were in residence in my skull, a very dinky percentage compared to how many killers I'd, uhm…killed.

"Do try and keep the fuss to a minimum, will you?" Wexford called after me. He was anchored to his spot, good-natured and filled with aplomb as ever.

"Why, I'm not going to fuss at all," I said, looking back at him. "This killer? They might squawk a little as I take them out of the picture, though."

Wexford seemed to favor me with a very chill look, probably something befitting a government minister in charge of lots of people and without much desire for chaos. "Very good, then," he said as I cruised on out of there. "Best of luck."

"Leaving things to luck is for suckers," I said, making my way through all the fancy scientific equipment. I had a mission that didn't involve bushwhacking pitiful robbers. Maybe a shot at a real, genuine villain at the end of this. And who knew how long it could take? I almost smiled, but didn't, because it was kinda untoward to grin stupidly while contemplating the deaths of dozens of people.

You've got that bounce in your step again, Harmon said. *Purpose at your back. Wind in your sails.*

"Nice sailing metaphor, Lord Nelson."

Before we go… Zack said, a little quietly, *don't you think maybe you ought to make that visit you've been putting off?*

I sighed. He was right. There was a certain stop I'd been holding off on for months, and one I oughta get out of the way, especially before leaving on an open-ended investigation that could last…well, hopefully a while. "Sure," I agreed finally. "One last stop and we'll be on our way." And I said it with a song in my heart, back to work—real work—at last.

7.

The old headquarters for Omega in London looked about like I remembered it. It was another brick building in a district filled with them, but the difference between it and the ones around it was that this one had a well-cultivated look of being abandoned. Which I figured was a desired effect, since who wants to make your secret metahuman gangster headquarters the kind of locale that people are always popping into and out of, like a Walmart? Or Asda, I guess, over here.

I strolled up to the back door, pushing my way through into the abandoned entry. In spite of appearances, I didn't for a minute believe that this place actually was abandoned. It was an old trick I'd learned about disused places—the floors were dirty, but not dirty enough to hide that they'd been walked on, and recently. There were security cameras up in the ceiling too, small, but present, in spite of the fact that some of the walls were torn open, wiring removed, graffiti spray-painted over the ones that didn't have massive, gaping holes in them. The whole thing was a passive effect designed to inculcate the impression that this place was not worth wasting your looting time on, if that's what you were here for.

I flipped the light switch in the entry, and the bulbs popped and hummed as they came on—well, two out of four, at least, in the central fixture. It was good enough, though honestly I could have seen just fine without it.

Making my way to steel elevator doors, I stared, wondering if they'd even work. I pushed the button and was rewarded with the hum of elevator cables springing to life, motors carrying a car toward me from somewhere above or below. It was hard to tell which. When I stepped inside, I pressed the button for the right floor from memory, wondering exactly when Omega's security precautions were going to start coming into play, because so far I'd waltzed right through the front door with zero resistance.

Stepping out as the doors slid open, I found myself in an open space, a bunch of old, weathered cubicles stretched out over the floor ahead. The lights in here were dark, and a deathly silence pervaded the place, but it looked different than when last I'd been here. For one, it had been cleaned up since then, the image of an abandoned place left on the floor below. Here it was all office, cubicles and rows of ordered neatness, but the lights were out and silence was thick.

I was pondering the layout, looking past the big reception desk, when I caught sight of the first movement in the shadows to my right. I spun in time to see a giant walking out of a side corridor, big and bulky and five times my height. It looked like it was crouching low to avoid scraping the ceiling, and low, heavy breathing scraped out of the place where its mouth would be. Glowing red eyes gleamed in the semi-dark, piercing and fixed on me as it moved into my path.

Another pulled itself out of the shadows to my left, like a boulder unfolding from sleeping on the battlefield and turning into a rock giant of the sort you might expect to find in a cheesy fantasy novel. I couldn't see its features, but it was craggy and misshapen, like a cliff face pulling itself to life.

There they stood, twin pillars of death, leering down at me with those eyes, those scary-looking eyes. They breathed in the dark, then got louder, howls echoing through the open space, and I could sense the malice of these giants, these things that meant to destroy me, as they swooped down to attack.

8.

"Karthik," I called past the horrors menacing me, threatening to descend and destroy me, frightening figures in the dark, "knock this bullshit off."

With that, they vanished, the wide, open space before the cubicles suddenly lit brightly, a young man behind the reception desk who was all too familiar guarding access to the warren of offices behind him.

"Sienna," Karthik said, his black hair slicked back, dark eyes watching me tentatively, "I'd say it's good to see you, but…"

"You don't have to lie on my account," I said, keeping my hands at my sides. I didn't want to tell him that he'd almost gotten me with that effect he'd created. Those giants had been freaky real, something I vaguely remembered about Karthik's earlier creations, but seeing something this sweeping and intimidating? I didn't remember him being able to do that sort of grand terror convincingly before. "Looks like you've upped your game. With your Rakshasa powers, I mean."

Karthik smiled tightly, taking the compliment in the way it was intended. "Thank you. Coming from you, this means…quite a lot. You seem to be gaining some power yourself."

"I dunno about that," I said. "Gaining attention, maybe. But I'm still basically the same Sienna you knew before. Nothing new to report, power-wise." This was a lie, but why would I share with him that I'd added telepathy to my list of abilities? Especially when he was already acting like I was the enemy.

My oh my, Harmon said, *Omega is certainly up to a great deal of mischief.*

Anything that should concern me? I asked. This was one of the reasons I'd avoided paying a call on them. Karthik and his boss had fought on my side during the war against Sovereign, and I had a vague sense—no, strike that—I knew they were up to no good, and while I was visiting this place as a fugitive from the law, I didn't particularly want to have to bust up their little operation. Which I would feel obligated to do if I knew they were up to real, honest-to-goodness bad.

Mid-level criminality, I'd say. They're mostly steering clear of killing, if that worries you. Mostly.

My jaw involuntarily tightened. *Aren't we all.*

"What are you doing here?" Karthik asked, arms folded in front of him.

"Social call," I said. "I was in the neighborhood…or leaving the neighborhood for a spell, thought I'd stop in and say hi."

Karthik was trying to be inscrutable, but he was failing miserably at it. "Is that so?" I would have bet dollar to donuts that he'd known I was in London all along. Which would have been good, because good, American donuts were tough to get in London. Not that I could eat them on my current dietary regime.

"That I'm leaving? It's so. That I'm being social? Well… I'm making the effort." I gave him a tight smile of my own. "For old times' sake, or something."

Karthik just stared at me, smokily, for a moment. "What do you imagine is going to happen here? Should we…go get a beer and talk about old times? Sit at the pub until midnight and reminisce about all the friends we lost during the fight?"

"That's what war buddies do, isn't it?" I shrugged. It was hard for me to put much care into it, having now received the frosty reception I'd suspected would be mine if I came here. Mission accomplished, and now I could strike this thing I'd been dreading off my list. "Never mind, it doesn't matter. I won't stay, I'll just say—stay out of trouble, Karthik. You and Omega. I'm on this side of the Atlantic now, and as long as you guys keep your mischief out of the serious realms, I'll pretend I don't see you, kinda like you pretended not to see me when I came in here." He did not react to my veiled threat, just stood there like a stone. I could see others behind him, in the cubicle farms, their heads up above the walls, watching our conversation. I think they got the message, even if he didn't. "All right, well, I'm done. So long, Karth—"

"Sienna." The voice that called my name came from the other side of the room, echoing through the cavernous space. It was filled with meaning, poignance—meant to get my attention and stop my turn and stalk off.

It worked, too, though not because of the voice itself, but because of the speaker, whose history with me stretched back farther than almost anyone else yet alive. I turned and looked and found him standing in front of the office at the far end of the room, the one that had once been my own, when I was—briefly—the head of Omega. He wore an old tweed jacket, his beard was growing in, grey all the way through, and his eyes were so sunken as to seem skeletal.

Janus.

9.

The old office wasn't too far off what I remembered—wood paneling all the way around, bookshelves filled with old tomes that wouldn't have been out of place in any of England's innumerable museums and libraries. They were old, dusty and leather-bound, and they made the office smell of old books, which was one of its more charming points.

Against it: the mighty desk in the middle was like an island designed to separate visitors from the person who sat behind the desk, which Janus did now, retreating behind it like it would protect him from my wrath. I doubted he had any illusions about that, though, since the previous occupant of his chair had been me, and the guy before that…

Well, he'd come to a bad end at my hand, sitting in that very spot, in fact. Janus probably wouldn't have forgotten that, since he'd come into the room as I was beating Rick Gerasimos to death with pieces of one of the visitors' chairs.

I sat down in the chair across from the desk, eyeing it. It wasn't quite like the one I'd beaten Rick's skull in with, but it wasn't far off. Janus must have sensed what I was thinking, because he had a wary look on his face, one that made him look even older than when last we'd met. Though, given the circumstances of our last meeting—wherein I rescued him from being tortured to the breaking point by a psycho who wanted all of Omega's vast, centuries-in-the-accumulation fortune—I couldn't blame him for looking a bit past the sell-by date.

"The papers have shown you flying over many of the major European cities," Janus said, preambling our conversation as usual with occlusionary bullshit, designed to keep from getting to the nub of the matter. That was Janus for you, always taking the long way around to the point, if he got to it at all. "What brings you to London?"

"Cut the crap, Janus," I said. "You know I've been here for months. You probably even know why I'm here. In England, I mean, not here in your office right now."

He didn't nod, probably because he didn't want to tip me to the fact that he undoubtedly had sources all throughout the British government, even at the levels that Wexford operated. Instead he shrugged, lightly, addressing a matter of no consequence to him, like the most lethal meta in the world wasn't leering at him right now. "I hear rumors only."

"You hear everything always."

"You give me too much credit." He settled back in his chair, leaning slightly. "I am not what I once was. Time has taken its toll."

"I imagine that angry Englishman with a knife took a few pence of skin as well," I said, and though he didn't flinch, I had a suspicion that he tensed slightly. No one could have gone through what Janus had without being left with a psychological scar or two. If he'd been human, it would have been real scars, had he survived what was done to him.

"Why have you come to see us, Sienna?" Janus asked, drawing closer to what I imagined was the concern of his day.

"Why didn't you move your headquarters, Janus?" I volleyed right back.

"It would be a shame to close down such a storied facility, long in our care," Janus said. "And also…real estate prices in London are insane, and our building is not in the best of upkeep. Since Omega's fortunes have…declined…" He looked at me only for a second, but it was enough to convey to me that he knew I'd absconded with said fortunes once the thief that had tortured him had transferred them to a bank in Liechtenstein. "…moving offices is not a practicable idea…at least not at present."

"That's interesting," I said in a manner that made clear it wasn't. I doubted money was the holdup, because Janus's empath powers meant he could push around a loan officer at a bank to make just about whatever he wanted to happen, happen.

"I sense you don't believe that," Janus said, watching carefully for my reaction.

My eyes narrowed before I could control them. "You don't sense shit from me, Janus, don't lie."

For the first time, he smiled, faintly. "So it's true. You have a telepath in your head now. Harmon?"

"Or someone," I said, because copping to being involved in the death of a US President in front of a criminal didn't sound all that wise to me. "The good news is, now you can't push me around emotionally anymore." That was what empaths did, sense and direct emotion.

"You assume I ever did," Janus said lightly. Another lie. We both knew he'd done it, at least some. I wasn't entirely sure how much, but I was positive that he'd influenced my feelings during the war. Best case scenario, he used a light touch. Worst case…hell, he could have run me for some of it and I wouldn't have known.

"I assume you did, yes." I leaned forward in my chair and he seemed to shift back, like he was anticipating me smashing my chair and then mashing him with it.

"If that is what you believe, who am I to contest the great Sienna Nealon?" He disarmed me a little with that one.

"Of course you wouldn't argue the point. Or deny it flat out."

"What purpose would that serve?" Janus put his hands across his belly and interlaced the fingers. "You are steadfast in your judgments, Sienna. I have always respected that about you. I was the God of Doorways, the God of Transitions, and I aided many people in walking through to a new place in their lives, a new state of being. You, though? You don't wish for my help. And you definitely don't wish to change who you are. And so here we sit, across the desk from one another, and without knowing your feelings, I can tell you this: the reason you have avoided this meeting and that I have not sought it as well, even after you have been here for months, is…you have made your judgments. You have chosen your path. You are who you are, and whatever coinciding of interests there might have been between us before? It is long over now." He spoke gently, softly, reassuring—like I remembered him, which kinda put the lie to the idea that he could only manipulate my emotions through his power. He was smooth; he had other means to build trust.

"When you're right, you're right," I said, and got to my feet, sliding the chair back slowly. No reason to age Janus a few more years by making him think I was standing to bust his skull, after all, when I had no intention of doing any such thing. "Do I even need to warn you about the line you're walking?"

"I should think it would be unnecessary," Janus said. "But if it would make you feel better to threaten me, I will not take it as anything other than a definite statement of your position in this matter."

"I will rip up Omega by the root if I find you stepping over the line, Janus," I said. I figured I might as well make it blindingly clear, though I probably could have been a lot more subtle and he still would have gotten it. "I will salt the earth around you, and I don't care if you threaten me, if you call the government to bomb me, try to get them to murder me, hire every mercenary on the planet to kill me—"

"I am fairly certain that has been tried with little success."

"—come after my friends, come after what's left of my family—you could give it a go, and I would still fly to wherever you hide yourself, torch your entire organization, and leave nothing left but scorched ground and your tears."

"Which could only aid your salting efforts."

"Keep from being huge dicks, will you, Janus?" I made my way to the door, figuring I'd made my point about as clearly as I could without smashing furniture or busting heads open. "I don't really want to cause the level of carnage a conflict between us would require."

"Nor do I," Janus said, and here he narrowed his eyes. "But allow me to deliver a similar message, though perhaps a bit more understated—Do not seek us again here, Sienna." He put his hands on his desk and rose. "Now that we are clear where each of us stands, this Omega facility and any others are off limits to you. We are not friends, and we will never be friends, and thus you have no reason to be here or anywhere else that we call home."

"You think your flimsy warning is going to stop me if I catch a whiff of evil from an Omega facility?" Hands on my hips, eyebrow up, kinda surprised he was being so brazen. But then, Janus was always a plan-within-a-plan kind of guy. He probably had one for killing me right now, though if he executed it I would probably execute him before they managed to take me down.

"You will not 'catch a whiff of evil' from us, as you say." Janus stood up, fingertips leaving the desk. Now he was tall and commanding, though not exactly a giant or anything. "And if you think you do...I might suggest you are scenting yourself, for your activities of late have been...most concerning. You are not the girl I once knew, who had to be coaxed into killing to save the world. Your innocence is long gone, and the warrior that has replaced that girl...she walks in the grey, not nearly as pristine and righteous as her intentions might suggest."

"That's the problem with becoming the instrument of war that you and Winter and others wanted me to become," I said, holding my ground in front of the door. "You make someone into a weapon powerful enough to destroy the enemy, you just never know where they might point that power once that enemy is destroyed." He shifted uncomfortably behind the desk, and I deemed this a good place to leave our relationship, hopefully forever. "Goodbye, Janus." And I walked out, wishing that I would never, ever, have to return.

10.

When I got back to my hotel, my encounter with Janus still running through my mind on an uncomfortable loop, I found a package already slipped under the door from Wexford's little servants. It was a cover identity from Scotland Yard, including government ID. I had to give the man credit; he had his bases covered.

So, you're really going to do this, huh? Zack asked quietly as I stuffed a few things into the overnight bag that was... basically all I owned at this point. I was getting to be a real ascetic. A very few valuable possessions were locked in a bank vault back in Minneapolis, and everything else was essentially clothing, wigs and toiletries. But that was what happened when you could spontaneously combust and burn up all your possessions. And frequently had to. Less was more, anyway.

"Why wouldn't I?" I asked, stuffing one of the wigs into the bag. "Wait, aren't you one of those voices in my head that's constantly pushing me to work because it's a good thing for me?"

Yeah, shut up, Gerry Harmon said. *You know how antsy she gets when there's no case.*

You know how antsy a heroin addict gets when he hasn't had a needle in a while? Zack fired back.

"What the hell?" I asked, straightening up next to the bed, dropping the wig. "Comparing me to an opioid user? Not cool, man."

40

Sorry, Zack said, but he was not sorry, not subtle, and kinda sullen.

"I can quit any time I want," I said with a faint smile, taking his addiction metaphor and running with it. "But not literally, because then the UK would probably let America come right on over and shoot me or something."

Zack just shook his head within mine. *You should have a life.*

"Kinda tough when the cops are after you."

People do it all the time. I've lost count of how many stories I've heard about fugitives being caught with a new family.

"Way to put that criminal justice degree to work showing me where I'm getting it wrong," I muttered.

This wasn't supposed to be your life. Remember? I could feel the earnestness flow. *Last time we were here, in London, you walked away with a sense that you had to change things or else you'd burn bright like a comet and crash to the ground. In the years since, you've done nothing—or almost nothing—to change it. Now you're worse off than ever, and chasing that next hit to feel alive. How long is that going to last?*

"Until I find the next job, I'd imagine?" I was being too cute by half.

And the next and the next and the next. We aren't just put on this planet to work and work and work, Sienna. There has to be... His voice cracked. *There has to be more than just living to work.*

"Lemme know if you figure out what it should be," I said, brushing all of this crap off as the musings of a man who had no idea what he was talking about. "Because I haven't gotten it, other than—y'know, a desire to pound the faces of people who upset the order of folks actually trying to do just that."

Zack just shook his head in the darkness of my mind. *There has to be more than you just being a silent sentinel against the forces of...whatever. Crass stupidity and wanton criminality.*

"And yet...there's not."

Your friends...you haven't even talked to them once since you came over here.

"I've been busy," I said, not even bothering to get defensive. "We're good. We left it in a good place. I made my peace with them. And I've talked to Zollers!"

Once. Two, three months ago. And you didn't even contact any of the people you know here—Janus, Karthik…that British detective you acquainted yourself with last time you were here.

My cheeks burned at the realization I was discussing a former lover with another former lover. "Those guys are all busy living their lives. And as for my friends, well…a conversation with Zollers goes a long way," I said, finishing my packing. I didn't have much, and once I'd put my new Scotland Yard ID in my pocket, I was basically ready to go. "Besides…I don't feel isolated and alone. I feel…fine." I didn't have to consider that very long before adding a caveat. "Ish."

There she is, Harmon said. *She's ready. And she doesn't need you distracting her right now. Remember what happened last time?*

"Yeah, remember what happened last time someone distracted me or lied and withheld important info while I was on a job?" It was kinda neat how Harmon had tried to distract from that, given he was the one who'd most recently caused me havoc while on a job. I could almost see him smiling innocently in my head, like, "Nothing to see here." I slung my bag over my shoulder. "Zack's probably right," I offered as a concession. "But I'm on the case now. It's time to get things done, and we'll worry about this other, personal stuff…y'know, later. Right?"

There was a chorus of assent, and I could hear almost all their voices. There was a slight prickling in my mind, though, a feeling that something was not quite right, that somebody was not quite present. I heard Eve, Bastian, Gavrikov, Harmon, Bjorn—even Zack chimed in, reluctantly, but present, nodding his sullen approval for my course of action.

I shrugged, tossing off that feeling that something was missing, that someone was not quite all there, not quite on board with this, but I didn't spare much thought to wonder who it was or why they were absent in their enthusiastic, choral support for my current endeavor.

I didn't even bother casting a last look over my hotel room as I opened the door to leave. When I came back from Scotland I'd change it up again, stay somewhere else. Wouldn't want to stay here too long, or establish a pattern someone could trace. I needed to keep moving, keep going. "Scotland ho," I said under my breath as I closed the door on another transitory chapter in my life, wondering if there was something going on in my head that I'd missed.

11.

Wolfe

Republic of Athens
453 B.C.

The caves were dark, dank, filled with the occasional howl and yell of the tormented. The air seemed to crawl across the skin like claws, gently scraping the flesh as it passed.

Wolfe took a breath of the stale, dank air. There was a tinge of salt that he could taste, wandering its way through his nasal passages through the stink of all the people that had made their way down here over time. The smell of fetid bodies, both living and dead, meandered through his sense of smell as well, and it reminded him of...

Food.

There was no cure for the smell. The caves were lit by torch, which carried a scent of its own, that burning smell, but one not nearly strong enough to overcome all the other scents this place held. The crash of the waves behind him, where the caves met the sea, echoed madly, was nearly deafening to his enhanced hearing, but he struggled his way through it.

He was the guard of the gate to this place right now—the sentinel to keep others from passing into this realm, this...

Underworld.

"Wolfe," Frederick called, causing Wolfe to open his eyes,

to blink in the darkness. A slow look over his shoulder confirmed it. Frederick wandered his way, a dark-haired shadow picking around the bones that had not been disposed of properly by the handful of slaves that worked in this place. "The master calls."

"And I answer," Wolfe said with a nod. It didn't bear thinking about, doing anything but subserviently coming when bidden. Wolfe respected strength above all else. It was the way of his family, his way…strength meant you could take what you wanted, and he had built his own strength prodigiously to ensure that no one could take from him what he did not wish to yield.

But the master…the master could take from him in mere seconds that which no man had prised from his grasp given years. And that was why he was the master.

Wolfe threaded his way past Frederick, bumping shoulders hard with his brother. They both growled, keeping it low, where others would not hear. Wolfe smiled silent satisfaction; Frederick's had been the shoulder turned aside this time. It was not always so, but it was so more often than not. Of the three of them, Wolfe knew he tried hardest to strengthen himself, to leather himself against threats. Was he not the one who ground his skin against the rocks outside the cave for hours? Slammed his head against them only to let them heal, stronger against that sort of wounding in the future? Frederick and Grihm had taken some of it upon themselves in turn, certainly, but Wolfe…

Wolfe had led the way. Not that they appreciated him for it.

He descended into the darkness, torches lighting the way into the abyss of the cave. Bones crunched underfoot, more…spillage…from ill-fated servants doing an ill job. Wolfe did not care, but the master was furious when he crunched bones. Which was probably why he seldom came this far toward the entrance of the caves. It had been years since last he'd emerged; Wolfe remembered it very faintly, as he remembered all such good times.

And it had been a good time…at least for Wolfe and the other brethren of Hades. Perhaps not so for the nearby village who'd suffered their…visit.

The darkness lightened, a cluster of torches ahead flickering in a symmetrical pattern. Two to the right side of the throne, two to the left. Wolfe did not slink, but he did ease his walk. His normal mode of walking was to pad upon his feet, to stalk and hunt. There was none of that here. He approached straight of back, a subject summoned into the sufferance of his king, lest insult be given where none was dared.

He could not see the throne in the middle of the torches, but he did not need to. To stare into the shadows was, in itself, enough. He could see the shape, sense the presence, and that was quite enough, yes. Wolfe sank to a knee, bowing his head. "I am summoned, and I appear. What would you have of me, oh great Hades?"

"Wolfe…" The very voice caused his bones to quiver, as Hades himself turned his full attention upon him. It could be an uncomfortable feeling, if the man truly focused and used his power to reach out and tug at your soul, to read it for himself the way others might parse a manuscript. It was a heavy and unbearable feeling, like the breath of death itself was coming down the back of your neck. It was a thing for which there was no defense, and Wolfe had felt it only a very few times. Those were quite enough for him.

"Yes, my lord?" Wolfe asked, keeping his head bowed.

"Look up," Hades commanded, and Wolfe froze in place. He gradually adjusted his sight upward, afraid he might be looking into the face of death—in more ways than one.

But when he raised his eyes, Hades himself was not standing before Wolfe. No, not Hades. Nor Persephone, either, though she had the same dark hair that marked her mother, but those eyes…

Those eyes were purely her father's.

The woman before him was one that Wolfe had seen only in passing, a shadow in the darkness of the caves. That was the way of Hades, of his bride, to keep their offspring close, in the back of the caverns, in the family quarters, for lack of a better word, where Wolfe and his brothers and all but a few servants were not welcome. He had heard the cries in the dark, the people brought into those places who never left, save as sprinkled bones. He could smell her, the scent of her, unwashed for the most part save for in the sea water brought in by the slaves in buckets every so often. It was a pungent aroma, the scent of her, but in spite of her life spent in the dark, in the captivity of this place…

Her chin stuck out defiantly, and she looked at him…as a master looked at a slave.

"This is my daughter," Hades breathed, his voice like a drumbeat of intensity in Wolfe's soul. Wolfe lowered his head again, drive to show deference like a weight pushing it down. "You have not seen her before, yes?"

"Perhaps in the shadows," Wolfe allowed. There was no counting how many offspring Hades and Persephone had now, but it had to be many. The cries of childbirth all ran together in his mind, and there was no telling how many of the children had survived into adulthood. Considerably fewer than had been born, naturally.

"Good," Hades said. "No one should know our numbers."

Wolfe did not feel a need to offer counsel on that; the man who was known as the God of Death had no need of his opinion on this matter or any other.

Only his service. "I have a task for you," Hades went on. The shadows moved before him, behind the woman.

"Anything you request, my lord."

"You will escort my daughter out of this place," Hades said, and faint disbelief chilled Wolfe's ears. "Wherever she wishes to go…you will follow, and ensure her safety."

It felt as though all the air had been drawn out of the cave, as though some Aeolus had swept in and done the inconceivable, pulling it out with their power. To evince such disbelief at Hades's words, though, did not bear consideration, and so Wolfe held his silence until the understanding of what had been said had fully seeped in, the shock passed. "I will follow her for so long as you command it."

"I command it until I say otherwise," Hades said. "Go with her. Go with her wherever she desires. She is to see the world, the world beyond these feuding cities and states, to make report of it all…and bring such knowledge back to me here, so that I may consider…all that will come next."

"As you wish," Wolfe said as the woman before him moved, swaying. His eyes flitted up and saw a face like carved marble, chin strong and extended, jutting out as if daring him to strike at it as a target. Her eyes blazed even in the darkness, and she moved, right toward him, without a hint that she would consider slowing if he did not move out of her path.

Wolfe smelled the challenge, and knew what waited in the shadows behind her. Had this been Frederick, he would not even have been so bold as she. But she did not slow, did not stop, and she was so close he could smell her even more intensely now, beneath the ragged cloth robe she used to cover herself—

He moved aside, as befit his station, and she swept past, clearly having either expected him to do so, or perhaps ready to make him do so if he had not moved. Wolfe moved deftly, sideways, and then came to his feet once she was past. The faint, low rumble of amusement from the throne did not cause Wolfe to burn as it might have had it come from anyone else. Strength was strength, and the strength of a man who could rip the very soul from his body with a thought was nothing to be trifled with. It commanded respect…or it would command your death, and Wolfe was clear on which he was willing to give.

"I will do as you command," Wolfe said, keeping his front facing the throne as he made to follow the daughter of Hades. She continued her pace unabated, and he was unable to show his back to the king, so he quickened his pace, trusting his feet to be nimble and keep him from tripping over any of the assorted stalagmites that had grown in this cave over the years before their arrival.

"You will faithfully serve me as ever you have," Death said, his laughter now spent. "This I trust." And he said no more, the shadows growing still as Wolfe retreated, until he had passed the chamber wall and was free to turn, and chase the daughter of Hades.

She moved swiftly, not waiting for him, perhaps trusting he

would catch her, which he did just as she was reaching Frederick. Wolfe heard the subtle growl in the darkness, his brother's hackles raised at the approach of a servant.

"Quell yourself," Wolfe said, hurrying forward. "That is no mere—"

But it was too late. Frederick had sprung forward; servants died all the time in this place, and no child of Hades had been seen at the cave mouth in…ever. Nor had Persephone, either. It simply never happened.

Frederick's mouth was wide, his anger rising at the thought of a servant challenging him in the way of his brothers. There was little malice behind his movement, merely a desire to establish the dominance of his power. Frederick swept in at her—

And she dodged, deftly, on the balls of her feet, swifter than him.

Frederick's eyes grew wide; servants did not outmaneuver the brothers three. Doubt surfaced, easily read in his movements, and he held himself away from her, still, assessing, thinking—

She did not think. She did not consider. She struck, like a snake at a wolf's paw, lashing out and grabbing him by the throat. Frederick struck back, furious, battering at her hand, where it had him. He was taller than her by several heads, but she did not let loose of him. Wolfe could see her grip like iron upon him, her teeth bared as she let out a growl as savage and feral as any Frederick had ever loosed.

It was a matter of seconds and Frederick loosed his first whimper. He had realized, Wolfe knew, realized what he faced, who he faced, and had restrained himself in the face of the daughter of death. Now she had clutched him at the neck and he hung there, limply, upon his knees, whimpering like a dog.

She spat in his eye, and he whimpered further, his muscles jerking until she surrendered her grip on his throat. Wolfe hung back, unwilling to interfere in this contest which had already—clearly—been decided. Frederick fell back on his haunches and sat there, head down, breath coming in quick, juddering movements. He did not speak, but his bearing was

49

more than just a man who had surrendered himself to yield to a master…

It was the bearing of a dog in pain.

She stood over him, straight-backed and scorning, and there was no touch of sympathy in her gaze, no empathy for her lesser. Her hand was fixed in a claw, ready to snake out again and take hold of him. Frederick's hands touched his throat, protecting it from her strength, from what she had done. She did not speak, but merely stared at him for a full ten seconds before she moved again, toward him, and Frederick scrambled aside without a hint of shame at yielding his ground to her.

Wolfe followed her as she went, bold, unafraid, toward the crash of the waves in the distance. The mouth of the cave was ahead, and she plunged toward it with steady steps, her back exhibiting no fear that Wolfe could read.

He paused at Frederick's side; his brother would not look at him, not now. Not in defeat. "What did she do?" Wolfe asked, uncertain. There had to be more to Frederick's reaction than mere embarrassment at being thwarted by one of Hades's children.

"When she touched me—" Frederick's fingers, long and shaking, held court over his throat, a shield from harm that already been visited "—it was like him. Like his power to fix itself on your soul and rip it from you. Her touch…" His eyes flashed in the darkness. "Be wary of her touch. For it will steal you from yourself. It will be your death, if you do not heed me."

Wolfe studied him, the fear of his brother, and nodded once. "I will be wary," he said, and followed the daughter of death from the realm of Hades, and into the world, his brother's words ringing in his ears.

12.

Sienna

I remembered in my youth reading a book about the grand old city of Edinburgh, in the days of yore, when there was no sewer system and people bathed once a year, usually on New Year's Eve. They said you could smell it before you could see it, and I believed them. How could you not, with all that mass of accumulated filth?

I quietly thanked the heavens for the development of the sewer system and indoor plumbing as I came in sight of the city itself, flying down out of a low-hanging cloud and catching my first glimpse long before I caught my first smell of the place. It was an impressive view, with a massive, massive castle just sticking up in the middle of the city, a bulwark and fortress to be defended in times of struggle. It reminded me of those books Reed read about mighty battles between forces of orcs and men and whatnot with swords. I tended to like watching those sorts of things unfold on a screen, Netflixing my way through the great battles of epic fantasy rather than reading them the way my brother did.

And Edinburgh…it looked like it had a history of that sort of massive battle, the kind of thing that might inspire the tellers of those sorts of stories.

It didn't take me too long to use my phone's GPS to find where I was supposed to be. It was on the east side of town, a hill that stuck out from the landscape, dotted with monuments—a tower or two, a Greek-looking temple that was about a quarter done, if that, and simply ended at the edge of it, like they'd just sort of run out of interest or money before completing it. And then, at the edge of that hill, I found what I was looking for—an old graveyard, laid out on the base of the hill and sloping down, old stones in neat rows, old vaults up at the north like little interconnected castle courtyards of their own. I wondered if the wealthy and notable were buried up there, but I didn't wonder too hard about it.

I landed in an alleyway nearby and put on a wig, then stowed my bag on a nearby rooftop that had no access. My work done, myself mostly presentable, I then hoofed it up to the Old Calton Burial Ground, a graveyard by any other name, entering through the southern gate, and worked my way up the hill toward the visible police presence in the vaults to the north of the site.

It was a pleasant summer's day, clouds overhead threatening rain in the future, but for now I could see the sun hinting at its own presence behind a clutch of clouds. A breeze came rolling through the graveyard, light and low, and as I sauntered uphill toward the waiting men and women in the yellow jackets emblematic of UK police uniforms, I wondered how long they'd been standing around up here. Hours, probably, since it had been at least a couple since I'd had my briefing with Dr. Logan and Wexford, and the murder had clearly been discovered in advance of that by some time.

A couple of the cops caught sight of me and started to move to intercept, coolly, probably wanting to head this civilian intruder off before she could cause any damage to the crime scene. I pulled my ID and advanced on them, easily within meta killing distance, and they let me approach because I wasn't in human killing distance, at least not in their view. I flashed Scotland Yard badge, hoping I was rocking the blond wig the way I thought I was. "Sarah Nelson," I announced as I closed on them, and they actually relaxed, perhaps even more foolishly. "Scotland Yard." I did an accent and everything, trying to make myself sound British. I'd been practicing.

"Ye're the special metahuman investigator from London?" One of the cops was a guy, the other a girl, and they both looked funny in bright yellow. Like a fire hydrant back home. "Aye, wondered when ye'd get here," he said, taking the lead.

"Been waiting long?" I asked, trying to keep from accidentally appropriating their accents. I had this mimicking tendency that I tried to keep under control and occasionally failed at, which had been really embarrassing one time in Texas.

"A few hours," he said, and the last word came out almost like 'ewers,' and it took me a second to decode that, even though I suspected that as far as Scottish accents went, this was probably relatively mild.

"All right, well…let's get to brass tacks," I said. "Who's in charge of this investigation?"

The two cops looked at each other, then back to me, clearly perplexed. "Well…you are, of course," the woman answered.

"Oh," I said. "Well. Cool." I didn't know Wexford had arranged for me to have that much sway, but it was a nice perk to find yourself unchallenged and in charge when you had a job to do. "Care to give me the grand tour?"

The woman nodded, and the man took whatever meaning passed between the two of them in stride. I assumed it was a sort of, "I'll go; you guard here?" kind of exchange, which was born out a moment later when she started to lead me away from their post in the middle of the asphalt path and up the hill toward the vaults.

"How old is this graveyard?" I asked, trying to catch a glimpse of one of the tombstones as we passed. Some of them were pretty tall, monuments over my head in height. I caught a date of death as 1891 on an upright stone as we went by. So not medieval, at least.

"Old," she said. "Opened in the 1700s. This way."

We threaded our way up to one of the vaults, which wasn't really a vault in the traditional sense. More of an enclosure, like an archway into a small, ten foot by ten foot space that was open air above and lacked any sort of gate. I wondered at why someone would build such a space, but assumed they must have had their reasons because people did all sorts of weird stuff that I couldn't understand. I mean, seriously, how else did you explain ice hockey? Slapping a puck around with sticks on a frozen lake? Where did that come from?

"Here we go," I murmured as we entered the vault. The victim was impossible to miss, laid out as he was in the corner to my right as we entered, staring at us, eyes unmoving, like he was a silent sentinel of the entrance.

"Groundskeeper found him this morning at around six o'clock," the lady cop said. "Said he walked by and saw the poor fella staring out at him. Nearly had a heart attack."

"Staring corpses tend to put a little fear in most of us," I said, looking right in the dead body's eyes. His skin was relaxed, his face frozen in a rictus of pain, a grimace that was permanent. I suspected a good mortician could maybe fix it, and would have to, if the family wanted an open casket funeral. Otherwise, this dude's friends and family were going to be staring at one scary expression during the funeral and viewing.

He was not a small guy. Probably over six feet tall, maybe getting close to 6'4" or 6'5", and big, not skinny and bony. His body was all curled in on itself, like whatever incubus or succubus that had done the job had forced him into the corner and kept him there, trapped, as they ripped the life and soul out of his body. Judging by the expression, he'd felt every second of it.

"Victim's name is Adam Perry," the lady cop said. "Resident of Edinburgh. Hadn't been reported missing yet, as it seems he doesn't live with his family."

"He looks young," I said. "Young enough to be out on his own, living the good life." I wondered what the hell the good life was, having not really tasted it myself. "What did he do for work?"

"Worked in a shop part-time, I guess," she said, holding up a pocket notepad. "According to the PC who interviewed his mum."

"So the family knows?" I asked, staring at the earthly remains of Adam Perry with more than a little pity.

"Aye," she said. "They're grieving, I'd imagine. They've no

idea who might have done it, though. As I said, he didn't live with them. Had some roommate though, apparently, and they haven't been talked to yet, either."

I frowned. "Because you can't locate them?"

"Aye," she said. "Nobody's home at his flat."

"I'll need the address for his residence and his mom's—err, mum's," I corrected, causing the lady cop to frown at my slip, "residence." I forgot everyone called moms mums around here, like they were a flower.

"Aye," she said again, scribbling something in her notebook and then tearing out the page and handing it to me.

"So, just to recap," I said, pocketing the note, "we have no idea what the victim was doing in his last hours—other than when he ended up here, probably screaming based on that look on his face." The lady cop shuddered at my diagnosis. "We have no idea how he met his killer, and…do we have any idea how any of the other victims met their killers? Is there a pattern?"

She shrugged. "We weren't even certain there was a killer until recently. These deaths…the pathologists can't mark them as anything other than unnatural, mysterious. It's not as though they've got a gaping stab wound in the side of their head, or they're missing a liver, or they've been given a Glesga smile." I interpreted that last word to mean Glasgow since I was very familiar with the term 'Glasgow smile,' being something of a sick puppy who dealt with even sicker ones. "There's no clear mark here, or at least not one we've been able to see until one of our boys in the lab tumbled to this—this metahuman business going on." Here she evinced some distaste that was evident in the way she said the mere word 'metahuman,' like it was some sort of bitter curse. Which, to someone who had no good experiences with my kind…it reasonably was. "Are you seeing a lot of this type of thing lately? Metahuman stuff?"

"More and more," I said. It was true, after a fashion. There was a rising number of metas in the US, and I had no reason to believe the same wasn't, perhaps, true here across the pond in the UK. After all, why would the nation of Revelen choose to upset the proverbial apple cart of order only in one country or the other when they could destabilize the whole world? "You getting many meta crimes outside of this? You know, lately?"

"Seems to be rising," she said, intent look on her face as she stared at Adam Perry's contorted face. "Got a reason for that? Because I'd heard metahumans were nearly wiped out, at least according to that last president over in the US when he blew the lid on all this…" I sensed she was going to say something stronger, but she finished with "business" again. Better than 'garbage' or 'bullshit,' I supposed.

"No clue," I lied. "Way above my pay grade."

She snorted. "Well, if the Londoner doesn't know it, I suppose no one does." She seemed to be trying really hard to control herself after spitting that out, but I caught a metric ton of irony all strung through her statement, and a pretty decent amount of derision in the term 'Londoner.'

"I should probably get on with this, then," I said, taking a gander at the paper she'd handed me. "Unless there's anything else you want to point out here?" She shrugged, like she was done with me, but then there was a catch in her expression, like she thought of something. "What?" I asked, curious.

"It's probably nothing," she said, dismissing herself more than me.

"No, I'm curious. What?" I genuinely was.

She seemed to take my interest with a bit of skepticism. "I've probably watched too many of those TV programs about serial killers, but…" She looked around, as though we were being eavesdropped on by someone outside the vault. Apparently satisfied that no one was going to hear her thought, she continued in a whisper. "It's kind of an odd place to drop this one though, isn't it? In the middle of a graveyard?"

"You're thinking it might have some symbolism?" I asked. "Death among the dead?"

I could see the very slight enthusiasm she had for the theory cool in her eyes. "When you say it like that, I suppose it sounds foolish."

"You could be right. It's hard to say." I folded my arms. "Were any of the other victims found in a graveyard?"

"No," she said, shaking her head. "Apartments, in shops, in alleys…wherever was convenient, I imagine."

"Probably not a hidden meaning in this one, then," I said with a forced smile. If she was disappointed that I'd taken the air out of her theory, she hid it well. I started to leave, offering this as my parting wisdom: "To paraphrase Freud, 'Sometimes a corpse is just a corpse.'"

"Well, this fellow is leaving kind of a lot of them around here," she called after me, apparently quite content to stay with the dead. "I hope you do something about him."

"Oh, I will," I said, emerging back into the clouded sunlight and picking my path out of the graveyard, heading along the path to the wall and the gate, which was blocked by the other cop who was watching me make my way toward him. "I always do."

13.

The thing that I could tell was going to suck about solving a crime like this in a smaller city like Edinburgh was the travel time. In a big city like London or New York, I could fly everywhere, knowing I'd be seen but equally certain that if I was seen, the cops had sooooooo many places to go looking for me that I could linger around for a while, playing my "hide and change on rooftops" trick for days and days without my schtick wearing thin.

Edinburgh was a lot smaller than either of those metropolises though, and thus, as I was flying overhead, like a bird, or a plane, I garnered a lot more attention because the buildings weren't that big and neither were the city bounds. I'd read it had a population around 1.3 million for the metro, and that was a pretty small haystack in which to hide the flying, fire-shooting needle that was Sienna Nealon, especially when I was trying to solve a crime while undercover.

And so I swore, as I flew toward the address on my GPS, the one where Adam Perry's mother was probably crying big fat tears right now, I probably was going to have to start taking local transit rather than making my life easy and convenient by jetting from place to place. Such was the problem with smaller city life, and woe was me for having to take the damned bus. Succubus on a bus? More like, "suck you, bus." Bleh.

I crossed the city, heading past the castle and jetting south toward a newer district of town. I kept low, which was difficult because being built somewhat on a hill, the altitude changes when I came over the central hillock where the castle rested meant I had to partake in a dive toward the rooftops to try and keep my exposure to a minimum. I was pretty sure people below, on the streets, were probably seeing me zoom overhead, and that was annoying.

But then I saw a shock of red hair on a rooftop out of my peripheral vision, and someone waving at me, and that kinda drove home the point, for good, that flying was right out as a mode of transportation if I didn't want to completely blow my cover to tiny, infinitesimally small pieces.

I sighed as I set down in the southern portion of the city, by a totally different castle parked in the middle of a city block just below what looked like it must have been the old town. It had turrets, a big bell tower in the middle, and a sign that declared it was Heriot's, whatever that meant.

Across the street there was a newer building, the kind of seventies glass monstrosity that embraced a square box aesthetic, which was, incidentally, a sort of look I hated a lot. I emerged out onto a street from an alley after jumping a wrought-iron fence, my wig firmly back on my head and as straight as I could make it.

The bustle of the city at midday was not quite chaos, but it wasn't a placid country road, either. There were people moving to and fro up and down the street, and I saw the street sign on the corner of the building nearby that the English (and apparently Scots) favored over the freestanding signs we Americans preferred. Lauriston Place, it read. Well, I was in the right place, or at least close, I reflected as I consulted my GPS.

It suggested I needed to go a couple blocks west, and I heeded its advice, passing old residential buildings that had been here for an indeterminate period of time. Hundreds of years, for all I knew. Once a building got past a certain age, I could only diagnose them as old, and these looked kinda…well, old.

Some of them were obviously apartments, or flats as they called them over here. Three to four stories, with that weathered look of grey stone up top and a whiter stone to facade the first floor. They had numbers, fortunately, and I read them off like a silent countdown until the GPS indicated I'd arrived at my destination. My stomach rumbled as I stood on the doorstep outside Adam Perry's mother's flat and announced my presence with a heavy knock.

I could hear Ms. Perry's movement inside before the lock clicked and the door opened. Standing there was a woman who was very slight, unlike her son, cheeks and eyes red from the trauma of the morning's events and news. My heart went out to her, but I kept my composure and said, "Ms. Perry? My name is Sarah Nelson. I'm the investigator from Scotland Yard."

"Oh," she said, and crumpled a little bit, like my mere presence was a fresh stab wound. Hell, it probably was.

"I just need to talk to you for a minute," I said in my quietest, most sympathetic voice. "I'll make it quick." *Harmon,* I said in my head, *let's make it quick for the sake of this poor woman?*

Aye, Harmon said in a terrible Scottish accent of his own, way heavier on the brogue than anything I'd heard in Edinburgh thus far.

Ms. Perry invited me in, reluctantly, allowing me to pass through the blue door that served like a shield between us. I tried not to be too abrupt or invasive or whatever, but just being here made me feel like an intruder in her grief, and I hated it.

"When was the last time you saw your son?" I asked, delicately, while hoping that Harmon would dump her memory for anything super important so we could GTFO ASAP.

"The day before yesterday he popped by for tea," she said with a sniffle. "After work, ye know."

"And he worked at…?" I prompted her.

"One of the tourist shops up on the Royal Mile. Not too far from Scottish Parliament and Holyrood House." She sniffled, dabbing at her eyes with a tissue that had seen better days. "He sold kilts and kitsch to tourists." She was clearly holding back a desire to weep, probably for my benefit. And I appreciated it; raw displays of human emotion, especially sorrow, got under my skin like little else.

"Did he have any enemies?" This was probably the stupidest question I could ask, since he had putatively been killed by a serial killer. Assuming a random choice of victims, Adam Perry's biggest sin was probably being in the wrong place at the wrong time. But even serial killers had grudges they wanted to settle, and occasionally you'd find one that had a clearly drawn motive for killing the people they chose.

"Everyone loved him," she said, shoulders heaving as she continued to contain that emotion.

I didn't challenge this hagiography, and after a moment Harmon said, *She believes this is true. She doesn't know of anyone who would have wished him ill, at least not on the level of malice required for murder.*

Does that mean she knows someone who was otherwise disgruntled with him? I asked.

I pulled a list of names, Harmon said. *But based on what I'm seeing, at least her knowledge of the conflicts, there's not much here to concern yourself with. I'll keep it for you if you want to poke at any of them later.*

Thanks, I said, and aloud, "Do you know what Adam's daily schedule was like? Did he go out anywhere at night?" I'd forgotten to ask the cops at the scene if anyone knew a time of death on him, which was something I'd need to ask the coroner later. They probably already had one estimated, if I had to guess, and just based on what I'd seen of the corpse, I would have guessed between 10 pm last night and 4 am this morning. Wide window, but it was better than one that judged to days.

"He went out some, yes," she said, bristling, like I was attacking his reputation. "He was young."

"Did he have any pubs or clubs that he…favored?" I asked. Getting an idea of places he might have frequented could open the door to a hunting ground this killer was using to select their prey. That'd be a hell of a boon in my search.

"I'm afraid nae," she said, her head sagging. "I…I did not ask."

"All right," I said, mentally narrowing down the list. "What about friends? Who were his closest ones? I might need to talk to them."

She sniffled slightly. "I give a list to the nice constable who stopped by. I suppose I could make it up again—"

"There's no need if you're already done it once," I said, and to Harmon: *Get the list.*

Already "downloaded," as it were. His closest friend worked with him at the tourist trap on the main stretch of road in this flea town. So thankful I never had to make a state visit here.

You're such an ass, Harmon. It seems nice so far. Then, back to Ms. Perry: "I've taken up enough of your time, ma'am. I'm so sorry for your loss."

She nodded at me, red eyes so swollen I thought they would explode the moment I left her flat. Out the door I went, apologizing and offering condolences as she nodded and made a squeaking noise in her throat that suggested her emotions were reaching critical mass and she was not going to be able to hold them in much longer. For the sake of her dignity, I sighed in relief as she closed the door on me, a little more abrupt than was perhaps polite, but judging by the sobs that strained their way through afterward, I couldn't find it in my heart to blame her.

So saddddd, Eve said, almost crowing.

"Shut up, Eve," I snapped. "Don't you have any humanity?"

Why…no. I think you took it along with my body and my life.

Don't let her fool you, Sienna, Bastian said, and I could sense his smile. *She didn't have all that much before she died.*

"It has been a while, and I've obviously known her longer in my head than I ever did IRL, but I do recall that, Roberto."

I walked down the Edinburgh street, catching a few stray looks either because I was talking to myself or because my blond wig commanded attention. It definitely wasn't because of my height, which was average for a woman, or my looks, because the attention I was getting was the type of brow-furrowed looks that said, "That girl is crazy," and not, "That girl is crazy *fine*!"

At the nearest alley I dodged inside, just across the street from a hospital. I made a mental note of its location because I figured I'd end up sending someone to it at some point, and it felt like a point of interest I should know on that basis alone.

Once I was in the alley, I tried to get my bearings, figure out where I'd left my bag of goodies. I'd tagged the location on the map app, which was good, because although my memory was decent, unfamiliar cities were kind of my kryptonite, at least from a rooftop perspective. They all tended to look somewhat the same, at least in Europe, a strange kind of uniformity of architectural style that looked nice but made it a real hell to navigate by air sometimes.

Stuffing my wig in the inside pocket of my coat, I looked left and right down the alley. A light rain was falling, sprinkling my skin, but not really enough to even wet my hair effectively. "Come on, Scotland," I muttered, "you can do better than this."

I rose into the air and started to orient myself to fly toward the castle again. I'd absorbed enough about the layout of the city to know that the touristy stuff was definitely near the castle, down the road that practically led out its gate, so that seemed like the place to start. My stomach rumbled again, and I realized that I kinda needed breakfast. Well, lunch now, I supposed. Still felt like breakfast time because it was…back home.

My next move—after breakfast or lunch or whatever they served here—was going to be doing some old-fashioned investigating. And I didn't mean drinking an Old-Fashioned while sitting around thinking. I sighed as I rose, wishing I could just call Jamal or J.J., but unfortunately the only way I had to communicate with them now was dreamwalking, and it being morning in America right now, I was unlikely to get a response, even on the off-chance I could have fallen asleep.

As I reached rooftop height I saw a flash of movement, a blaze of red hair and someone shouted, "Sienna!" as I went past.

Shit.

Someone knew I was here.

14.

I flew around hard in a loop, circling the building and watching for attack from below or above. Usually when someone shouted my name these days, bad things tended to follow, like bullets and explosions.

None of those came winging my way; just the continuing light rain that was now beginning to wet my hair as I made my circle around the building where someone had shouted at me as I passed out of the wet alleyway. Looking down, I could see the person who'd commanded my attention, just standing on the rooftop and waving like a maniac—with both hands, like she was on a desert island and signaling a plane for rescue.

I can usually tell when someone's attacking me or of a mind to by the fact that they've got a gun, or an expression like they're biting down on a rancid beet. Their body language, their facial expression, they're all a dead giveaway when someone intends you harm.

This gal, though…her body language suggested she might just pee herself in excitement at the mere sight of me.

What the hell. I was already getting wet anyway.

I came down to the rooftop slowly, the redhead waiting below coming into focus for me the closer I drifted to her. I kept a nice distance, about twenty feet or so, at the least. "Hello," I said coolly.

"Ohmigosh," she said in a light Scottish accent, and her voice told me she was just as pleased as punch to see me. She blushed wildly. "I can't believe it's really ye." Yeah, she said 'ye.' Her accent was a little heavier than the other Scots I'd met thus far in Edinburgh, but not indecipherable. "I mean, I saw ye fly over before, but just—so quick—I thought maybe my eyes were deceiving me."

"Nope. Your eyes are firmly telling you the truth. Still, presumably," I said, trying to gauge this person who'd flagged me down. I had a feeling it was someone who'd want me to sign her yearbook. Or maybe something more private and awkward.

"I am such a huge fan of yours," she gushed. "I saw you over there—" she pointed back toward the castle, where I'd flown over before "—and I followed. I'm sorry. I just—this is Edinburgh, we don't get that much excitement around here, at least not since they finished filming the Avengers movies here."

What do you even say to something like that? "Uhh… that's nice…"

"I'm so sorry; I'm making a right fool of meself," she gushed, pale skin flushing to the roots of her red hair. She covered her mouth in both hands and went chokingly silent for a moment. I was just about to ask her if she was okay when she squeaked. "So sorry."

Harmon stirred in my mind. *I can't read her.* He was calm at first, then, *Uhm…this is bad.*

Stifle yourself, Gerry, I said, and then, to her, "What's your name?"

"Rose," she said, flushing deeper, which I had not believed possible. "Rose Steward. I'm—I'm just such a fan, you have no idea. I was, uhm…manifesting right around the time you—came out, I guess you could say. I was so confused, and just…unsure of my place in the world. And all the sudden on TV, there's this girl who—she's got powers, like I had powers—and it was like, uhm…someone shining a light on me, like a voice telling me—I'm not that weird—I'm not alone in this, totally—" She went a deeper hue of red and fell silent for a moment. "I'm sorry. That probably sounds—so bloody stupid to ye—"

"Ah, no," I harrumphed, trying to control myself, my emotions, because she'd, uhm…stirred a few. I remembered really well what it had been like at the Directorate, a freak in the middle of a sea of people who seemed to have a really good lid on their own powers, their own weirdness. It was part of them in a way that it was alien to me, which made me feel like even more of an outcast. "No, it doesn't sound stupid at all."

"Well, enough about me," she said, finally returning to her regularly scheduled shade of milky pale. I could empathize with that too, because it was my shade as well. "What brings the great Sienna Nealon to Scotland?" She put what was, to her, probably an appropriate amount of awe into her question. Unfortunately for those of us not so enamored with me, it sounded…uh…worshipful.

"Business," I said tightly. I wasn't ready to give away the farm on this just yet, especially to a total stranger. "What kind of meta are you, Rose?"

"Empath," she said, going red again. "When I found out who ye were—well, it's—never mind." Her redness cleared. "You know, whatever business you're here on, maybe I could…give ye a hand—"

"I don't think so," I said, drifting a few more feet away from her in order to give the psychological impression that the request had pushed me away, because…well, it had. We'd been having a nice polite conversation at a safe distance, and then she'd basically made a request to get closer to me, one which I immediately answered by getting farther away. It didn't take a PhD in behavioral psychology to work out the obvious sign behind that movement.

She took a step forward, apparently missing the carefully buried symbolism in my movement. "But—I'm dead useful—"

"I'm sure you are," I said, "but I'm worried you'd just end up dead, and useful to no one, because that is a thing that happens to people around me sometimes." Her face couldn't have fallen any harder if it had leapt off the top of the castle with her attached to it. "I'm sorry, Rose. I work alone. And…I'm probably not who you think I am in your mind."

"You're a hero," she said in worshipful tones, like she was about to take a knee and throw a prayer at me as though we were in Ancient Greece and I was one of the old gods.

"I'm a fugitive from justice, actually," I said. "I've caught more bullets than a backstop at the FBI range. Been burned more times than the collective crotches at an LA wax parlor." I cringed. Where the hell did that come from?

Rose made a funny face at that one, too. "All…right…"

"The point is," I said, quickly getting back on track, "I work alone. And I'm sure you've got a life to attend to, so…" I shrugged, and started to rise into the air, intent to get back to breakfast and then catching a murderer. "So long, Rose." I waved.

"Wait!" she called after me, but the wind stole the next thing she was going to say. I didn't dare look back, for fear of encouraging her; just turned my back on this girl who admired me, and flew for the High Street up on the hill.

15.

I found a breakfast place—well, a cafe that served breakfast among other things—and sat down inside the sparely appointed dining space, waiting for them to bring me my food. I'd ordered a standard Scottish breakfast, figuring I'd try some of the local cuisine, and while I was waiting I sat in silence in the empty cafe, listening to the owner grouse at the young man who'd taken my order as he did a fry-up or whatever they call it when they make breakfast.

You know, Harmon said, once again taking up the role of meddler-in-charge in my head, *you could have not shut the door quite so hard on that poor girl.*

I didn't roll my eyes at him, but only because the server was crossing the cafe right then on his way to the front door and I didn't want him to think I was being a huge jaghole for no reason, so I smiled tightly to keep up appearances. *I'm getting sparkling personality advice from you now, Harmon? The man who never gave a damn about another living soul?*

That hurts, he said, though he plainly wasn't hurting much as he said it. *I tried to save the world, I'll have you know.*

I'm sure Wolfe was trying to save the world, too, I said, *one partially digested human carcass at a time. Not even a grunt from the old boy. Man, he must have been really up his own ass today.*

Well, what are you trying to do? Harmon asked, keeping his tone quite level given that I'd just insulted Mr. World-Saver President by comparing him to a prolific serial killer. *Solve a local murder. But you don't want local help?*

You couldn't read her mind, I said. *You really want someone around whose mind you can't read?*

Oh, please, Harmon said. *You saw this poor, sad little puppy, didn't you? That girl had no capacity to lie. If you'd set down on the rooftop next to her, she'd have been beset by a severe case of incontinence all over your boots.*

"These are new," I said, "so I guess it's good I kept to the air." Realizing I'd just spoken aloud to an empty room, I shut my mouth and bit my lip to keep it from happening again.

You could have used some local intel, Bastian added, apropos of being an interfering busybody dickhead.

And you could use a muzzle, I offered in return.

You lack the desire to hurt us that you once had, Eve opined, because why not? I wasn't actually muzzling anyone, and hadn't for a long time.

Remember the good old days when she used to suppress us with narcotics? Gavrikov asked. *Or simply lock us in that mental box she'd constructed.*

"Good times," I muttered, then bit my lip again.

You have too much heart for that now, Harmon said. *You got in touch with your humanity.*

Talk about the top of a long list of regrets, I said.

Maybe you should have been a little nicer to the girl, Zack offered.

Et tu, Zachary? I sniped back at him. He just shrugged. *What is the deal with all of you today? I'm trying to catch a serial killer here. This isn't a time for me to get all lovey dovey with the hero-worshipping natives in the local population. That's a good way to get that poor girl killed like—well, like any of you. Or Breandan. Or Mom. Or—*

Yes, we know, Harmon said. *Long list of dead bodies.*

Mostly my enemies, thankfully, I said. *But still…this poor girl? She has no idea what she'd be getting herself into.* I shifted uncomfortably on the hard chair. *Hell, I don't know what she'd be getting into, except that there's a serial killer somewhere at the bottom of this. That's probably not healthy for most people.*

Metahumans are not most people, Bjorn chimed in, because it was clearly asshole day. *You need to begin thinking about your legacy.*

That was the most absurd thing I'd ever heard, especially coming from him, and I was pretty glad that the owner was back in the kitchen doing his cooking and not visible where he could see my face, because he would probably have thought I was having a damned spasm or something. *Really, Bjorn? You're going to talk to me about legacy? What the hell did you leave behind in—five hundred or a thousand or however many years you lived? Other than a mess and a crap-ton of victims, I'm hard-pressed to figure out what kind of mark you left on the world. I mean, your brothers are known, and, like, legends, but who the hell are you? Really, I mean. No one remembers Bjorn Odinson—*

I left my legacy out there, Bjorn said with a deep-seated sense of satisfaction that stirred a sense of nausea in me as the owner emerged from the kitchen and set a plate in front of me with a grunt. Eggs, the yolks hard like they'd been fried to death, a couple of big, greasy sausages that I immediately slid to the far end of the plate. Yorkshire black pudding, which I also slid to the far end of the plate, intent on not eating it since it was, in fact, a blood sausage (I looked it up on Wikipedia last time I'd had one and found it gross). That left the fried tomato, some mushrooms, my haggis, which I'd wanted to at least try, as well as something they'd called a "tattie scone." It looked the most appealing, so I ignored the harrumphs of Bjorn in my head as he puffed up himself about his legacy or some such bullshit and took a bite.

I was in instant heaven. It was rich and buttery and delicious, like the Scandinavian dish lefse, a potato bread that you ate with cinnamon and butter, a Minnesota staple—except this was about a thousand times better. "Ermagerd," I muttered between bites, "I need these in my life. How are tattie scones not a thing the world over?"

Try the haggis, Bjorn muttered with a snicker.

I shrugged and did. "Not bad," I said.

It's sheep's heart, liver and lungs, he said, guffawing loudly within me.

You think I didn't know that? I directed this thought at him with a heavy load of amusement and it shut him up. *Please, Bjorn. I once chewed up a human being in my dragon mouth. You think a sheep's stomach is going to make me queasy? Haggis is like that little piece of Minnesotan insanity, lutefisk. Except lutefisk is even more disgusting—*

What's this...lutefisk? Gavrikov asked.

It's fish aged in lye, I said. *Minnesotans eat it at Christmas. Old Viking tradition, supposedly from back when they'd get raided. They'd take their fish and dip it in lye so that it was so disgusting no raider would dare take it, and instead sate themselves by pillaging the women of the village and eating the kids or something, I dunno.*

That sounds appropriately revolting, Harmon said.

It kind of reminds of a death cult thing, honestly, I said. *They want you to try it, but I don't think anyone really enjoys it; they just sort of eat it to prove their group insanity.*

I scarfed down the rest of the tattie scone while the voices in my head argued about the most disgusting cuisine choices they'd ever tried. Wolfe, thankfully, was silent, because he would have been the winner in a walk, I was sure, leaving the rest of us as big-time losers in that discussion.

Speaking of...I was just about to wonder what was up with Wolfe, so uncharacteristically silent, when the bell at the door tinkled and what I can only describe as five toughs—or tough guys—came strolling in.

Unlike Rose and her clear lack of aggression, these guys were full of it from feet to neck. And they weren't just directing it aimlessly, like guys looking to cause trouble. Their body language screamed one thing, because they were all tense, shoulders hunched, their gazes flitting but focused on one centering point—

Me.

"Well, hell," I muttered to my plate, "I didn't want the sausage, the blood sausage, the eggs, the fried tomato, the— you know what, this Scottish breakfast is really a mixed bag. But the mushrooms were good, and so was the toast, and the haggis decent—but that tattie scone—"

The toughs were sharing cool looks among themselves, not saying a word, like they were able to communicate telepathically. Which prompted this gem from Harmon:

Sienna...these aren't ordinary thugs.

I looked them over. They seemed exceedingly average, maybe even a little below. I couldn't even pick out a ringleader, just one guy in a knee-length coat that was holding himself awkwardly. Not like flasher or pervert awkwardly, just...stiff. "I'll say. Look at these clowns. They're like a bunch of losers that wandered in out of the junkyard after they got bored sodomizing each other with old struts—"

No, Harmon said, and the alarm in the president's voice sent a chill through me in the warm cafe, *their minds...I can't read them, either.*

16.

The bell above the cafe's door jingled a little as one of the toughs jostled it. It clanged through the confined space, a sound that focused my attention on the matter at hand—my imminent attack from these brutes.

You're having a rough day in regards to reading minds, I said to Gerry Harmon, in my head. *First Rose and now them? Are the two related?*

No, he said. *I could tell if it was an empath involved in this; they're like a black hole. This is...different. Their minds are fragmented and—just bizarre, like trying to read a book through a crystalline glass. I'm not getting anything that makes sense.*

"Uh huh," I said aloud, mostly because it caused the toughs to look around, disoriented by my inner monologue brought to life. They were trading glances, looking for the action that would send them into motion. It'd be like pulling a trigger, and when it was tugged, these jackasses would all spring into motion at once, like balloons during a balloon drop.

Except they'd all be heading for me.

I had a plan to deal with that, though. I was still seated, because I figured standing up would be the thing that pulled that trigger, and I was waiting because it lost me nothing to try and get a full read on the situation and let things unfold in due time. It gave me more time to plan, which revealed insights like:

In this situation, a confined cafe on the Royal Mile in

Edinburgh, using Gavrikov's flame blasts would likely result in the entire place going up, probably faster than I—or the Edinburgh fire department—could put it out. Which would be bad for the cafe owner, bad for the street, and probably bad for me since I was trying not to cause a stir.

For similar reasons, going dragon was right out. Not that I was ever eager to pull that particular dragon rabbit out of my hat, and not just because it ruined whatever clothing I might be wearing at the time. Though with my reduced wardrobe, that was a concern, no lie.

Telepathy, my newest ace card, had also been pulled from the deck, which was annoying. *Have you ever run across anything like this before?* I asked Harmon.

No, he said flatly. *This is new.*

And you're sure it's nothing to do with an empath's ability to block your powers?

No, he said again. There was certainty, which was nice, because the thought that Rose had betrayed me after I'd known her for all of five seconds…well, that would have hurt. Mostly her, when I beat her sensitive little hero-worshipping ass, but it would have hurt. Also my knuckles, probably. Because punching like a champ does not come without some cost.

In terms of available options, this left Bjorn's mind games—assuming they'd work where telepathy didn't—the Wolfe strength, which was handy for ass beatings, and Eve's light nets, which were the best non-lethal weapon in my arsenal.

"Okay," I said as these boys started to edge closer and closer to my corner table, taking a wide set of approach vectors so that they came at my corner table from all the available angles, "what can I do for you fellas? You want a little blood sausage?" They didn't say anything. "Or just blood?"

They angled closer, and the communication between them had ceased, just stopped like they no longer had the ability to turn their heads. I took them all in with a careful glance. If they were humans, this would be relatively easy. If they were metahumans, on the other hand…

Well, this would get messy. Really, really messy.

The one with the long coat was closing on me, right in the middle of the pack. The one closest on the far right intersected a table and chairs along his path and reached out, flipping it out of the way with a hard push that sent it out the front window.

It was easy for him. Like tossing an apple over his shoulder.

Shit.

Metas. Or at least one.

I decided that another step closer was too much to allow from these guys now that I knew they had powers, so at last I whipped my hand up to start the fight, and shit kinda flew off the chain in earnest, a few things happening all at once.

Aiming low with my right hand, I launched a light net that caught the meta who'd just tossed the table right across the knees. It wrapped him up like one of those bolas in the old cartoons, and his arms pinwheeled comically while his eyes grew to the size of hubcaps. I didn't wait for the fall, because I was already launching another one, this one out of my left hand and at the guy who'd sauntered between me and the outcrop of wall that sheltered the kitchen from public view. It caught him right in the middle of the chest and plastered him, hands crossed over his heart, against said wall, a dark spot on the drab yellow paint.

Swiveling my attention between the extreme right and extreme left of the attack was kinda risky, yet, I deemed, kind of important. Now I was left with three foes, and all of them were squarely in the center of my vision. No flanking risk, which was just as dangerous to me as it was to anyone, because although unlikely, I could still be killed by a really well-placed punch to the back or side of the head.

Or worse, I realized, as the guy in the middle, the one with the long coat, swept a shotgun out of the depths of his long coat at metahuman speed. He raised the barrel so that I could look right down it for the briefest of seconds before I saw the flash as it fired, and at this range…I knew it wouldn't miss.

17.

Wolfe

Republic of Athens, Greece
453 B.C.

The air was hot and thick and heavy, warm like blood sliding down Wolfe's skin. He was crouched, shoulders hunched, the smell of prey in his nostrils. This was as it should have been—no cave, no grinding flesh against rocks. This was the way of the Wolfe—to hunt, to feed, to kill.

They were lingering in a copse of trees, green cover and underbrush keeping them well hidden as they watched the movement at a spring ahead. The water tinkled lightly, a quiet noise pervading Wolfe's consciousness. A breeze rolled through, rattling branches and swishing the leaves.

The daughter of death waited silent just ahead of him. She didn't hunt on all fours, but she was near-silent in movement, a quiet that even Wolfe could appreciate. She'd shed the rags that she'd worn in the caves, dirty, naked flesh unashamedly on display without care for how it looked or how Wolfe leered at her. He couldn't help it. She wasn't a prey animal as the others were, a thing to be destroyed, used, eaten, cast away. There was something about her…

She caught his gaze flitting over her, cold iron look that directed his own away, back to the thoughts of the matters at hand. The smell of prey filled his nose again as he concentrated, leaving the scent of her sweat, her body, out of his mind.

He wrinkled his nose. This was not the prey he would have preferred, but…at least it would be fresh blood, fresh meat.

The daughter of death reached up, taking hold of the tree branch above. Silently, she climbed, bough after bough, dirt-streaked skin rising above him as she strained to lift herself up without making noise from rubbing her feet against the branches. Wolfe watched carefully, waiting for her to look at him so he could swiftly turn away.

She did not look, though. She was far, far too intent on her prey, ahead, at the banks of the spring.

It was a stag, antlers high and wide, an impressive trophy for men, presumably. Wolfe had no interest in trophies. If he had, his chamber in the cave of Hades would have been filled to the brimming with human skulls. Servants would not have been able to walk in without bones crunching underfoot—already a peril.

The daughter of death balanced expertly upon a branch above, testing it with her weight. She stood extending her hands out, perfectly balanced as she walked along its length to a point where it began to bow, the first signs of strain presenting themselves. She stopped there, bare feet perched expertly as if tethered to the tree branch, knees slightly bent, the light, curly, dirt-streaked hairs that covered her legs up to her bottom standing on end as she waited, tensed, on the bough.

It came in an instant. She dove and landed on the back of the hart before it could scarcely stiffen its body. Wolfe cringed slightly at the impact. It had surely not been without discomfort, that landing.

Anchoring her hands to the sides of the stag's neck, the daughter of death held on as it reared back on two legs, fearful noise stampeding forth out of its nose and open mouth.

Wolfe bounded ahead, the sign given, and slashed one of the does that had been lapping up water at the edge of the spring. It took two steps and folded, guts squirming from the wound like worms as it collapsed from his strike. It tried to stand again but faltered, landing on its face as he sprang forward, ready to aid his charge.

But she seemed not to need it. The stag was already faltering on its back legs, and as it fell he saw its head hung at a strange angle. She hadn't even waited for her power to work, assuming it even did on such lesser creatures. She'd seized it by the antlers and broken its neck.

"Halt!" a high voice screamed at the edge of a thicket across the spring. A rustling came, and a moment later a woman emerged with a fine spear, hunting leathers covering her taut body. Wolfe went to all fours by instinct. Seeing her spear, and a bow slung across her back, he could sense the conflict brewing and did not wish to chance it unwinding into a fight without him being ready for it.

The daughter of death tensed as well, her kill clutched in her hands. Wolfe could read the lines of her body in that movement, catlike and ready. If the woman with the spear chose to throw it, the daughter of death was prepared to raise the stag as a shield in front of her. It was a canny move, and Wolfe prepared himself to advance if needed, to kill the woman with the spear before she could unsling her bow.

"Who are you?" the woman asked. "Who are you to hunt these grounds?" Her manner was brusque, tense, and she held herself stiff and steady, the spear high and ready to loose. Wolfe recalled her voice from days past, and a slow dawning of recognition trickled over him, though he did not stand.

The woman's gaze flitted from the daughter of death, tensed over her kill, to Wolfe himself. At the sight of him she did not relax, nor barely even acknowledge him. "A dog of death, is it? One of the three brothers? The cerberus?"

"You know who I am, then," Wolfe growled. "And I know you as well, huntress Artemis."

"You have no license to be here, dog," Artemis said, a low fury matching Wolfe's growl. She was no light goddess, ready to shrink from violence. She was the Goddess of the Hunt, and she knew the threat she'd seen displayed here. Her spear throw would certainly pierce through the stag; she would see to it. Wolfe was leery, now. If it had been just him and the goddess, perhaps she'd be dinner, but given this…situation…

"*She* has reason to be here," Wolfe said. The daughter of death was still frozen in place, ready to move, ready to defend, probably prepared to counter attack once the spear had been loosed. He had his doubts that it would miss, given Artemis's power of reflex. She did not miss, as far as he knew, and she would not waste her spear on him now that she knew who he was. "This is a daughter of Hades."

"Then she, too, should be in your realm of caves," Artemis said, the fury in her voice giving way to a hard iron. Her resolve was unwavering, and this would not go…well, Wolfe reflected, a slow ebb of worry, nearly unfamiliar to him, bubbling up like the waters of the spring.

"You have no right to deny a goddess her kill," Wolfe said, trying so very hard to find words that would not further inflame the situation. "She is not a mere human trespassing on your lands. She is a child of Hades, one of your own, whether you like to admit it or not, whether you shun her and all her kin—"

"I am aware of what she is," Artemis said, the tension ready to spring loose like a taut rope. "Of who her father is. There is a reason you were sent to those caves—"

Wolfe's mind raced. "Not all were sent." If he could not stop this nascent conflict, the daughter of death would surely take a spear, perhaps a fatal one. Hades would be… displeased, and further, he would have to kill Artemis upon the spot, which would doubtless cause…conflicts with the other gods. "Her mother is Persephone. Persephone was not exiled."

Artemis turned her head and her full attention to Wolfe for the first time since this had begun. She measured him, saw him, and he could sense the fear behind her eyes that he had missed before, when she had failed to look at him. Within them he could see her own worry. That a daughter of death had gone beyond the bounds she thought proper was perhaps worrisome, but Artemis must have known that her throwing of spears or slinging of stones or hailing of arrows could not stop him. It was all there, right on her face beneath the high cheekbones, along with something else, some other worry—an advantage she held in reserve, but was now unwilling to play, perhaps…

Wolfe sniffed. There was other prey here, and he could sense it. He did not dare to smile, did not dare to make this a threat other than veiled. "Surely you must realize, Goddess of the Hunt," Wolfe said, patronizing her with her title, "the lengths to which Hades would go to avenge a daughter."

Artemis stiffened, eyes catching ablaze like dead brush on a hot, windy night. "You would dare threaten—"

The brush rustled to Wolfe's right, and there was a girl, no more than seventeen, only a shade younger than the daughter of death. Her face was hard as carved marble and her bow was drawn back, ready to loose in Wolfe's very ear. That would undoubtedly hurt, possibly even kill him. It was very canny, and as he looked sidelong at the new threat, he tried very hard not to pay it much attention. This was not a fight that they would win by fighting. "He would die," the girl said, her own muscles as tight as Artemis's, her voice confident and strong, the unchallenged, undoubting words of a teenager who had yet to collide with hard reality.

Wolfe looked at the girl out of the corner of his eye. That was what she was: a girl, no more, really. He would have to throw himself sideways, into the arrow, and hope to absorb it somewhere he could take it. He'd not practiced taking arrows, and it might pierce him. If it did so through the head, he had to hope that it would be a non-fatal wound, something he could quickly heal from. He was under no illusions, though—this girl would probably kill him, which meant he would need his vengeful, parting strike to kill her, his dead hand in motion to cut her head cleanly from her body through sheer momentum even if his heart were stilled.

"Your child will die," the daughter of death said, voice a low rattle. She did not look at Artemis's daughter; she stared down Artemis herself. "She will be struck down by the hound's teeth, his claws, even should she claim his life." The way she spoke sent little chills creeping down Wolfe's naked flesh. "Do you value your daughter's life, Artemis, huntress?"

Artemis did not flinch, but there was a strange, obvious pullback, as though she recoiled within. "Of course I do," she snapped.

"Hades values his daughter as well," Wolfe said. "His vengeance…would be a terrible thing. Mine…will be more immediate."

Artemis slowly lowered her spear. "The daughter of Persephone cannot be denied the embrace of sky and earth, nor of its bounties," she said at last. "Your mother is not exiled; merely unfortunate in her spouse. And you, in your father." The huntress bristled. "'Twas not a choice for any of you, and thus we should not inflict unjust punishment as though you committed some crime. Come, daughter." She looked sternly upon her own, spear still held in a tight fist at her side, ready to be thrust up at the first hint of betrayal. "I bade you come, Diana."

There was no slack in the twine of Diana's bow. She held it steady, ready to let it loose in Wolfe's ear. "I have heard tell of this beast, mother," Diana said. "It and its brothers are a blight to our eyes and our lands."

"That may be so," Artemis said between gritted teeth, "but Zeus is a pestilence and we do not deal with him thusly."

Diana's eyes narrowed and she kept her focus perfectly honed on Wolfe. "Perhaps someone should."

"If you do," Wolfe said, lightly, "I imagine my master would gladly lend a hand in such endeavors."

The girl recoiled, slack appearing in the drawstring at last as she brought down the bow. "I would not enlist so perverse and foul an ally in any endeavor I undertook. I would sooner seek actual death than treat with Hades or his spawn." She spat for emphasis.

"You are seeking that now," the daughter of death spoke low and true.

"Come now," Artemis said, eyeing the dirty daughter of death. Wolfe watched her for malice, but even Diana began to retreat, soundless footsteps as she made her through the underbrush toward her mother without stirring so much as a leaf. Her control of her body was perfect, and she moved effortlessly, the bow still clenched in hand, arrow nocked, ready to raise should the need arise. "We need not jibe at one another."

"Your offer is fair," Wolfe said, eyeing the daughter of

death, trying to convey that message to her. Did she not realize how close they had both been to ending? Only the sanity of Artemis had prevailed over the hotter heads of these young goddesses.

"And what is your name, beast?" Artemis asked, with little heat. "Which of the three brothers are you?"

"Wolfe," he said.

"You are the Wolfe?" Artemis rippled with surprise. "I was given to believe you were the one without reason, and yet here you reason your way through this strife with a tongue of silver the like of which would impress mine own son, no stranger to such negotiations himself."

"The son of Apollo must surely be golden-tongued indeed," Wolfe said. He had not met the boy in question, though he'd heard of him. Wolfe was seething inside from the veiled insults, but would not dignify her backhanded compliment by betraying his mission now and getting the daughter of death killed.

"And what is your name, daughter of Persephone?" Artemis asked. No longer was there threat, but she still spoke warily, and never once relinquished her weapon or pointed the tip in any direction but at her perceived foes. "Tell me, so that I may let my brethren know to let you pass unimpeded in future encounters."

The daughter of death spoke quietly, when at last she broke her silence. "You may let them know of my coming, and that my name is Lethe." Artemis nodded at this, and began to withdraw from the glade, but not before the daughter of death left her with one final command, one that the goddess took without blanching, an insult that found its mark and yet still did not provoke the elder goddess to action. "Tell them of my coming, and warn them—warn them, huntress…that they should not dare to cross me, lest they find themselves in the poor graces of death."

18.

Sienna

The shotgun blast hit me right in the center of my chest, pellets tearing into my clothing and drawing from me a scream. "Aughhhhhhhh!" I shouted to the heavens, "Nooooooo! It hurrrrrts!" I howled out. "It hurrrts soooo bad! Arghhhhh!"

Your acting is terrible, Harmon said with plain irritation.

You deserve all the Razzies for that one, Eve agreed.

I clutched at my chest where the buckshot had struck me, and then pulled them away like a magician making a flourish, my three audience members staring, momentarily frozen by my display of dramatics. "Just yanking your crank, guys." Pellets tinkled to the cafe floor like rain outside. "I've built up my immunity to shotguns. Try again."

One of the three remaining guys, the one to my right, reached into his waistband and yanked out a revolver, an old one that looked like it had maybe seen better centuries.

"Shit," said I. "I thought you people didn't have guns in this countr—"

I ducked as he pulled the trigger and the revolver roared. My table went over as I tried to put it between me and him. It splintered, not exactly doing a yeoman's work in absorbing the bullet. My calf caught it instead and I let out a cry that was way, way more sincere than my fake acting at the shotgun blast. Because it hurt.

There's nothing like getting shot in the leg to focus your attention. Mostly on the pain, sure, but also on the fact that the next bullet could kill you dead, even if you're me. "The table, it does nothing," I muttered under my breath, huddled behind it uselessly. It was concealment, but damned sure not cover, because it wasn't going to protect me from anything but sunlight, which wasn't a concern in Scotland anyway.

Trying to turn lemons into lemonade, I said, "Wolfe," and didn't wait to hear if he'd pull out of his recent torpor in order to get to work pushing that bullet out of my leg. Instead, I kneed the table with the other one, hard, and sent it sliding across the floor toward my assailants.

While it did that, I used my power of flight to go real low, zipping across the floor about a half inch off the ground and into the smaller, two-person table that had been right across from where I was sitting. When I got there, I reached under the nearest chair in the set and took hold, hurling it. The table I'd thrown had forced two of my foes to jump to avoid getting kneecapped, or maybe groincapped, which would have been hilarious. This included the shooter with the revolver, thankfully.

"This girl likes it rough," said the third, appearing above me. He raised a fist and brought it down, probably attempting to cave my head in with his punch, because it whistled toward the ground like a car dropped off a roof. (I've done it. It does whistle.)

"Boy, do I," I quipped in reply as I let his momentum carry him down. He smashed his fist into the tile, where it shattered, spraying me with fragments. Sadly, not of his fist, which remained intact and apparently unharmed, judging by the fact he didn't grimace. While he was at the low point of his swing, though, I reached up and grabbed him by the cheeks and said, "A fine judge of character you are." Then I slammed his face into the ground. "Distances, maybe not so much though."

I lifted his face enough to see that he had that glazed-over look in his eyes, blinking them furiously like he could just shrug off the concussion I'd just given him. With a hearty shove—and I do mean hearty—I sent him flying through the front window without ceremony. The sound of shattering glass did my heart good, and the sight of his ass tumbling out onto the Royal Mile didn't exactly make me weep either. "Three down," I muttered.

The revolver blistered the air behind me and I caught another round, in the stomach this time. This was the price you paid for getting caught up with the unarmed, superpowered idiot while someone was trying to shoot you. Taking two slugs to the gut wasn't exactly a highlight of my career or life, but honestly, it wasn't even the worst thing that had happened to me this year.

"Asshole!" I shouted, channeling my pain into anger and whipping this table at the shooter. He and the guy holding the shotgun were still in the fight, and I got a bad feeling that since I hadn't heard the shotgun discharge lately but the guy was still holding it, that it was going to be used as a club to beat me to death. It'd probably be good for that, too, because it was useless for anything else presently.

The searing sensation tearing its way through my belly reminded me of a time when Wolfe had stuck a finger in my guts and lifted me up. They say a stomach wound is one of the most painful ways to die, and I could vouch for it, paralyzing claws of agony worming their way through my central nervous system, making it damned impossible for me to concentrate on the important business of filleting these bastards and using their entrails to hang them as a warning to the next round of thugs to come after me in this godforsaken country that you really shouldn't mess with Sienna Nealon, ever. Or at least not at breakfast.

I was trying to marshal enough presence of mind to fling the last chair at them, but I was coming up short. Pain had quite literally shut down my body. I couldn't even lift an arm to chuck the damned thing, and my eyes wandered, barely responding to my commands. I was shaking, my body—not quite convulsing, but at least locking down as my abdominal muscles flexed in an attempt to push out the murderously painful bullets currently afflicting them. My unconscious reaction was about to be the death of me.

I couldn't cast a light net. Couldn't detonate for fear of killing people. Couldn't go dragon, couldn't summon the presence of mind to use Bjorn's power...

I was tapped out. No options left save one.

"Time to die," the man with the revolver said. I looked up, his face so blurry that all I could see was the gun barrel leering down at me, pointed right at my head.

This, I couldn't survive. And as I watched and shook, transfixed on the approaching doom, his finger began to tighten on the trigger.

19.

There are some moments in life where time just slows way the hell down. From my friends who actually went to school, I'm told the last ten minutes before the bell rings for summer is especially like this. The moment before a first kiss, when you're nervous as hell, wondering if it's even going to happen. Yeah, slow as molasses on a Minnesota January day.

The moment before some Scottish goomba pulls the trigger on you? Yeah, it moves surprisingly slow. But fast at the same time, a hellish two-fer of contradictory clock movement. I actually had the thought about saying, "Wait!" in hopes it would buy me a second to come up with something that would buy me another second, but then I thought…to hell with it. I'm not gonna beg this schmuck to spare me for a tick tock.

"*Wait!*" That shout wasn't me.

I looked up, the guy with the gun looked up, the guy with the shotgun behind him looked up. It was just one big festival of looking up, and we all saw the same thing, presumably. Unless I was delusional from the pain, which I didn't rule out.

There was a flash of red hair and MY HERO—Rose grabbed the guy with the revolver and swung him around. The gun belched loud, lipping a six-inch flame out of the barrel as she took one in the side and grunted hard. I couldn't see the shot, but I could see her face and it went a couple shades paler than it had been before as a hideous red wound opened up at her ribcage.

Credit where it's due, though, the girl soldiered right through it, knocking the revolver aside and then thwacking the tough in the neck. It looked like it hurt, but it was hardly the most effective of blows, merely knocking him back a step. The armchair quarterback in me wanted to ask her why the hell she'd done that, but I got my answer a second later when the man with the shotgun capped off another round—

Right into the back of his friend's head. Rose had shoved him right into the line of fire. Human shield 0, Scottish Rose 10. Or at least 5, with a deduction for the fact that she took a round and also got revolver man's brains all over her ensemble. In the Sienna games, we do deduct points for that.

"Go team," I warbled, the pain in my belly subsiding at last. I rolled to my knees as Rose came back at the wild shotgunner, snatching the weapon out of his hands as I got to my feet. She kicked him in the throat and her form was spot on, clearly some training shining through. She whirled and delivered a lightning strike to his neck, capitalizing on the damage she'd already done.

With a guttural sound, Mr. Shotgun staggered back, clutching at his throat. It didn't look quite right, mostly because it had a serious crease right where his Adam's apple should have been, a perfect gutter that you could catch water runoff with. It reminded me of one time when I'd seen crime scene photos of a guy who'd decided to hang himself from a bridge, enduring an eighteen-foot fall before the rope had caught him. It had probably been a quick death, what with the snapping of his neck, but it hadn't left a very pretty corpse. Definitely a high collar suit or a closed casket required for that one.

Mr. Shotgun fell over backward, still trying to figure out how to breathe through a windpipe that had been closed like a Minnesota road during summertime. He never quite figured it out, bucking wildly for a few seconds as he struggled, increasingly desperately, for breath that just wasn't coming.

"I could probably do a tracheotomy and help him," I said, "but to hell with that guy." I clutched at my stomach as a couple bullets popped out and fell from my shirt to the floor. They were still stained with red.

"Are you all right?" Rose rushed to my side, like I hadn't just popped the bullets out, but kept herself from hanging on my arm or something similarly deleterious to her health.

"How'd you find me?" I asked, just managing to get upright. *Thanks, Wolfe,* I said. He didn't answer.

"I leapt the rooftops after you," Rose said, wisely keeping out of my personal space. "Lost you on the Mile, but…hard not to notice gunshots in Edinburgh, and people flying out windows onto the street."

"I bring chaos with me," I said. "Like I pack it in my very suitcase." I stretched gingerly and looked at the red mark on her side. "What about you?"

She looked down, and her eyes went wide. "Oh. Oh my. That's…"

"Definitely more than a flesh wound," I said, and she nodded along, sickly. "How strong is your meta healing?"

Rose went so pale it looked to me like her hair was on fire. "Uhmm…I don't know. I've never tested it before."

Sirens blared down the way. "Well," I said, "we should probably get you…uhh, sorted out, or whatever you people say up here." I glanced at the guy thrashing on the floor. "I just need to do one thing first…"

I knelt down and put my hand on his head, holding him to the ground. Rose clutched her side, still pale, but also curious, her head cocked to the side, watching me. "What are you doing?"

"Draining his memory of the events leading up to this little soiree," I said, pushing through his mind quickly. I didn't want to be in there as he died, after all, and I damned sure didn't want to absorb him wholly. It took a few seconds to get to the memory I wanted, and I was a little out of practice ripping memories out of peoples' heads, but since people were dying and these goons had just come to kill me, I wasn't thrilled to walk out without a lead.

And a few seconds later, I got one.

I tumbled through his mind to a few hours earlier, and a vision of where he'd been just before this. I sensed it was the beginning of the story, or as near to it as I could find. Harmon wasn't wrong; this guy's head was weird, his memories cast in a kind of strange light, like his brain was diced or something.

He was shaking hands with a man and feeling funny about it—staggering a little afterward, like he would have now if he'd been awake when I went to take my hands off him. He shook his head when it was done, looked back up at the man who'd touched him, and I got a clear look at the guy's face.

"I want ye to kill Sienna Nealon," the man said. His skin was smooth, he had a five o'clock shadow, and his head was cleanly shaven. His eyes were a little sunken back in his head, but not too badly. He had a lean and hungry look, and when he smiled, it looked predatory.

"Come on, let's go," I said, dropping the thug's hand as I re-entered the real world of the cafe, with the tables strewn across the floor from my battle and glass shattered in the front. Rose was still standing there, pale and clutching her side. I beckoned her toward the door and she came, hobbling smoothly along in my wake, stain on her shirt almost as red as her hair.

When we got out onto the Royal Mile, I looked left and right. The cops were coming, but they weren't quiet in sight yet, which worked for me. "Come here," I said, and when Rose wandered close enough, I snaked an arm around her waist. She made a yelp of alarm at the suddenness of the movement, and then we were aloft, as I pulled her into the sky, seeking a suitable place to doctor her wound and also to think, to ponder, to study a little closer the face of the enemy that I'd just pulled from that tough's mind.

20.

I stopped just down the High Street, way down the hill from the castle and not far from a building that looked like the seventies had birthed it after an ill-considered night with Frank Lloyd Wright. Which was really gross when you considered he'd died in 1959.

"That's Scottish Parliament," Rose said, catching me giving the building a grim eye as we came in for a landing. Past it I saw a funky-looking castle building, or something similar, and before I could ask, she said, "And that's Holyrood House, the Queen's residence in Edinburgh."

"She has a lot of houses, doesn't she?" I asked.

"She's the queen," Rose said with a shrug and a far-off look that suggested to me that shock from the gunshot wound was setting in.

"Come on, let's get you doctored," I said, and led her over to the center of the building we were standing on.

I led her far from the edges of the roof, where people could see us, and then stopped. She was about as easily led as a baby lamb with a rope around its neck, and when I gestured for her to, she gingerly sat down, cringing all the while but being a good sport and not whining about it.

"Looks like a through and through," I said once I'd had a chance to give it a once-over.

"A what?" she asked, politely baffled, like she was just asking something inconsequential. If it'd been me, I would have been a little more, "Arghhhh, what are you talking about, arghhhhhh, stop bullshitting and say what you mean in plain effing Englishhhhh!" But not Rose. She looked like she was holding her breath, probably a strategy to minimize the pain. I wasn't going to tell her not to, because for all I knew it helped that she wasn't putting pressure on her diaphragm, which would maybe translate to her ribs, one of which was likely busted by that bullet.

"It just means there's a secondary wound, an exit where the bullet came out," I said, lifting her shirt and peering at the entry wound and then the exit wound. Yep, it had come out, and it looked pretty much like a straight shot through. I could even see Edinburgh faintly through the other side of the gunshot wound when I stared in. "Ouch."

"Is that good, then?" She was so damned polite, that lamb on a rope analogy was sounding more accurate all the time.

"It's good in that I'm not going to have to dig around in your chest cavity to retrieve the bullet," I said, still staring through, trying to see if her healing had done much with this thus far. It didn't seem to, though the hole wasn't bleeding profusely, just a small trickle. That was a good sign. "Depending on how strong of a meta you are, you can heal faster or slower, more completely or, erhmm…"

"Less completely?" she offered weakly.

"Not necessarily," I said. "Someone with less of a natural healing ability will still heal from something like this, but they'd need more aid. For example, my healing ability can push the bullets right out of me in most cases, the tissue growth is so sudden and so powerful. Not all metas can do that as they heal. Some would heal with the bullet still inside them."

"Really?" she asked, sounding faint in the sense that she wasn't talking very loud or forcefully, and also in the sense that when I looked up, she seemed like she might keel over from lightheadedness.

"Yeah," I said, figuring it was better to continue my lecture and give her something to focus on other than being shot. "Although I do occasionally have to watch out. For example, one time I got lung shot and the bullet didn't come out. Which was a problem, because when I healed, the bullet got pushed into the lung instead of out of my body."

"Oh my," Rose said, wobbling where she sat. "What happened?"

"Oh, it hurt a lot, rattling around in there until I had someone pull it out."

"Someone?" She evinced a certain measure of worry in this, and I couldn't decide whether it was for my wellbeing or her own, and ultimately decided it didn't matter.

"Yeah, I had a curious friend practice surgery on me," I said. "Figured I didn't need an actual doctor, and I didn't want to go under general anesthesia, so I just had them cut an incision, break a rib, and pull it out." Needless to say, that had hurt a lot, and Augustus, so enthused about maybe pursuing an MD with his paid-for college, quickly changed his tune after about twenty minutes of following my curse-screamed requests that he get on with finishing the incision and breaking the rib. It was not our happiest day of the friendship, but I felt a lot better when I heard the bullet thud on the ground outside where we'd decided to do the surgery. I Wolfe'd back to health a few seconds later and knew by the look on Augustus's face when I rose that he wouldn't so much as look at a hospital again without feeling like he'd need to shit a brick.

"Is there anything ye can do for me?" Rose asked, still holding her shirt rolled up just below her armpit. This girl clearly did not believe much in wearing sexy underthings, because what I noted of her bra strap was pure function, and it totally clashed with the top band of her undies. A girl after my own heart, not even bothering to try and bring sexy back.

"Well, we could get some bandages and dress the wound, if you want," I said. "It'd kinda be a formality, just give it some space to heal, but it's the best we can do here. I mean, if you're an empath, I think you'll probably heal mostly overnight anyway—if I had to guess. Not a lot to be done to speed it up unless you've got a friend who's a Persephone."

"A…whut?" Befuddlement flashed over her open face.

"Like Kat Forrest," I said.

"Ohhh." Yeah, everyone got that. Rose wavered, then leaned toward me, cringing from the effect the motion had on her side. "Is she as, ahh…daft…as she appears on TV?"

I held in a chuckle. "Kat?" I pondered how best to answer that without insulting my friend. "She's actually fairly smart, like book smart. But she does—I don't know, fail to think sometimes? Doesn't take full advantage of her higher brain functions? Something. It makes her look…daft, I guess, for lack of a better word…but people who think she's a total idiot tend to underestimate her at their peril. You can drop your shirt down. I'm going to look for a pharmacy and get you some bandages."

"All right." Rose nodded. "Then what?"

I took a moment to compose my reply. "Then you should get home and rest overnight, give that a chance to grow back."

She stared at me, blinking, like she didn't quite get it. "But I'm going with you."

I stared back at her, and maybe it was me who didn't get it. "Rose, you've been shot."

"But you said it'd heal."

"Yeah, by tomorrow—and probably. It could take a day, two days—I don't really recall for someone with your power. Been a while since I dealt regularly with an empath."

"But is me loafing around my flat really going to make it heal any faster?" She was wheedling now; I recognized the tone even without knowing her well. This was the same thing Augustus did when he wanted to sway me to a particular course of action or way of thinking, the same earnest manner. "I could be out helping you."

"Rose—"

She landed a hand on my wrist, then seemed to think the better of it and pulled it away. "Sorry. But truly—I can help you. Please."

I studied her face. As sincere as she was, she was also holding in the pain from a gunshot wound, which was no small amount, as I'd discovered—again—just minutes ago. Still, she was here, and she was actually holding herself together, not being a giant baby about it, which was a major mark in her favor. The guys I hung out with back when I had friends and a life? They would have probably been screaming their heads off in her situation. And here she was, holding her shirt up on a rooftop to show me her bullet wound, and not only had she not screamed once, she was trying to come with me on my investigation, even though she looked like she might keel over any minute now.

"I've got a bad feeling about this…" I started to mutter.

"I'll be nae trouble at all," she said, pulling the shirt down gingerly, its dark colors effectively masking the fact she was bleeding on it. "And if I start to—well, pass out, I'll go home then, I promise."

"Duly noted," I said, remembering my earlier admonishment that I work alone. But this girl had taken a bullet for me, and she didn't seem—well, dangerously obsessed, even though she was a little overenthusiastic. I vaguely recalled having heroes at one point in my life, probably far in advance of her having heroes. By the time I was her age, I'd already had my dreams crushed nicely, and all those illusions of heroes beaten squarely out of my head by having my mentor force me to kill my own boyfriend to absorb his soul.

Sure, I could teach Rose the same lesson, albeit more gently, by being a huge ass right now, but…

Shit, if she wasn't put off by the fact that I was a wanted felon in the US, most of the things that I would do in the course of a normal week weren't going to crush her dreams and vision of me as some hero worthy of emulation or worship. The only thing I could do that would kill those now would be to be a ginormous ass to her, and since she'd just taken a bullet for me…

Yeah, I wasn't going to do that.

"You can come with me," I said, "since I've just rebuffed an attempt on my life—with your help," I added. "But there will probably be another one." My mind raced, wondering about the bald man with the vicious smile that I'd seen in the stolen memory. "And another. You know what, we can probably expect them to continue until this is done, actually. Maybe beyond, even." And though I didn't voice it aloud, the thought occurred to me that now that Rose had cast her lot with me, if I sent her away they might go after her in an attempt at revenge, or else to use her as a hostage against me.

As tough as she seemed, throw five of those guys at her in a surprise attack and I doubted she'd walk out the other side alive. "So…you'll need to be careful." I understated it for her because there wasn't much point in scaring her off, especially since I was going to need to keep her nearby in order to protect her from what was doubtless coming our way.

She put up one hand like she was about to take an oath and put the other one on her heart, movements which made her cringe momentarily. "I swear I will stay out of yuir way as much as possible and do only helpful things."

I stared at her, processing what she'd just said. "You know…that might be the best thing anyone's ever vowed to do to help me."

Flushed with triumph, she grinned, and then the corners of her mouth were pulled down by pain. "Well, I'm just glad you took me on as your sidekick." She paled, like she'd insulted me by saying that. "No, err, not sidekick. Umm, err…lackey?"

"How about partner?" I asked, figuring I'd offer her the sort of olive branch that could maybe make the pain fade away for a few brief seconds.

Based on the glow that radiated off her cheeks when she extended her hand to me, that did it. She reached out and pumped my hand once, pulling away after only a second or so of contact. Very smart. "You won't be sorry." She cringed again as the motion agitated her wound.

"But you might," I said with grim amusement as I stood to go fetch some bandages. "Wait here. I'll be back in a few. We'll patch you up and get going."

"Uh…not to be intrusive but…now that we're partners…" I looked back at her, and she was having a hard time containing the excitement, the pain, and a few other emotions. I just hoped the control issues didn't extend to her bladder. "Where are we going next?"

"To investigate," I said simply, and walked to the edge of the roof, ready to step off.

"But investigate what?" She had that air of befuddlement. "I mean, it's Edinburgh. Nothing really happens here."

"Murder, Rose," I said, and her eyebrows sailed north.

"There's a serial killer in town." I pictured the face of the smiling, cold, bald-headed man. "An incubus, I think—the male version of me. We're going to find him—and we're going to take him out."

21.

Once we'd gotten Rose all patched up, with a minimum of fuss, it was a short trek to the souvenir shop where Adam Perry had worked. It was on the High Street, had a predictably Scottish name, and had more tartan kilts on display than all the battle scenes in Braveheart combined. When I expressed this opinion to Rose, she made a face like I'd stuck a dirty diaper under her nose, and it was not related to the pain.

"Braveheart," she said with unbelievable scorn. "D'ye have any idea what a fiction that film was? Start to finish, I tell ye."

"That's nice," I said, not really giving a damn.

"I mean, I dinnae ken how you can get the story of William Wallace so bluidy wrong." Her Scottish brogue was coming out hard now, and she was ranting in spite of her wound, something I had a feeling would pull her up short here in a second. "Oof," she said. There it was. I looked back and she was cradling her side. She talked with her hands, I'd noticed, something she'd probably unlearn in the next day or so while healing.

"Take it easy, okay?" I said as we walked into the shop, which was wide open to the air. The better to take in the tourists, my dear. "That's not a pinprick you've got there."

I'd bought her a cheap coat from the store next to the pharmacy before I'd come back to her, and she wore it now. Luckily it was raining faintly, enough to cool everything off. I didn't know if Scotland got miserably hot in the summer, but there was none of that in evidence right now, at least, which was nice because it made the two of us in coats not look ridiculously out of place, even though I was sweating under the wig.

There were about five clerks on the floor of the shop, all girls, all late teens or early twenties, all pretty. I would have thought that strange until I saw the shopkeeper, who was an old guy with a bald head and a slight paunch to go with his ungainly long limbs. It was like he was skinny at the extremities but put on all his weight in the middle, where he could better pack it. He had his head down over the till, counting his money, and I sauntered up and flipped some of my blond wig-hair over my shoulder to get his attention.

It worked like I thought it would. He stopped paying attention to his money long enough to flash me what he probably thought was a dazzling, charming smile, but which to me reminded me of every lech I'd ever known. "What can I do for you, my dear?" I worked hard to control the eye twitch that threatened to manifest itself when he called me 'dear.'

Die, was the answer I didn't say out loud. Instead I put on my best phony smile and said, "My name is Sarah Nelson and I'm with Scotland Yard." That wiped the smirk off his face almost as effectively as if I'd told him to die, maybe more so.

He swallowed visibly and said, "Angus Macdonald. On advice of counsel, I'd—"

"Relax. I'm not here about you," I said. "I'm here regarding Adam Perry."

Macdonald turned as red as the tartan kilt behind him, without the benefit of the black crosshatching for contrast. "That lazy arsehole? Well, if you see him, tell him he's sacked. This is the third time he's failed to show up for work. Can't hire good help around here anymore, I swear—" He moderated his tone as he caught the wounded looks from a few of the pretty shopgirls. "You know what I mean, girls. You're all fine. It's those others I was talking about." The sad thing was, a couple of them actually bought his BS.

"I could tell him," I said, "but I don't think the message would get through. He's dead."

Macdonald's eyes widened slightly, but he whispered, "Dead?"

"Right," I said, "so I guess he's going to continue his pattern of showing up late for work. Very late, in fact, because he is now, by definition, late. The late Adam Perry."

There was a high-pitched titter from behind me and I looked back to see Rose holding her side, the laughter she'd snorted out having aggravated her wound. "Sorry," she whispered, clearly trying to keep a lid on the pain. "That was…just funny is all."

"Who's this now?" Macdonald asked with all the restraint of a starving man who'd just had a plate of tattie scones slid in front of him with a sign that said "DO NOT EAT" on them.

"That's my sidekick—I mean lackey—I mean partner," I said, trying to remember what we'd settled on and feeling pretty chagrined about screwing it up. Now it was my turn to apologize, so I turned to Rose and said, "Sorry," but she was flashing me a thumbs-up like it didn't matter, grinning again.

"So how did the dumb-arse die?" Macdonald asked, embracing the sort of manners that had probably made him very popular among the orcish hordes he'd probably descended from. "You know, out of curiosity."

"Well, it damned sure didn't seem like it was coming out of the milk of human compassion," I said, "but he was murdered, in fact." I let that one sink in for a moment before delivering the coup de grace, which wiped the smugly satisfied look off his face. "I'm searching for likely suspects right now." I pulled out a little notepad and pretended to study it. "So…it seems like you and Adam didn't get along terribly well…"

The brief flicker of panic in his eyes was worth it. "Look, I had nothing against the lad—save for that he was a terrible employee and a moron." He held up his hands. "That's hardly worth killing him over, though. Firing would be much easier."

"Mmhmmm," I said, staring at the blank page of my

notepad. "Tell me...if you fired him, would you incur any negative financial benefit?"

"I had nothing to do with this!" Macdonald said, long arms extending out from his head in a wide shrug. "I didn't even know he was dead until you told me!"

I made a show of writing that down, careful not to look at him. I swear, half the time when I'm working I'm really just tormenting irritating people I encounter.

Only half? Zack offered warily.

Hush up, you.

"Did Adam work yesterday?" I tossed out a real question, figuring I'd take a break from raising the shopkeeper's blood pressure.

"Aye," Macdonald said with a curt nod. "Until closing, and then he scarpered off to do whatever it is he does in his off hours."

"Any idea what that might be?"

Macdonald's scowl deepened. "Elspeth." He beckoned to one of the girls, a blond with pale skin, like most of the rest of the Scots I'd met since arriving. She padded over from where she'd been rearranging a stack of sweatshirts with Edinburgh logos on them. "Do ye know where Adam spent his evenings?"

Elspeth looked at him curiously. "Aye. He went to Ailbeart's."

I looked back at Rose and without even having to ask, she said, "It's a dance bar, club...it's where all of us younger folk go if we're of a mind to go out."

"Do you know if he went last night?" I asked Elspeth, writing down the name of the place on my little pad.

"Aye, he did," she said. "I saw him there myself." She craned her neck toward me. "What's this about?"

"Adam died last night, lass," Macdonald said gruffly. He clearly still was not feeling it, but he said it loudly enough that the other shopgirls stopped what they were doing. I took a quick temp on the emotional reactions. Three stood stunned. One didn't seem to understand what she'd heard. One burst into immediate tears.

For her part, Elspeth was the one who burst into tears.

"But I saw him just last night." She was whispering, as though speaking it louder would make it real.

"How did he strike you?" I asked.

"He didnae strike me at all, ever!" she said in protest.

"Not—I mean what was your impression of him last night," I corrected, as the tears streamed down her face. "I wasn't trying to suggest he beat you or anything."

"Oh." That didn't help the tears, but the question, rephrased properly, did prompt her to answer. "He was…quiet, I guess? Not quite himself, but he'd been like that all day." She blinked, thinking it over. "All week, actually." She looked up at Macdonald. "Wouldn't ye say?"

Macdonald didn't let that grudging look go so easily. "He was as much a dumb-arse yesterday as he ever was." After catching a withering glare from me and a couple suppressed sobs from Elspeth, he allowed, "Though I suppose he was less exuberant these last few days."

That was curious, I thought, jotting down a note that the vic had been subdued at work and at play. I couldn't see how exactly that would tie into murder by an incubus though, unless he'd been stalked or something by the bald guy beforehand. "Did he seem worried about anything?"

"No," she said, wiping her eyes and smearing her mascara across her pale cheek. "Just quiet. Distracted, even. Oh, God, Adam…" She started to lose it.

"There, there," Rose said, putting a hand on her shoulder. The crying juddered to a stop, for which I thanked my lucky stars. It took me a second to make the connection, at which point Rose smiled at me. She was using her empathic powers to quell the excess feelz in the shop. Whew. Between Macdonald the prickish and the five girls who were clearly keeping from going to pieces under Rose's influence, this place was turning into a Sienna Nealon nightmare, way worse than the cafe where I'd almost just died, really.

"Is there anything else you can tell me?" I asked, hoping against hope that Rose could keep back the surging tide of emotion running through this place. The fact that no one else had burst out crying would have been a minor miracle worthy of comment if I hadn't tumbled to her game. Good game, 10/10, would play again.

"I can't think of a thing," she said.

"Did he have a roommate?" I asked. "Flatmate?" I amended, realizing I should have asked this question of his mother as well but failed, probably because of the feeeeeeelz and the desire to hightail it out of there before it got any worse. Usually I came in after the vic's family had been told. Way after, if I had it my way.

"Yes," Elspeth said. "Graham. Graham Selkirk."

I perked up at that. "Do you know him?" She nodded. "Where does Graham work?"

"He worked at one of the other shops down the row," she said, sniffling lightly. When she caught my questioning look, I didn't have to ask; she just supplied the answer. "Graham died two weeks ago."

"How did he die?" I asked.

"He was a young man, like Adam," Elspeth sniffled, Rose's emotional hold over her clearly about to falter, tears streaming down her white cheeks. "But...but..." She sniffled, trying to compose herself and failing. "They said it was a heart attack."

22.

As Rose and I walked away from the shop I heard a chorus of wails begin behind us, drawing a deep cringe from me and a puckish smile of amusement from her. "You shouldn't take delight in the misery of others, you know," I said, like I had any room to talk.

"Oh!" I'd caught her red-handed and she blushed hard. "I'm not delighting—I wasn't smiling about that! It was just, you—when ye were dealing with them…I caught that wee hint of—"

"I don't like feelings," I said, cutting right to what she was going to say before she said it. "Which is probably why I'm not the hugest fan of empaths, just FYI."

"You've known some of us, then?" she asked, falling into line beside me, still cradling her side, as we walked past a shop whose signage promised that they sold the finest whiskeys in Scotland.

"I've known a few empaths, yes." I glanced at the whiskey shop, at the display in the front window, which gave way to a jewelry shop next door. Lots of silver, which interested me only marginally more than the whiskey.

"If you'll forgive me for saying so," she said tentatively, "most people, when I'm around them…I get a sense of their feelings whether I want to or not. But with ye…"

"You don't get anything, right? I'm like a black hole in the sidewalk?" I kept my eyes forward. Graham's shop was supposedly just up the hill, though Rose was lagging a little and I slowed so as not to leave her behind. I scanned the street, looking for watchful eyes or hostility, but not too many people were out in this misting rain that had begun again.

"Exactly," she said. "Which—I'm sorry, I've never encountered that before."

"I have a telepath in my head," I said. "Telepaths and empaths are—I dunno, polar opposites or something. They block each other pretty effectively. Empaths can't twist a telepath's emotions and telepaths can't read an empath's mind."

"Oh." She lapsed into a very brief silence, which normally I would have found comforting. For some reason, with Rose, her questions didn't bother me as much as they did with a normal person. "Do all metahuman powers have an opposite balanced one like that?"

I blinked, giving it some thought. "Uhmm…that's a good question. I don't know, exactly."

"Well…does yours?"

"Sort of," I said. "The opposite of a succubus or incubus is probably a Persephone. I can kill and absorb a soul with my touch while a Persephone can heal and give life with theirs. But they can also control plants from root and seed, which has no analog in my abilities, unfortunately. But I guess they're a sort of equal and opposite for my kind."

"That's really fascinating," Rose said, and I could tell by the way she leaned in that she wasn't fooling around. She was eating this all up, which was kind of…cool. Because most of the time when I was on a case with an unfortunate hanger-on, they weren't typically all that jazzed about it as a teachable moment. They were either trying to survive or else so used to my presence that they were jaded by me.

There's an old saying that you're never a prophet in your own land. For the first time ever, maybe, with Rose, I finally understood what that meant. Because here, in Scotland, I'd finally found someone who wanted to learn what I had to teach. Not that I'd made much of an effort to find pupils, but still…

"Can you think of other powers that have that sort of

relationship?" She was really getting into this.

"Hmm," I said, racking my brain. "You could almost say that a Hercules and an Atlas have a relationship to one another…a Hercules can swell or shrink their muscles, with some sort of converse relationship to brain power the stronger they get. Whereas an Atlas can actually grow or shrink their body, becoming smaller or larger, but their strength largely remains fixed, along with their brainpower…"

I got kinda lost in this new line of thought and almost missed it when Rose said, "I think that's where Graham worked." She was pointing at a shop that sold—guess what? Whiskey.

"Right you are," I said, dragging myself out of my nice little intellectual exercise. It was a pleasant change of pace from beating asses, giving some deeper thought to metahuman abilities in a way I'd never had cause to discuss them before.

"We can pick this up later again, if ye want," Rose said, and she sounded hopeful about it. Then she looked both ways and started to cross the Royal Mile, heading for the whiskey shop.

"I do want to pick it up again later," I said, taking a step off the curb to follow her to Graham's place of employment, and, with any luck, some answers.

23.

We didn't find any answers in the whiskey shop, unfortunately, just shelves and shelves of obscenely high-priced Scotch whiskey and a shopgirl who shrugged her shoulders at any inquiry about Graham, the type of person he was, what he might have been up to, etc.

She's new, Harmon informed me, not exactly knocking my socks off with surprise. *And kind of dumb.* Also not a huge surprise.

"Well, that was a bit of a dead end," Rose said, frowning as we stepped out of the whiskey shop and into the street, where the rain had, for the moment, stopped. Dark clouds still malingered overhead, and I eyed them with annoyance, wondering how much moisture my wig could absorb before it became completely unserviceable as a disguise. These were the moments when Scott Byerly was sorely missed. Well, now and sometimes late at night, when—

Never mind. You don't need to know about that.

Gross.

Anyway, as I stopped on the curb, trying to decide what to do next, Rose stuck up her arm on the unwounded side of her body, which still prompted her to cringe. Before I could ask what she was up to, a cab slowed and popped to a stop next to us. "Sorry," she said, genuinely apologizing, "but it occurred to me that we're going to the Ailbeart's next, yeah?" She waited for me to nod. "Well, if you want, you can fly ahead and I'll take the cab and meet you there, but—"

"You being flown right now is going to hurt like hell," I said, getting it at last. "Quick thinking on the cab."

She let a pained look flash through, and I could tell her side must have been really bothering her. As would tend to happen when you had a several-centimeter hole torn through flesh, internal organs and bone. "Just trying to be efficient. Like I said, I can meet ye there if you want to get a jump on—"

"No, I'll ride with you," I said, leaning down to open the door for her so she didn't have to. The cab was what I referred to as a shoebox car, the sort of thing almost all Europeans seemed to prefer, provided they had a car at all. It was some sort of small hatchback, and I fit into it comfortably enough next to Rose, who scooted in like I was chasing after her with a pitchfork and a torch. "Chill, Rose," I said as she settled into place. "There's no rush. I'm not going to bail on you if you take a few extra seconds to get into the car."

She laughed uncomfortably. "Just don't want to slow ye down."

I sat back as the cabbie started the car and Rose gave him the address, wondering about that last exchange with her. It was a little weird that she'd be worried about slowing me down while I was worried about her wellbeing. Weird for me to be worrying about a near total stranger, and not leaving her behind, but I consoled myself by knowing that I was looking out for her against whatever assassins might come her way now that she'd cast her lot with me.

"How are you feeling?" I asked as she cradled her arm close to her side. I spoke meta-low, so quietly that only another metahuman, with our enhanced sense of hearing, could have heard me.

"A little better, I think," she said, replying in kind. The cabbie wasn't even looking around, just watching the road without a clue we were talking, hopefully. "Still hurts, but nothing I can't deal with."

"That's good."

"Can I ask ye about this victim?" She looked at me very tentatively until I nodded. "Do you have any idea why he was killed?"

"Not the foggiest—yet. I was leaning toward random act until we found out his roommate had been killed too. Now I'm thinking—well, I don't actually know that I have a thought for it, unless Graham is secretly the killer and he's faked his own death." I made a mental note to stop by the Edinburgh PD shortly and get the file on Graham's death. Assuming they'd realized it was a homicide and done any legwork on it. Heart attack ruling made that…unlikely. I would have called them, but…hell, I still didn't know how to dial British numbers in my American phone. I probably should have had my bankers in Liechtenstein find someone to buy me a British one, but I'd been loathe to contact them lately, now that the American heat was so high on me. I was always worrying that a drone was overhead at any time, ready to pump a Hellfire missile right up my tookus.

"Hmm," Rose said, going back to her own thoughts.

"This doesn't seem like a very big town," I said, looking out at some of the old stone buildings of Edinburgh as they passed. We were turning to go down a hill, crossing a huge bridge with pedestrian traffic swarming on either side. I could see the glass roof of something out my window. It looked vaguely like either a train station or else a hell of a conservatory. "Did you know either of these guys?"

"No." She shook her head. "I'm not from Edinburgh originally."

"Oh? Where'd you come from?"

"Small town on the west coast. Of Scotland, I mean—"

"I didn't expect it was Seattle you were talking about."

"I only got here a few years ago." She smiled weakly. "Right about the time you came to fame, actually."

"What brought you to Edinburgh?"

"Not a lot of people left in my town," she said, taking her own chance to look out the window.

The cabbie turned the car onto a main drag, one I'd overflown earlier in the day. I watched with interest, and noted a street sign: Princes Street.

"This is new Edinburgh," Rose said, apparently noticing my attentiveness to the scenery. "The old town is up on the hill, spreading out from the castle. They used to have city gates and everything, plans for a defense because it'd get, ye know, under siege from medieval invaders. Once that threat was out, people started building out here, and the wealth moved off the hill and into this nice, new area."

"Only a stone's throw away," I said, looking back over the bridge we'd crossed. On the opposite side from the train station, there was a park that stretched off into the distance, couched at the base of the hill between the old town and the new. "Almost literally." I peered out the back window. "That park is huge. It's like Edinburgh's version of Central Park in New York."

"It wasn't always so nice," she said with a slight smile.

"Oh?"

"The reason it's not built on? It used to be Nor Loch until they drained it," she said, still smiling. "The city's at the top of the hill, lake at the bottom…all those people, no indoor plumbing…that refuse needed somewhere to go when they tossed it out their front doors and down the hill…"

"I bet that was a smelly place to swim."

"Yeah, I'm kinda glad it's gardens and park now," she said. "Not sure a swampy sewage reservoir would make this city as nice a place to live."

I snorted. "Well, it's gotta go somewhere." Ahead, in the distance, I could see the hilltop monuments I'd spied when I'd landed in Edinburgh for the first time, and I could tell that the Old Calton Burial Grounds, where I'd looked at Adam Perry's body, was not terribly far.

The cabbie turned left off the main road, and suddenly we found ourselves making a few turns, enough that I lost my sense of direction. Pretty soon he stopped the car and said something fairly low himself, but not so bad I couldn't understand him. "£8.24." It was the first thing he'd said since we got in the cab, and I thought I was in love. I didn't know how many cabbies had tried to make conversations with me over the years since I'd started riding in cabs, but it was a lot.

I paid the man with a wrinkled £10 note and got out after Rose, who had a little more spring in her step. She probably was healing fast, though I'd need to check on it after we finished this interview and potentially got back to more serious business. I didn't bother waving at the cabbie as he pulled away, because his code of silence and stoicism probably would have prevented him from waving back in any case.

Ailbeart's was all done up in a blue storefront, funky with glittering letters. It looked like it might have been a pub at one point but taken a bad left turn to cater to schoolkids. I shook my head and followed Rose's lead to the front door, which, to my surprise, given that it was mid-afternoon, swung wide when she pushed.

"In the non-evening hours it's just a pub," she said as we found ourselves in a dark space, my eyes swiftly adjusting to the cave-like atmosphere. I could see the dance floor that gleamed to my left as I headed to the bar, which was to the right. The whole place had been sandwiched into the first floor of another of Edinburgh's ubiquitous European-style apartment buildings, the kind I tended to see all over the damned place over here. The only thing that varied was the facade, and only slightly.

There was only one guy behind the bar at this hour, and not a patron in the place. Seemed like a good argument for it being a high school establishment, with the caveat that in the UK, a high school establishment included liquor.

"You're frowning," she said, informing me of something I did not realize but should have guessed, since it's me and I assume I frown a lot.

"Was just pondering your drinking age and remembering how irresponsible I was at eighteen."

"You didn't drink at age eighteen?"

"Oh, I did," I said, remembering the time I'd gone on a mission with Kat and Scott that had resulted in drunkenness and some truly terrible decisions, like nearly sleeping with an Omega incubus. "And regretted it."

She got a wry smile. "Couldn't hold your liquor?"

"Couldn't think very well after imbibing it, actually."

I steered us toward the bartender, who, like the shopkeeper in the last place, was doing a bit of leering as we approached.

He focused his attention mostly on Rose, and I asked, meta-low, "Is Edinburgh suffering from a higher than normal proportion of leches? Or are these last two just poor ambassadors for their sex?"

"I haven't been anywhere else but my village," she said, "so I guess I'm not sure if there are a lot more leches elsewhere than here, but these two aren't what I'd call normal, wearing their gawking on their sleeve like this."

"Good."

"'ello, dollfaces," the bartender said in an actual British English accent, one that didn't really seem totally out of place in Edinburgh but was distinctly not Scottish. It actually sounded almost Cockney, but like it had faded over time. "Can I get you a drink? Ladies' night is tonight, two-for-ones, and I'm more than happy to start you off a little early."

I debated whether having a drink would make him chattier or not, and ultimately decided my usual, bullheaded approach was the way to go with a guy like this. Why change things up for the sake of an ass? "My name is Sarah Nelson and I'm with Scotland Yard."

He froze, but only for a second, then picked up a glass and a rag and started polishing it. "Whatchoo want?" he asked, not exactly the height of civility.

"I'm here about Adam Perry."

He paused for a second. "Oh. That sod. Should have known; you two are a little older than our usual crowd. What'd Adam do now?" He evinced just a hint of relief that we were here about someone else.

I decided not to be merciful in dropping the hammer. "Got murdered."

That hit him like a brick in the face, but he evinced only momentary surprise before tossing out, "What's that got to do wif me?"

"Well, I assumed you murdered him, of course." I smiled sweetly, and watched the panic form in his eyes as he tried to come up with an explanation.

"Look, I don't know what you think is going on here, but I was here, at the bar, until late." He spoke with the air of a man desperately, desperately trying to get me to believe him, a man who hadn't quite tumbled to the fact I was toying with him. "I have witnesses. Dozens of them. I'll make a list—"

"Do that," I said, and watched him dive for a paper and pen like he was a brave soldier jumping on a grenade to save his fellows. Though, in this case, he was about to throw me a dozen names to save his own ass, so…

"Perry wasn't even here that long last night," the bartender said, writing feverishly. "You want these guys' mobile numbers, too?" He didn't even wait for me to answer, pulling out his phone. "Of course you do. You just give them a call, they'll tell you, I was here until late. Super late. Like break of dawn."

I shared a look of pure amusement with Rose, who seemed to be getting a kick out of this as well. "It might take me a little while to call them all. You okay with us staying here while we do?"

He stopped writing in the middle of a name. "Staying… here?" He looked like I'd tossed him in front of a train, and I wondered if I'd caught him in the middle of a lie or if he'd just been caught by surprise that we'd want to bask in his presence for any longer than we had to.

"Of course," I said, keeping my malicious glee buttoned up inside. Rose was trying to hold in laughter, shoulders shaking in silent mirth, mixed with the grimaces of the pain that was probably rolling through her from the stress on her lungs and rib cage. She wasn't whimpering, so give the girl credit. "Like you said, we're a bit older than your usual clientele, which means we weren't born yesterday. I know the minute I walk out that door you're going to be making frantic phone calls to your pals, making sure they confirm your alibi, and I want to talk to them before you get a chance to screw up their young and impressionable heads."

He swallowed visibly. "I don't think they'll take your call."

"Good point," I said, and swiped his phone right from out of his grasp before he could do anything about it. I peered over the bar and grabbed the list of names, which probably wasn't done but was good enough to make a start on. "You just hang out right there while I go to work on this, all right?"

He visibly gulped, and it was adorable in the way that a rescue animal with a missing limb trying to hobble would be. Well, no, actually, it wasn't nearly that cute. He flushed and said, "I know my rights! You can't take my mobile phone like that!"

"Know your rights?" I snorted, picking out the third contact on the list to start with. "You probably don't even know how to make a Blue Hawaiian."

He almost took a step back, his honor visibly affronted. "Rum, pineapple juice, Curacao, sweet and sour mix—maybe a dash of vodka if you're feeling adventurous."

"Great," I said, "make two of those in the non-adventurous variant." I glanced at Rose for confirmation, and she shrugged, then nodded. "Ladies' night is about to begin early with a two-for-none special."

His shoulders sank and he got sullen, but he sprang into motion. I nodded at him, and Rose nodded back at me, getting the message, which was to watch him so he didn't try to hock a loogie in our drinks or something even more revolting, while I made some calls checking up on his story.

The phone rang and then gave way to a male voice saying, "Whassup, bruvnor?" in a gangsta Scottish accent.

"I don't know what that bruvnor thing is," I said, "and I'm not your bartender buddy, but he's standing right here. My name is Sarah Nelson, I'm with Scotland Yard, and your pal is facing a long stretch of jail time."

"Whaaaaaaat?" The voice on the other end of the line wasn't quite picking up what I was laying down.

"Do you know who Adam Perry is?" I asked, figuring that plunging ahead would eventually enable me to drag this idiot along when his brain started to catch up.

"Yeah. Lurch-looking motha. Who is this?"

"I told you, Scotland Yard. Adam Perry is dead."

"Whot? Lurch?"

"Yes. He was found in the Old Calton Burial Ground this morning."

There was a faint snickering on the other end of the line. "Dead in a graveyard. Who'd have thunk it?"

"Focus, imbecile. Your bartender pal? He's in hot water for

this. Where was he last night?"

"Well, he was with me at the bar—me and a bunch of others. We were there almost until dawn."

"Do you remember what time you left?" I asked.

"Hang on, yeah. I think I checked my phone when I did. 5:10. Somewhere around there. It was a late night." He chuckled.

"Thanks for your help," I said, and hung up on him and plunged back into the directory, picking another name from the list at random.

They answered on the third ring. "Yo, what going on, barman?"

I went through my schpiel again, this time my subject picking it up a lot more quickly. I guess I'd inadvertently dialed the brains of the operation. It took me a few seconds to get to the question at hand: "Where were you last night?"

"At the bar, until late, with the person whose cell phone you're calling me on. He didn't do it; he was partying with us all night."

I was starting to get that feeling, but then, I'd had a suspicion the bartender was no more than a run-of-the-mill lech all along. "Remember what time you left the bar?"

"Sometime around five, I reckon, because I collapsed at home about five-thirty and the bar's about twenty minutes away from there."

Thanking him for his time, I hung up and made my way to the bar. "Your story checks out," I said, as the bartender set two icy, blue-filled glasses down on the polished oak.

He wavered a little at the end, spilling just slightly out of mine as he let out a rather obvious breath of relief. "Told you," he said.

"Great," I said, taking a sip. It was pretty good. Nice and sweet too, probably because he was used to getting high school girls drunk by hiding the liquor flavor until they were too smashed to resist his charms.

"Fantastic," he said, clearly relieved to be done with that. "Now drink up, ladies, and be on your way."

"Ready to be rid of us so soon?" Rose asked, sipping from the straw in a faux-seductive manner that was exactly the kind of thing I would have done if I'd been feeling less lethal and more playful with this jackass.

"Quite," he said simply.

"Yeah, we're nowhere near done," I said, and his shoulders slumped as he realized we weren't going anywhere anytime soon. "Now, maybe now you can tell me about Adam Perry…and what you know about what happened to him last night."

24.

"Look," the bartender said, and I could see the beads of perspiration strung across his forehead, which I suspected was not so high about five years ago, "Perry is a bit of an odd fellow, okay?"

"Define 'odd' for me in the Edinburgh sense," I said, taking another sip of my drink.

"I don't know," the bartender said, making his misery at our mere presence obvious. He looked like he wanted to tuck his non-vestigial reptile tail between his legs and slink off somewhere, like we'd become a completely intolerable burden he couldn't wait to escape.

I have that effect on people, I'm told.

"He's just strange," the bartender went on. "Watches oddball TV programs and blathers on about them endlessly. *Doctor Who. Battlestar Galaxy*—"

"*Galactica*," I corrected. Rose and the bartender both looked at me and I felt myself redden. "What? My brother's really into that show."

He didn't look like he believed me, but he didn't challenge me about it either. "Anyway, he's just—strange. Who comes to a place like this to talk about *Battlestar…*" He looked at me, prompting.

"*Galactica.*"

"Right, who does that?" He shook his head. "Doesn't make much of an effort with the ladies, you know. I don't get it. All this prime tail and he's trying to talk up the blokes

117

about stupid spaceship shows. What's wrong wif a man who does that?" He frowned, like a thought was occurring to him for the first time. "I wonder if he was…ohhh. Yeah. Probably wasn't interested in the ladies, now I give it a think. He had this little sixteen-year-old, draping herself all over him, and he couldn't be arsed." The bartender made a face of pure disgust. "It's just wrong, unless he's—you know. Then it all makes sense."

I rolled my eyes, not bothering to hide my own disgust, because that little factoid only concerned me insofar as it gave a possible additional reason why an incubus might have been able to target Adam Perry. "Maybe he just wasn't into underaged girls."

"Whatchoo talking about, 'underage'?" The bartender leaned forward. "Sixteen ain't underage." He paled rapidly, and looked to Rose for confirmation, like he'd just woken from a bad dream. "It's not underage, is it?" Without waiting for an answer: "I always heard the age of consent was sixteen, I swear it!"

I worked hard to control my blush, which was good, because this was one of those little things that might have outed me as an American, where the overall age of consent was more or less eighteen, with a few exceptions for people in an age bracket near to eighteen—something our bartender friend hadn't been for at least two decades. "You're a classy guy, ace." His eyes were still flitting around left to right, hard, trying to suss out whether he was in trouble. He wasn't, at least with the law, but I started to get the feeling that those sixteen-year-olds succumbing to his charms weren't doing so naturally. "I was talking about how you ply those sixteen-year-olds with liquor and maybe worse in order to get them into bed. Because we all know they're not here for your shining good looks and sparkling personality."

He gulped. It was the most beautiful thing he'd done since we arrived. "Look…I helped you with this Adam Perry thing. I'm not guilty of that—"

"No, you're guilty of other stuff," I said, standing up. "Maybe worse stuff, depending on how you look at it." I was starting to get really mad, because he'd just tacitly confirmed

118

that he was getting sixteen-year-old girls drunk in order to sleep with them, and the expression on his face made it blazingly obvious he was guilty as hell.

"Hey," Rose said, and her hand was resting on my arm. Her lush green eyes were mischievous, but also warning. She could probably sense I was about a half-second from taking up the honor of those poor, unfortunate sixteen-year-olds that this sleazebag had taken advantage of by lighting the bar on fire behind him and then tossing him into the shattered glass just to watch him try to crawl through it and the flames. It would be sweet.

I backed off a notch. Not because Rose could touch my emotions, but because I was here on a job, and getting revenge for the girls this douche had done wrong would, by necessity, need to include as little property damage as possible. For all I knew, he didn't even own this place. Besides, Rose seemed to have something in mind, so I paused and let her lean forward.

She concentrated intently on the bartender, squinting at him like she was pushing into his mind—or feelings, more accurately. "Whenever you look at a sixteen-year-old girl, you know what you feel?" The bartender shuddered, jerking his hips back like he was protecting his nuts from attack, even though Rose was only leaning over the bar. "Yeah, that's it…unbridled lust. Well…" She smiled, and it was the most malicious thing I'd seen from the sweet Scot thus far. "Let's put a bridle on that, shall we? From now on, when you see a sixteen-year-old girl that's lovely to your eyes, you're going to experience a different emotional reaction. Something more akin to…how you feel when someone has kicked you right in the bollocks."

He flinched back again, harder this time, dropping both hands to his groin and gasping like one of us had struck him. I raised an eyebrow and he came back up, horrorstruck. "What'd you just do to me?"

"Not a thing," Rose said sweetly. "I didnae even touch ye. And whenever a sixteen-year-old girl gets close enough to do so in the future—" She reached out for him as if to illustrate the point and he leapt back, jarring against the shelf behind him and knocking off a couple bottles of whiskey. They shattered to the floor and he flinched. "Well," she went on, "you'll have a similar reaction to what happens any time I get close enough to ye."

"That was the Macallan eighteen-year-aged!" He was still clutching himself for protection. "Do you have any idea how much that costs? The owner is going to take that breakage out of me arse!"

"Is he now?" Rose leaned forward and reached out for him again, on her tippy toes over the bar. At her mere motion, he flinched back again, involuntarily, and hit the shelves again, this time dislodging a vodka bottle and two of gin. They all came crashing to the floor and he was powerless to stop them, still cupping his privates like they were about to be assaulted by the Luftwaffe or something. "I bet he'll be really mad when he sees you've broken those as well."

"Please stop!" He shifted down the bar, trying to escape her, and by extension, me. He retreated toward a door to a backroom, lingering there for a moment, almost in tears. "You can't do this to me!"

"Oh, but I just did, luv," Rose said with a smile, settling back on her stool. "Consider yourself lucky I didn't mess with your reactions in other areas as well. Say, dial up your interest in other activities, ones you might find repellent just now." She waggled her fingers at him.

He swallowed visibly and without further comment darted into the back room, slamming the door behind him. I let out the cronish cackle I'd been holding in all this time and Rose gave a solid chuckle, then cringed at the pain it caused her.

"That was well done," I said. "Did you really mean it? That he wouldn't be able to react—uhhh—how he reacts—to sixteen-year-old girls in the future?"

"He'll jump back from them like that every time," she said, taking up her Blue Hawaiian and pondering the contents suspiciously. "So long as I'm alive, anyway."

"Hmm," I said. "How'd you do that?"

She shrugged, taking a sip before answering. "Lust is an emotion. Fear is an emotion. All I did was plant a little block that killed his lust at that stimulus and replaced it with a dead fear that any comely young lass he meets is going to kick him right in the boys." She took another sip, long and cool. "Which, honestly, should be their reaction, if they knew him for the snake he is."

"I'll drink to that," I said, and started to raise my glass.

"Och," she said, almost choking on hers. "We should have toasted." She brought up her drink, the liquid sloshing gently within. "Shall we raise our glasses in the usual Scottish way?"

I stared at her blankly and raised my glass. "Uhh...'To the boy who lived'?"

She almost snorted her drink. "No...something a bit more appropriate to the moment, and a bit more traditionally Scottish...Alba gu brath—it means, 'Scotland forever.'"

I thought about it, then raised my drink once more. "I can get behind that." And we clinked glasses.

25.

We took a cab to the Edinburgh PD, which was called Police Scotland, probably in an effort to provide some kind of national police force. It sounded a little funky to an American used to dealing with local PDs and sheriffs' departments, but it probably made sense given how many jurisdictional nightmares I'd seen, with all the interdepartmental pissing matches.

I'd decided to make an effort to swoop in and take whatever file they might have assembled on Graham and see if they had anything new on Adam Perry, though I doubted the coroner would have done much with him yet. Or that there was much to be found, really. What were they going to say? "He got eaten by an incubus, and also had an addiction to pe-jazzling." If that was the case, I didn't need to know about it.

The Police Scotland building was a strange brick thing, bisected with a glass facade couched right in its middle, like some sort of church mixed with an architectural experiment involving lots of masons. Walking through the main entrance, we were confronted immediately by a waiting area, which I ignored, and stepped up to the window where a desk sergeant waited to direct visitors. She was a very librarian-esque woman, stern, serious, someone's pissed-off, maiden aunt, and the primness of her expression was like a ten-thousand-watt sign letting the world know that the level of nonsense she would brook was somewhere between zero and none.

"Can I help you?" she asked with the light Scottish brogue I'd come to expect in this town.

"Sarah Nelson, Scotland Yard," I said, flashing my ID. "I'm working on the murder investigation and I need to check up on another victim that may be related."

She kept pretty buttoned down. "Do you know who you're here to see?"

"Well, I was told I'm actually in charge of the investigation, and I'm not here to see myself because I could do that with the aid of any mirror in town, so…" I held up my notebook. "The victim, Adam Perry, had a roommate, Graham Selkirk, who died recently. I'm here to talk to whoever is in charge of that investigation, if there is one."

If the discussing of possible multiple homicides discomfited the maiden aunt desk clerk, she showed not a whit of it to me. "You'll probably want to talk to Detective Inspector Clements. Let me ring him up and see if he's available."

"Or if he can make himself available," I said. "Urgently." She raised an eyebrow at this. "You know, before more people die," I added calmly.

She took this in stride, or, since she was sitting, in utter stillness.

I turned to Rose as the clerk spoke into the phone in hushed tones. I could have listened in—and did—but I didn't really care what was said provided I didn't catch a whiff of someone giving me the runaround. To Rose, I said, "I'm wondering about the connection between these vics. That's cop slang for victim," I added, trying to give it a conspiratorial air.

"I kinda worked that one out for meself," she said, leaning in to my little conspiracy of two. Rose was a good sport. "If one roommate dies after the other, d'ye think that means they were in league in some way with this…incubus fellow? That maybe he was using them for some purpose the way he turned loose those blokes at the cafe on you? Or were they just innocent victims?"

"I don't know," I said, waiting for Maiden Aunt to hang up with Detective Inspector Clements, who was quietly cursing this interruption to his afternoon nap or something. "I know he drained Adam Perry, and given Graham's cause of death being suggested as a heart attack, probably him, too. Maybe this incubus did it for fun, maybe to cover up something once he was done with them, like you said. It'll be tough to know until we can establish a working relationship, if any, between them and the killer."

"The bartender seemed to think Adam Perry was interested in men—"

"Possibly," I said. "His opinion was filtered through the lens of his own, nasty pedo experience, which makes him unreliable in this department. Perry could have just been really shy and introverted toward the opposite sex." I dipped back into my head for a second.

"That's a fair point," Rose said. "How will we figure out which it is?"

"Well, first we have to find out if it matters," I said. "Meaning, I need to look at the pattern of victims. Serial killers often choose victims for a reason—either because they're part of a pattern than they can see, or because, hell, they're convenient and won't necessarily be missed. Our incubus has had less reason to worry about raising suspicion until now, because every one of the deaths he's caused have been ruled natural up until Dr. Logan's research turned the tables around on it. That might have emboldened him to worry less about the convenience factor, or he might have been paranoid enough to stick to working in relative safety. It's hard to say from what we've seen of this puzzle so far." I lifted a hand and rubbed my temples and then the bridge of my nose, my go-to move for stress relief. "I hate to sound like a computer, but I need more data."

"DI Clements will see you now," Maiden Aunt said as she hung up the phone. She hit a buzzer and a door to my right made a not-subtle unlocking noise. "Straight through the door and he'll meet you just on the other side in a moment."

"Thanks," I said, and went for it, beckoning Rose to follow.

Maiden Aunt harrumphed, clearly meant to get attention for some reason. "Excuse me."

"You're excused," I said, not intending to give her any more of my time than she'd already absorbed, like an incubus stealing minutes of my life. I opened the door and held it for

Rose.

Maiden Aunt was on her feet, outrage increasing second by second. "I'm sorry, but your…*associate*—" and boy did she put some mustard into that word "—will have to wait out here."

"Listen, Dame Saggy Smith," I said, causing Maiden Aunt's mouth to gape in outrage, "I don't know what they've told you about me, but when I came here, they gave me carte blanche." I indicated Rose with my palm up. "This is my carte. Now blanche off." And I tilted my head to suggest Rose get inside, which she did with all due haste, and then I closed the door on Maiden Aunt before she could start in to sputtering.

"That was a bit harsh, wasn't it?" Rose asked once we were in the interior hallway.

"I didn't say a single swearing potty word," I said, "and no one lost a soul or their life, so…no, that was mild."

Rose snickered, and a second later a harried fellow came around the corner dressed in a well-pressed suit. He was middle-aged but still had his hair, dark and full, above a brow that was just starting to evince signs of his age. He stopped when he saw us barreling down the corridor toward him, and waited as I strutted up.

"Sarah Nelson," I said by way of introduction. "This is Rose, my associate."

"DI Clements," he said in precise tones, another Edinburgher who lacked much of a brogue. "What can I do for you, Ms. Nelson?"

"In our investigation, we turned up a second vic," I said. "Roommate to Adam Perry, name of Graham Selkirk. Got anything on him?"

Clements furrowed that brow, the subtle wrinkles of his advancing age turning into deep canyons as he contemplated this. "Aye; came though a couple weeks ago. I actually interviewed his flatmate at the time."

I followed him around the corner to the bullpen, which seemed to be a fixture of police stations the world over. I liked the air, the noise, the general feel of being in them, so to me this was a plus. It felt like home. "You interviewed

Perry? And you didn't put two and two together when the news came through that he died this morning?"

"The Perry case never hit my desk," Clements said. His expression said that he was probably sincere, in a lazy, didn't-care-about-anything-but-his-immediate-job kind of way. "And Selkirk got ruled a heart attack by the coroner. It's out of my hands now."

"I suppose you wouldn't want to step on any toes higher up by declaring it a homicide," I said, both acknowledging the somewhat precarious situation he was in but also kinda calling him a lazy chickenshit for not doing any digging, all at once. But subtly. "When I got this case," I said as we settled in the area around Clements's desk, him taking his chair and not offering either of his lady guests one, "I was told that Perry was not the first victim they'd tagged for this perp. Did any of those land on your desk?"

"Aye, for a time," Clements said, looking into a pile of paperwork in neat little bins on the corner of his desk. Paperwork, too, seemed to be a universal police burden, which was probably why they needed bullpens—to do the piles of paperwork. He selected a folder and pulled it out. "Bianca Kelly." He laid it down, then carefully picked out another. "Elizabeth Sutler." Threw it on the pile. "Petra Evans." And added it to the other two. "These are just the ones we can confirm, in the last two weeks, which was where I started digging before the people upstairs yanked it out of my hands." He smiled benignly.

I stared at Clements and he stared back. He hadn't totally slacked off. He'd started to work on this thing before it got bumped up to Logan, Wexford, and, eventually, me. I picked up the folders, opening the topmost, the one belonging to Petra Evans. "Anything in particular stick out at you?"

"Like I said, I didn't have much chance to dig," he said blandly. "But no. This connection you're mentioning between Perry and Selkirk, it's the first such I've noted. Evans lived with her husband up in Dunfermline, across the Firth of Forth—"

"The what of what?" I asked.

"Firth of Forth," Rose said. "In Fife."

I looked from her to Clements. "You're both just fucking with me now, aren't you?"

Rose chuckled. "A firth is an estuary, leads to the sea. Forth is the river. Fife is the county across the river."

"Right," Clements said, "so, Evans lived across the Firth of Forth."

"In Fife," I tacked on, because if they were having a good laugh at my expense, it was coming later. So far they were dead serious.

"Aye," Clements said. "Bianca Kelly was a nurse in a private practice here in Edinburgh. And Elizabeth Sutler was a tech worker. No connection between them. Sutler was abducted from outside her workplace. Kelly was taken from a public park. Evans…we're not sure, but it looks like she might have had her car stolen at the same time, because it turned up behind a Marks & Spencer at Craigleith Retail Park."

"Forensics?" I asked. "On the car, I mean. The killer could have used it for a spell and…absorbed her for the joy of it."

Rose cocked her head at me. "Is it fun? Absorbing people?" Realizing we had an audience, she added hastily, "D'ye think?"

"So I've heard," I said, a little clipped.

If it made it through Clements's well-practiced aura of giving a damn about nothing, he gave no sign and offered no comment on it, instead sticking to my question. "The car didn't make it to forensics before…" He gestured at the folders now in my hands.

"It left your desk, tragically committing suicide, at least in your eyes," I said. His narrowed at my swipe. "I need forensics on all this stuff, ASAP."

He shrugged almost indifferently. "Can't."

I stared at him. "Why, pray tell?" I asked, with so much more patience and forbearance than I really felt he deserved at the moment.

"It all got shipped, didn't it?" Clements asked. "These files? They're my copies." He nodded at them. "The rest are making their way through the bureaucracy even now." He kept a really steady, annoyingly so, gaze on me. "Figured you would know that." It carried a bite of accusation.

I didn't let it rattle me, because unlike some amateur poseur, I'd been faking being federal law enforcement for years before I became an actual one—albeit on a different continent. "Bureaucrats," I muttered under my breath, loud enough he could hear it as I paged through the folder. In practiced English and affecting a little bit of a heavier accent, I added, "They didn't tell me nuffing."

Clements's smoky eyes were watching me closely for a moment longer, and then he relaxed an inch. "They do that, aye."

I looked up. "Didn't even tell me about Perry until I was almost here. 'Surprise,' they said. 'Head to this crime scene.'" I shook my head. "Anyway, anything else you can tell me, Inspector?"

Clements chewed his lower lip, clearly mulling over either the case, or whether he should spill the beans on something. I hoped for the latter. "There was one thing." He seemed somewhat committed at this point, so I waited for him to come out with it. "Evans and Sutler both went missing before they were found—on different sides of the city, I might add." He took a breath. "In the course of that part of the investigation, I contacted their mobile providers and tried to track their phones. Both went offline shortly before their deaths, but…I got an interesting point of reference from both of them." He turned to his computer and clicked it off the screen saver, then brought up Google Maps. "They'd both been recorded with a GPS fix at the same location—the night before each of the respective bodies turned up."

He zoomed in on a section of Edinburgh that I could tell from the overhead wasn't near the castle or the old town. It looked a little grungier from overhead, and Clements clicked the cursor on a building in the center of the screen. "Right here. Both of these women, seemingly unrelated to each other by work, circumstance, acquaintance, yet…" He chewed that lip again for a second. "Less than twenty-four hours before they die, their cell phones turn up in this building, right here."

"What is it?" I asked, peering at the screen.

"High rise up by the Firth," he said. "Both of those cell phones—it wasn't a precise fix, but they were up a few floors."

"Did you happen to get out there to take a look?" I asked.

"I appended it to the report," Clements said with a shrug. "But I didn't get this back until after—"

"The files flew from your desk, never to be seen again," I said, leaning in. "All right. I guess I know where our next stop is." I looked back at Rose, who nodded. She looked nicely determined. I approved. "Hopefully..." I said, giving voice to what I wanted—well, sort of, "this will put an end to it."

26.

"Stop here," I told the cabbie about three blocks from the apartment building that we'd gotten from DI Clements. He dutifully pulled over while I took in Rose's querying look. "If this guy has people watching, I don't want to give him a heads-up we're coming. I'd rather come in quietly, through the back alleys, looking for any watchers he's got set out so we don't come stumbling into a trap that's set for us before we get there."

"Ah," Rose said. "That makes sense."

"Of course," I said, handing the cabbie another £10 note and shutting the door so Rose didn't have to, "given my luck we'll come walking into one anyway no matter how much of a precaution we take, but still…" I thought about it for a second, the cab pulling away in a low hum of tires against pavement. "Actually, maybe we'd be better off just running it from here."

Rose got a pained look. "Uhm, all right." Good sport that she was, that was the end of her complaint on the matter.

We jogged along the street toward our destination, a multi-story red brick building that looked like it had seen much better days. There were older buildings along the street, residential, and a couple other towers nearby, lining the avenue with a distinctly old-timey feel, like they'd been built decades ago and let to go mostly to seed.

"Gahhh," Rose breathed, clearly laboring under some pain. I hadn't checked her wound yet, not wanting to tell her to put up her shirt in any of the cabs we'd been in. It would have felt awkward, and also like the opening scene of a really cheesy porno.

"You gonna be okay?" I asked, trying to set the pace at a run that would make an Army drill sergeant weep with joy if his charges were hitting this pace, but low enough that she wasn't completely screwed.

"I don't do a lot of cardio," she said. "So it's not the wound, it's the laziness, I'm afraid."

"Suuuuure it is," I said. "I saw you pull out the martial arts in the cafe when you saved me. You're practiced, and that doesn't exactly take no stamina."

She blushed. "I do a little, it's true. I took my inspiration on that from you."

"So it really is the wound," I said.

She clenched her jaw shut. "A little," she finally conceded. "But I'll be damned if I let you go busting in there all by yourself."

And I'd be damned if I left her behind to be picked off by any flunkies of Mr. Incubus, to be used as a hostage against me later. "Kind of you," I said. "By the way…what were you doing up on the roof when you first saw me?"

"Oh," she said, brightening a little. "Well, I wasn't actually on a roof when I first saw you. I was down at street level, walking to my job." She blushed a little. "Erhm…which I maybe don't have now, since I forgot to call and tell them I'd be not showing up today." She shrugged. "Seems pointless to do so now, given that I'm hours late. Besides," she said, a little glimmer in her eye, "this is so much more fun."

"It has a certain allure," I conceded, not wanting to cop to the fact that yes, I was an action junkie, addicted to the thrill of the chase. When I wasn't working, I felt like I was in static motion, trapped in life. But when I had a case? The sun was shining, children were singing—ones with good voices, like a choir, not a bunch of randos with pitch and tone issues. Even pursued by my country and hounded by the law, I didn't feel alive, truly, unless I was working on something, catching a bad guy.

"It's the most thrilling thing I've ever done," she burbled as we crossed the street. The tower was ahead, less than a block now. We weren't running so fast we didn't appear to be human, or a blur or anything—though I could have done that if I wanted.

"Even the yak yak parts?" I asked, drawing a frown from her. "Where we just talk to people and try and get them to spill what they know about people?"

"Look," she said, almost pityingly, "what I do—did—for work is data entry. So yes, talking to people, even lecherous ones like that shopkeeper and the bartender? Much better than my average day of staring at a computer screen and hoping not to make too many errors." She shuddered. "At least my meta speed keeps me moving fast enough to keep ahead, but I'll tell ye—sometimes I have nightmares about sitting at the keyboard."

"Well, you'll get nightmares of another kind entirely from this job," I said. She nodded, signaling that she understood, but really…she didn't. No one ever did until they saw some of the things we saw in this gig. And trying to warn her about them? Forget it. They had to be experienced.

The front doors to the apartment building were Plexiglas, I realized as I held one open and let Rose pass through—once I'd made sure the lobby was empty. It wouldn't have felt right sending her in without gauging threats first, but the elevator lobby for the place was pretty empty, and nice and open too, with a few apartment unit doors leading off it.

"How the hell are we going to figure out which is the unit in this building that the cell phones for those vics came from?" I asked Rose as we ambled across the lobby.

She frowned, then seemed to actually give it some thought, speaking out loud. "Are most of your type, uhm…loners?"

I blinked, giving it some thought of my own. "The ones I've met? Yeah. My mom, Aunt Charlie, James Fries, Sovereign…pretty much all of them lived alone or wandered the world alone. I guess my mom was maybe the least anti-social of them, now that I think about it." Which was kinda hilarious.

"Then we'd probably be looking for a single-bedroom, right?"

She had a point. "Makes sense." I looked around, searching for a sign, an administration office, anything. A couple of hallways extended past the elevator banks toward the back of the building, into gloomy passages where the lights flickered and nothing good probably ever happened. I picked one, the one on the right, and started down it, looking for—"Bingo."

"Bingo what?" Rose asked, coming up behind me as I kicked in a door to an administration office. "Oh."

It ripped off its hinges and fell in, sending someone behind it sailing to their feet, screaming at a high pitch that reminded me of an opera singer. When I came through into the administration office for the place, I found it wasn't actually a woman, it was a guy with shoulder-length curly red hair and a beard that was impossibly twisty. He wore jeans and a baggy denim button-up shirt and he threw his hands skyward as I came in. "Take whatever ye want! None of it's mine—I don't care if ye take it all; just please don't hurt me!"

I exchanged a look with Rose as she entered, clearly darkly amused by his statement. "I didn't know anyone was in here," I said, a little chagrined by this development. The office was a lot bigger than what I had figured on too, doubling as a kind of janitorial space and maintenance and storage area.

"I can leave," he said, keeping those hands up and pointing toward the door. "No problem. I'll make my way right out—"

"Hold on there, Braveheart," I said, causing Rose to display a nervous tick just by virtue of me mentioning the movie title. "Since you're here, I might as well ask you a couple questions." I flashed the badge, and he relaxed, finally letting his arms slowly drop to his side. "We're looking into some suspicious activity—"

"Yeah, that'd be the sixth floor," he said. Definite, no budge.

"I haven't even told you what—"

"Yeah, it's the sixth floor. Trust me."

Rose had a hard time containing her amusement. "What d'ye see 'em doing up there on the sixth floor?"

"Oh, I don't *see* anything," he said, shaking his head. "Nothing at all. Nothing I'd be willing to talk about in a courtroom dock, that's for sure."

"Then why should we start with the sixth floor?" I asked, wondering if this was going to go anywhere good. I'd decided he was probably telling the truth; he was just so completely chickenhearted that once he'd dropped the dime, he didn't want it to blow back on him.

"Stuff is going on up there," he said cagily.

"What kind of stuff?" I asked.

"Stuff. Probably not good stuff. Noise-complaints-from-other-tenants stuff." He swallowed visibly. "That kind of stuff."

"If you say 'stuff' one more time, I'm gonna stuff something up your nose," I said. He gulped again. "I'm looking for a serious criminal here. Get specific with me or I'm going to become a lot bigger pain in your ass."

"There's a guy up there," he said, useful words finally galloping out of his mouth. "In 6B. Hasn't been here long; maybe a couple weeks. Don't get me wrong, there's always been a rougher element as long as I've worked here, but…" He swallowed again, and paled slightly. "Now we hear screaming sometimes at night. I heard someone got dragged up in the elevator. And the other residents? They're walking around like zombies half the time, can't hardly believe what they're seeing." He shook his head. "Anyway…sixth floor. 6B. That's what you're looking for, I'd guess."

I exchanged a look with Rose. "Sounds like 6B is where we're headed."

"Yep," she said, and we nodded, heading back through the door.

"Oh, and by the way," he said, catching us on the way out, "if you could leave my name out of this—"

"Your secret is safe with us," I said, heading back toward the elevators, "chickenshit."

"Do you blame him?" Rose asked once we were safely in the elevator, heading up to the sixth floor. It moved with a quiet hum, crawling up so slowly I could hardly feel it.

"No," I said, "but I'm not in a place in my life where I like to condone the sort of ordinary, go-along cowardice that enables serial killers, so…"

Her eyebrows rose, and she nodded, but did not say anything.

I was already moving when the elevator dinged, sliding out into the hallway and stalking along it toward 6B. It was the second door I came to in a wide hallway to the right of the elevator bank, ordinary, nondescript, but showing some serious wear. Almost like maintenance hadn't been doing jack on this floor for a while. (Though in fairness that probably preceded this scary incubus moving in.)

I took up position next to the door and Rose put her back to it across from me when I motioned for her to. Using hand signals, I tried to convey what was coming next, though who knew whether she got it or not? She nodded, at least.

That done, I launched off the wall and readied myself, blasting forward into apartment 6B with a kick that shattered the frame and carried me through into a living room that was utterly placid, looking out over a beautiful view of Edinburgh town and marred by only one thing: a man standing with his back to me, head bald and, when he turned to calmly look at me over his shoulder, a grin as wide as any I'd ever seen.

"Hullo, Sienna," he said in a light brogue, arms clasped behind his back. "I've been waiting for ye."

27.

"I've been looking forward to meeting you too," I said and shot a Gavrikov-fueled flame bullet out of my fingertip. It shot across the impressively appointed apartment, this little oasis of cleanliness with a prime view of Edinburgh. It was headed right for his chest, and he lifted a hand, reaching out for it, and catching it in his palm. He seemed to twist his wrist, then opened his palm again to reveal—

Nothing. No burn, no flame bullet, nada.

He'd dissolved it as easily as I'd created it.

The man grinned broadly. "I've seen that trick before."

I started to get a cold, creeping feeling about this. He didn't take umbrage when I lifted my hand though, and a second later I was blasting him with a light net.

The air around him distorted, like a mirror that someone was bending, and the light nets disappeared, leaving me with nothing but a view of his smiling face. "Ye'll have to do better than that."

"Oh, I'm just warming up, bub," I said, looking back at Rose. She was staring at him intently, working her powers, but after a moment she broke off, looked at me and shook her head. Empathy was a no-go, which meant—

I can't read his mind, Harmon said. *I'm betting he's the one that screwed up my ability to read the toughs he sent after you earlier.*

That means the Warmind will similarly not be of use, Bjorn said.

No light nets, no telepathy, no Warmind, no fire…what the hell am I supposed to do now? I asked the souls in my head.

136

Please don't go dragon, Bastian said, *unless you desperately need to.*

We're in a populated building, Bastian. Of course I'm not going dragon unless I have to.

You've still got my stunning good looks, Zack said, and, after a beat, *What? I'm not allowed to crack jokes during tense moments?*

I stared at my enemy, and he started to talk again, arms now clasped behind his back once more in the sheerest display of arrogance while fighting me that I'd seen since… probably Sovereign. "Now you see plainly what I am," he said.

"Yep," I said, racking my brain. *Seriously, guys. He's been juicing.*

He's been doing what you've steadfastly refused to do, Harmon said, adopting the air of a lecturing douchebag. *Acquiring power by any means necessary.*

"Thanks," I said, accidentally aloud, causing Baldy to cock his head at me curiously. "Sorry, wasn't talking to you."

Displaying momentary surprise, he said, "Quite all right," in a fairly sonorous voice. "Have ye heard a word I've said, or are you too busy being in your own head?"

"Well, it's pretty in here," I said, tapping my temple with a knuckle. "I mean, no offense, but your face is not exactly the stuff of ladies' fantasies." This wasn't entirely true, but I needed a distraction while my mind was racing, trying to decide on the best course of attack. I mean, if this guy had stockpiled a fire power, telepathy or empathy, plus…whatever the hell he'd done to that light net…

Who knew how many other powers he was sitting on? Lunging at him, trying to get in a hand-to-hand scrap when I had no idea how deep his metaphorical bench of powers was? Sounded like a formula for calamity, especially given we were in an apartment complex surrounded by people.

"Ye wound me," he said, not showing a lot of signs of wounding. "Don't you know…we're made for each other, you and I?"

I made a deep, guttural gagging noise and stuck my tongue out while doing it. He recoiled an inch or so, and I glanced back to Rose for solidarity. She too seemed to be wearing an expression of acute surprise that I'd do this in the buildup to the big fight scene we were about to partake in. "Why does every incubus say this same, tired BS?"

Rose didn't waste a second before answering. "I think a lot of men say this, actually, and with much less justification than he's got."

"Point to you, sidekick," I said, reeling myself back around to find Baldy right where I'd left him. "Look...serial killer guy...it's not that I don't appreciate your attention...okay, never mind. I actually don't appreciate your attention. Because you're a serial killer."

"So are you," he said calmly, lacking any sign of being affronted. "And you've killed more than I have."

"I'm not a..." I paused, trying to figure out how to best frame my argument. "I'm not a serial killer, okay? Just a... justice killer," I finished lamely.

"Is that who you are? The swift sword of justice, Sienna Nealon?" His eyes showed a spark of amusement.

"Most of the time, yeah," I said. "Who are you?"

"A worthy question," he said. "My name is Frankie."

I stared at him for a second. "No, seriously. Do you go by, like, Frank? Or Francis? Or maybe—"

"Frankie will do."

"God, I think this one's got Peter Pan syndrome," I said, just shaking my head at him, talking clinically like he wasn't here. I kinda wanted to get him pissed off enough to attack and start showcasing some of the abilities he had up his sleeve. My other alternative was to smash him through the windows in an attempt to fly him up above the city and drop him like he was a hot potato in hopes that he hadn't absorbed the power of flight. Yet. Other options involved hand-to-hand combat of the kind that would result in the certain destruction of this apartment and probably the surrounding floors, maybe even the rest of the building if he had the off-the-charts energy projection I suspected. Just having Gavrikov powers put him right at the top of the scale.

"Oh, I'm all grown up." He smiled, either not noticing or not caring about my insult. "Would ye like to see?"

I assumed one meaning for that. "Keep your pants on, Frankie. I don't know you that well."

"You always assume the worst of people, don't you?" Frankie said.

"Well, so far since arriving in Edinburgh I've looked one of your dead victims in the eye and been nearly killed by a gang of metas whose leashes I assume were being held by you."

"They weren't going to kill you," Frankie said. "They were going to bring you to me."

"Why?" I asked. It was really the only question that mattered, getting to the core of who he was and why he was doing…all this.

"I needed to meet you," he said quietly. "Needed to look you in the eye. See who you were…in there." He pointed at my head. "Oh, sure, we all see you on TV. Big, bad Sienna Nealon. You look taller on television, by the way—"

"I get that a lot."

"And it doesn't fully capture that sparkle in your eyes." He stared at me, that head still cocked, shining from the light cast in through the windows behind him. "I think you're sneering at the world, all the time."

"Well, I'm certainly sneering at you right now."

"Was your mother like this?" Frankie asked, and my blood turned hot with anger, leaving behind the cold calculation of how best to kill him. "Your grandmother? Because—that's the line through which the power was passed, right? Matrilineal?"

"Yes, my mom was hell on wheels," I said, struggling to be civil. If I could get close enough, I could maybe use my Wolfe skull to smash his face into a paste. He wasn't moving any closer, and he was out of the range where I could easily pull that off. "Whyever do you ask?"

"We're all related, our kind," he said. "Just trying to put the pieces together."

"If you're trying to say you're my secret brother, I already had one of those. And fortunately for me, he's not a psycho serial killer."

"No, I don't think I'm your brother," he said. "Probably up the family tree somewhere, though."

"That's special," I said. "Let me introduce you to how we do things in my family."

I launched at him, at last, keeping my movements low and close to the ground. Short, shuffling steps carried me forward, and I refused to commit to a stupid, grand leap that would leave me open for a deadly counterattack. Instead I rushed him almost half-heartedly, ready to start slugging him in the face, which—I mean, really, that was a Nealon family tradition. At least the way my mom and aunt did it. And my great uncle Raymond, sort of, come to think of it.

It was a good thing I stayed low, because Frankie started to glow a second later, and unleashed a burst that I only just dodged in time. It was a glowing, vibrating red, a power I'd never seen before, and one that seemed to rip out of the very floor in a wall of sheer force as it passed, an eruption that splintered carpet and ceiling and peppered me with the spray of debris from both as it tore through the apartment. Rose cried out and leapt out of the way just before it blasted out the way we'd entered, annihilating the door in the process and leaving nothing but splinters raining down.

"Shit," I muttered as I rolled across the carpet. What Frankie had just done in here was unleash catastrophic damage. I couldn't see very much past the wrecked door, but I could see that his wave of ripping force looked like it had continued on past the hallway, and the apartments above and below were visible through the scar he'd torn in the floor and ceiling.

Rose was getting up, separated from me by the small chasm that divided the apartment. She had a worried look, no disguising it. She held her side but got to her feet, shaking but determined, facing Frankie, as I found myself doing. Now that I knew at least a little of what he was capable of…there was no way in hell I could afford to turn my back on him. Not for a second.

"Is that how you do it in your family?" he asked with faint glee, as the building creaked around us, my stomach plummeting as I realized exactly how bad a trap I'd walked us into.

28.

Wolfe

Norway
322 BC

The battle was like something out of Wolfe's sweetest dreams. Fur-clad clansmen, an unfortunate lot of them, a hundred or more all bound to foot and horseback in a few cases, laid out like a pleasant feast for him.

Him…and the daughter of Death.

She did not speak as she fought, using the blade they'd picked up in their travels to the Far East, where the people spoke a strange language, and whose appearance and customs were so different from those of their homeland. They had been welcomed, though suspiciously, once they journeyed past the land of the steppes, the cold, and all the way to the far shores of a distant sea. The blade had been a gift from King Dao and was beautifully crafted, very different from the style of swords in their native land. She was beautifully lethal with it.

It danced in the hands of Lethe, sharply cleaving through the chests of those northmen who charged at her, screaming in their oxen language. Wolfe followed behind, his claws slick with blood as he danced through the battle, tasting the throats of those he ripped through, enjoying the slick feel of their guts as he ripped them out. They came for Lethe from the back as she cut through them at the front and Wolfe gloried in their attacks, gloried in the waves of them as he slashed through, rending their furs and their bellies, tasting their sweet life pouring out in his face and across his hair, matted by the ichor he continued to tear from them by force.

Lethe let out a scream of battle fury. He had heard her do this before, a sonorous bellow, and her attacks became frenzied, even more furious. She did not seem to be stirred to it by any particular sensation, save one—a battle so chaotic she did not have the proper time to use her power against her foes. Here, her sword rose and fell, cleaving heads and arms, limb from torso, torso to pieces. They came at her and came at her, and no mere seconds existed for her to grab one, seize them with a hand, and drain them dry the way he knew she loved.

Wolfe did not stop his battle fury behind her. He redoubled his efforts, wanting to buy her those precious seconds, to give her her glory. They had traveled now for so many years, through so many places—to the edge of the sea in the east, to the swamps and jungles of the southeast, where the air was hot and thick, like the vines that stretched from tree to tree. They had crossed mountains west of that which had seemed to go on forever, some taller than Olympus, going beyond the heavens, perhaps. In a land of people with darker skin they had learned new names of those venerated and worshipped. And coming back from that, crossing the endless deserts, they had found other things, other battles.

And somewhere in that space of years, sleeping out among the stars or sheltering with friendly tribes that desired gods for protection and worship…Wolfe had awoken to a truth that he dared not speak.

Watching the daughter of death in her lethal dance, sword blazing and shining in the cloud-covered sunshine, he saw her fury and joy, twin feelings that warred across her face as legions were slain by her hand. She wore no robes, no clothing, for they were an impediment to war, to the fight, to death. She was clad only in the blood of her enemies—across her supple flesh, her chest, her face, it stained her crimson from top to bottom, the fight having dragged on over dozens of dead and dying. The cries of the bitterly wounded were like sweet music in his ears; no singer could have serenaded him as sweetly.

Wolfe licked the blood off his lips and buried his hand up to the wrist in the guts of a dirty tribesman. He did not dare pause to take his own relief, to suck blood and taste sweet meat—Lethe disdained that craving of his, though she tolerated it and other, more base and carnal ones. He focused only on clearing the back as she moved forward, slashing through these bodies like her sword cleaved through the flesh of her foes.

And he watched every moment he could. Turned and watched her in every lull of the battle. The lines of her body, dripping with gore as she cut through foes, her skin dripping with delicious blood, delicious death…

Delicious.

The enemies were thinning. A horn was sounding in the distance. They'd had this fray behind a hill, where this army of tribesmen was lined up for other purposes. That did not bother Wolfe and it certainly did not seem to faze Lethe, who continued to pursue them, cleaving one enemy in half even as their line broke and they ran to the side, trying to skirt the hill's edge and escape in a mad panic, fleeing from whatever was before them—and now, behind them.

"Hark," Lethe said, her voice weary as she stopped, seizing one of them by the back of the neck in his flight. She gripped him there as he struggled, but only for a few seconds before he gave up the fight once more, though this time not in retreat. He jerked a few times in her grip, then slumped, her power exercising its dominion of his soul. She threw her head back for a mere moment, savoring it, then cast the body aside. It was plainly dead, and Wolfe slunk in as Lethe grabbed another, taking to the corpse she'd just discarded as a dog might to a bone thrown by its master. "Something approaches."

"I'll be quick," Wolfe said, sinking his teeth into the neck of the body. He liked them like this, fresh, her effect on them stilling them without making them cold. This man's heart was dead, true, but only recently, and a few last pumps of blood spurted across his lips before it went still. The meat, though…that was still warm.

"See that you are." Her disgust was contained by her wariness at the approach of possible danger. She had thrown her head back to the heavens, savoring her own drink, the tearing of the soul from the body of these savages. Another taken in, she shuddered, her body shivering in the chill of the autumn. She tossed this one aside too, but not at Wolfe's feet. She may have tolerated his savagery, but she did not enable his eating of enemy flesh. His other practices, though…those she did not seem to object to.

He lifted his head from the kill as he sensed something rising above the hillside. Horses and men, even a few women, the scent was of their flesh, of their skins—those they wore and those that were bound to them. Their weapons were wood and iron. The power seemed to waft off of them as they stayed there, looking down upon Lethe and him, no rush to battle, no sudden charge.

"Ho," the one in the middle called. He spoke again, in a language that Wolfe had no knowledge of.

"We do not know what you are saying," Lethe called back to him in their own.

The man paused for a moment. He was broad and carried a spear that was drenched with blood. Upon his shoulder sat a raven, and it cawed as if trying to answer for him. "It would appear we have the same foe," the man said in their own tongue.

Lethe took this in stride. "I have no foes. I merely saw goats waiting to be slaughtered, and waded in to take my prize from their flesh." One of the fallen groaned at her feet, writhing, trying to crawl, and she reached down, lifting him up by the back of his neck. All was quiet save for his quickened breathing, a heaving sound of squeals in the grim midday, until he finally went still and Lethe let her head pull back just slightly, savoring what she'd just done.

"Then you have done us a great service in your…craving," the man said. "I take it by your language that you are from Athens? Children of Olympus?"

144

"We were from near Athens, though not of Olympus," Lethe said. "But now we are of the world, and drink battle and carnage wherever we care to."

The man smiled, nodding. "I know the call to war well. My people heed it at every turn. My name is Odin, and these are my own kin—my wife, Frigga." He nodded to the woman to his left. "My sons—"

"I do not care about your family," Lethe said coldly.

Odin took this without comment or apparent insult, shrewdly studying her. "You are focused on your purpose. Let me offer you this—my people make war the way others might farm a harvest. I see in you a kindred spirit, one who seeks to channel the chaos, who dances upon the edge of honor and pain. Come drink with us this night in my meadhall. You will be our honored guests, feted by my army, the Einherjaren."

Lethe watched, inscrutable. Wolfe did not watch this Odin; he watched Lethe. She was having a reaction, a very subtle one, as most of hers tended to be. But she did not speak. The blood continued to drip down her body as she remained still as if she had joined the dead.

"If you desire war and blood and fire," Odin went on, "I could tell you of places—nearby, even—where you could find enough of it to fill your bellies and your spirits for the lifetimes of many mortals." He wore a broad grin, the others remaining silent in his party. "Of course, I'm sure you could find these places on your own, but..." He wore a canny look, and Wolfe could see a sort of devilish wisdom in his only remaining eye. "Is it not sweeter to fight with an army? To be able to savor the battle rather than being constantly buffeted from foe to foe?"

Wolfe's hairs began to rise on his back. "Daughter of death—"

"Do not address me now, dog," Lethe said in the most steely whisper. "You follow me, and I do not seek or need your counsel." She took another breath, chest heaving, gore sliding down her supple flesh, as pristine now as when he had met her centuries earlier. "Very well, Odin," she said. "We accept your invitation. A meal would be a...kindness.

Battle would be…" Her eyes grew hungry. "…welcome."

"I think you could find a happy place among our armies," Odin said. "I have seldom seen your kind before, and never in so…glorious a state." He looked her up and down, nostrils flaring. "Your courage is great, and you are a chooser of the dead; I see it now. Come. We feast," he said, and turned his horse around with but an effort, disappearing back over the hill before his line of followers did the same.

"I do not trust them," Wolfe said once the last of them had crossed over.

Lethe did not look at him, did not answer, and he saw the back of her hair where it was clumped and sticky with the gore of the battle. "You do not need to trust them," she said, "and it is probably wiser that you do not. For if they do not deceive, we will go with them for a time, and see if they in fact do have a stomach for battle that this Odin has promised." Now she turned, just slightly. "For if so…perhaps we might find a place among them."

Wolfe's nostrils flared, but he did not speak. The desire of her heart was plain, and she started up over the hill without turning back, not bothering to fetch the drapings she'd torn off when the battle had been joined.

There was nothing to be done for it, Wolfe realized. To dissuade her once her course had been set? Impossible. Her will was harder than iron, harder than stone, changing it as out of reach as the skies themselves. What else was there to do but follow? Wolfe reflected as he began to pick his way over the bodies of the slain, taking care to watch where he stepped only so that he could keep pace with his mistress, the one whose father had sworn him to her service…

…and the one who had stolen his heart.

29.

Sienna

Little pieces of Frankie's apartment hideout were still raining down around me. Bits of the ceiling dislodged by his use of one of the most destructive superpowers I'd ever seen were finding their way to rest on my shoulders, in my hair, flaking down like a gentle December snowfall in Minnesota.

Of course it was July, in Scotland, but that was beside the point. The point was that I was staring down a soulless incubus who'd been absorbing the powers of other metahumans and who had just turned loose a really damned epic one on me, one I'd never even run across before.

How many more of those did he have in him?

He leered with amusement at how I was suddenly still. We'd lapsed into this momentary quiet, me waiting for him to do something else, him waiting to see what I did, and Rose staying silent as a mouse across the artificial chasm Frankie had just made in the living room, because she was smart enough to know that drawing the attention of a man who could hurl death in the way Frankie just had was exceedingly unwise.

"Well?" he said at last. "What now, d'ye reckon? Shall we dance some more?"

"I 'reckon' we're gonna," I said. "But first, I might as well ask…what do you want?"

"Oh, I must have impressed you," he said with mirthful

glee, eyes gleaming. "Because you're the girl who always attacks, never retreats, and runs her mouth the entire bluidy time without ceasing." He slapped his knee a couple times. "Seems I've got you on the ropes, do I? Bet you didn't expect that."

"There are a lot of things I don't expect," I said. "Bottle flipping to become a trend, for instance. People thinking the Kardashians are worthy of emulation as they sell access to their lives and fakey personal drama in exchange for massive amounts of cash. The Spanish Inquisition. But then, no one expects that." He watched me warily. "You're right. You've gone and turned yourself into a bonafide badass, Frankie, the kind that's making me want to take a step back instead of leaping forward and trying to tear your head off. I'd salute you if I did that kind of thing. But you've got to realize what's actually happening here."

I tried to take in what was left of the room. There wasn't a lot in here to begin with; the furnishings had been pretty spare. A couch that had been torn in half by Frankie's blast, pieces of which were raining down even now, along with the damage to the ceiling and floor. Voices were making their way through the cracks beneath and above us, and that worried me, because I didn't need any hostages getting in the way of what I was going to try to do to this guy.

He didn't smile, didn't leer. I could see the cold calculation all over his face. "What's happening here, then?"

I took a breath and let it out slowly. "I'm not holding back because I'm afraid of you."

He cocked an eyebrow and started to smile again. It was a chilling thing. "Is that so?"

"That's so."

"Why are you hesitating, then?" he asked. Clearly he didn't believe me.

"Because," I said, frantically pushing the same question I'd been asking in my head for five minutes—getting no useful responses from anyone and hoping—just hoping—that the wildest psychopath in my head would finally weigh in with a plan that would solve everything, "I'm trying to figure out how to kill you."

Frankie's eyes flashed with anger, and I lunged to the left as he shot something completely different at me. This was at least familiar, in that it was a bolt of lightning that looked thicker than a minikeg. It blasted past, a few little tendrils branching off and running harmlessly through me to the floor, grounding themselves against the concrete below the carpet, sparking little fires in the process. I didn't even feel it, thankfully, as I came back down, and something blew past my face so quickly that all I saw was the light of the energy as it streaked past. I didn't see it impact, but I knew it had struck behind me and wasn't, thankfully, that shredding blast he had turned loose before.

I flung a handful of fire at him, knowing it wasn't going to do shit but hopefully distract him for a second, and it did. He threw a hand up and caught it, dispersing it harmlessly into nothingness as I ran a few steps closer, reaching the back of the couch. I bent down and grabbed it by its soft corduroy and flung it at him.

It was heading right for his face when it was suddenly bisected by a red blade that sheered it in two. The couch flew into pieces and one of them shattered the window to my right, hitting the wall beneath and flopping back inside.

He'd pulled a damned lightsaber blade from out of his freaking sleeve. Or more accurately, projected one out of his hand.

I had a blowout sale on light nets, throwing them at him like EVERYTHING MUST GO, and out they went. He moved his hands again, the air seeming to distort in front of his face, and they shredded into splinters of illumination right in front of his face. I got a few steps closer, though, and that was what counted.

Frankie swept his lightsaber blade at me and I was forced to parry sideways. I wished for a weapon—a sword, an axe, an eskrima stick—hell, a teddy bear would be more than I had in hand at this point. I started to sweep low, hoping to take his feet from beneath him, but he leaped over my attempt and came back down with his lightsaber and carved a three-foot swath in the carpet where I'd been standing a second earlier.

WOLFE, I shouted in my mind. *Come on, man, a little help here!*

Wolfe stirred in the back of my mind. *You will find a way, Sienna.*

I threw my head back, catching myself on my hands and making myself into a backward arch to avoid Frankie's horizontal slice with his lightsaber. It was a desperation move, and left me vulnerable for a second as I transferred my balance to my hands and kicked up. He didn't present me with his chin, dodging neatly out of the way and following up with a laser beam that I was forced to do a freaking gymnastics move to avoid, going airborne for a few seconds, which was a hell of a lot longer than I wanted to commit to being off the ground and hanging in midair.

Frankie spun and came back around, hand already glowing red. He launched off another round of that ripper beam and it came surging across the floor at me. I landed poorly, off-balance, and stuck my right arm out to steady myself—

Just as the ripper beam tore past with a wall of force.

A spray of concrete from the floor pelted my eyes and face, forcing me to turn my head away. Blood started to dribble down my right cheek where the debris had opened up a dozen little wounds. Some more painful ones were now howling at me, lower, in my haunches and flank as I realized that some of the projectiles he'd blasted with that wave of force were now embedded like bullets all through my right thigh and buttock, one even as high as my kidney.

But that wasn't the worst of it. Not by a long shot.

When the pelting stopped, I looked to my right, to where I'd thrown my arm out to help balance me. It had been there just a second earlier, before the wave of force rolled through…

Now it was gone, ended just above the elbow, bone exposed and blood squirting out, into the newly opened abyss to my right. I felt faint, blood loss coupled with fatigue and a sudden sense of hopelessness that came with being presented with a foe so devastating, so powerful, that I couldn't see a way to stop him.

I started to tilt, to tumble, my right leg failing from the

damage it had taken in the wave of pelting, and without a hand to catch me on that side I started to fall into the crack, slipping toward failure, toward a fall...and eventually, I knew, as I saw Frankie watching me, satisfied...into death.

30.

A tinkle of breaking glass caught my attention, along with the surprise that flashed across Frankie's face. I landed on my side, about to topple over the edge and into the chasm, but not quite there yet, and my brain sprinted for ideas, for anything—

Flight, you idiot, Gavrikov said, and suddenly we were aloft, floating instead of falling, the abyss hanging there, immobile, instead of yawning closer to me by the millisecond.

Fight, you idiot, Eve said. *There are no prizes for not sucker punching him now that he's distracted.* And my stump of a left arm lurched up, light nets spraying from it at the distracted Frankie. They peppered him about the head and neck, and caused him to stumble forward. He was bleeding out of his bare scalp, and shattered glass rested all around his feet, the pieces roughly cylindrical.

My eyes wandered for but a second and found Rose raiding the little kitchenette on the other side of the room, a couple of glasses in hand and one in the air. She'd thrown them at him, and her aim had been true.

Think, Harmon said. *And you're not an idiot. But you are going into shock, which is not really my department…*

Wolfe, I moaned in my head.

I am working on it. Succinct, to the point. But also much less than he normally would have chimed in with.

This is a tactical nightmare, Bastian said. *We're against a superior force, and our usual force multipliers are nullified. May I suggest the better part of valor?*

It took me a second to get that. *Retreat?*

Yes, ma'am, Bastian said, buttoned up as ever. *Unless you want to keep pressing your luck and see how many limbs he can deprive you of.*

This is not a wise battle, Bjorn agreed. *Best to seek advantage elsewhere and try again once you have it in your favor.*

Yes, let's get the hell out of here once we're sure he can't follow, Eve said. *Because if you try and fly off without losing him—*

It's gonna be a short flight with those ripper blasts coming at my back, I reluctantly agreed. *What the hell is that power, anyway?*

Something you're wishing you'd had the fortune and dishonor to steal, Harmon said. I couldn't really argue with that.

I came back to my feet, or at least back to vertical, my right arm still a shredded nub but the bleeding stopped. I took only one breath as I watched Frankie tearing at the light nets wrapped around the back of his head. Rose threw another glass at him, dead on—

But the second before it hit, it went sideways, smashing into the wall. Another followed at him a second later, and it, too, was pulled to shattering against a wall like it was drawn there by—

"Gravity," I muttered under my breath. Another power this guy had ripped off from others. Damn. How deep was his toybox? Because it was looking endless.

"Rose!" I shouted, and she stopped grabbing glasses to chuck at him so she could look up at me. "We have to kill him!" I was lying through my teeth here, but I needed something that would distract Frankie long enough to enact my true plan, and I hoped this would be it.

That was it.

Frankie ripped the light nets from his head, sheer strength tearing them loose from where they'd attached to his head. Chunks of his scalp came off with them, blood running down the back of his head like a waterfall had been turned loose out of his skull. He was wearing a look of pure fury, and his hands started to glow with the red energy that suggested he was cooking up a bigass bolt of that ripper power, and I had no doubts about where he was going to send it.

I shot into motion with my flight power, aiming for Rose. I didn't slow down as I collided with her, her eyes wide as coffee mugs as I snugged her around the waist and blew to supersonic speed out the hole in the window I'd made behind Frankie with the couch. As soon as I was out, I zagged hard around the building—

And just in time, too.

Frankie's blast of power rumbled by, ripping the toe of my right shoe off—and a piece of my actual toe, as well—as it flew past. I looked back, only briefly, as I cut the turn around the apartment building and booked it north, heading the hell out of Edinburgh proper and using the building itself as a shield against Frankie's attack.

His bolt landed in the middle of another building, falling upon it like an axe and cleaving it a mighty blow up the middle. It continued onward, the blast, for a hundred yards—two hundred—

I lost sight of it as we got farther and farther north, but faintly, in the distance, I knew the glow of red had worked its way farther through the city of Edinburgh, carving a trail of destruction that would kill who knew how many people.

And it was entirely my fault.

31.

"Take us down over there," Rose said, pointing past a bridge that extended over a wide river. I looked to my right and saw that it headed out to sea, and concluded this must be that Fourth of Fifth of Sixth or whatever the hell they called it. "In Dunfermline."

I looked left and saw what looked like a naval base of some kind, just past the bridge. "Where are we going?"

She shrugged as best she could with my arm around her waist and hers around my shoulders. "Anywhere we can to catch a breath, I'd guess. I have an apartment in Edinburgh if you'd like—"

"No, let's get the hell out of town for now," I said, thinking back to that crackle of energy running through Edinburgh like a damned earthquake fault, splitting buildings and—heaven help me—people, probably. "No need to stick around when I don't have a strategy to beat this guy—yet."

"You'll come up with something," she said as I started to descend toward Dunfermline. In another time, less harried perhaps, I might have admired her optimism.

Dunfermline was a strange beast from overhead, almost like a small town that had sprawled large, without the mega commercial sectors I expected for a town of this size. I thought of Eau Claire, Wisconsin, a city that seemed from above to be of similar size, but looked completely different than this one. Any American suburb would be replete with miles of retail shopping strips, Walmarts and Targets and

Home Depots and grocery stores as far as the eye could see.

I caught sight of a supermarket-looking building in the distance, a kind of mini-development of retail, the little sister of the gigantic strip malls that had taken over American highway exits, and I angled toward it. Rose wrinkled her nose. "You feeling the need for a quick stop-off at Asda?"

The store was coming into sight, and I realized with mild surprise that they actually had the little light bulb mark from Walmart in the top left of their signage. Apparently I'd found American retail's British cousin. "I'm feeling the need for a public place where we can stop off and catch a breather. Somewhere that it won't be immediately obvious we've come." I reached up to my head, searching for the wig that had been on it when I'd gone into my confrontation with Frankie. Surprise, surprise, it was gone now, lost somewhere along with an arm that had now regrown and a coat sleeve that never would. "Well, maybe not obvious for you. I'm going to need a disguise."

She eyed me. "I can think of a way to handle that. Where are you planning to land?"

I looked over the endless grey clouds that stretched over the horizon. "I dunno. Somewhere near the store, I guess. Or within walking distance, at least, since I left my bag back in Edinburgh and we're going to need some freshening up in addition to a disguise."

She lapsed into a short silence. "Should we call the police?"

"No," I said.

"Because they'll get themselves killed if they go after Frankie?"

"Yeah," I said. I was damned pleased she was sharp enough to pick up my reasoning without me having to explain it in infinite detail, especially because I wasn't in the sort of patient teaching mood I'd need to explain it without snapping right now.

I brought us down in a grove of trees behind the Asda mega market, or whatever they called it. It didn't look like a traditional Walmart, at least not from the front. As I'd overflown it I'd noticed a triangular, glass entry portico that people walked in through, which was far different from the usual square box Walmart approach with its door on either side of the parking lot, left or right.

"What do you need me to get?" Rose asked, already rifling around in her pockets and pulling out credit cards.

"Do they sell baseball caps here?" I asked. "Never mind, whatever. Get me a hat of some stripe and sunglasses. Baseball cap is preferable, but if you guys don't have baseball—"

"It's not our national pastime, but we do have it," she said, giving me an appraising look. "I'll find a hat that'll flatter ye as best I can."

"Good luck," I said sourly, and settled down to wait while she headed out of the trees and disappeared around the edge of the store.

As soon as she was out of earshot, I listened hard, trying to figure out if anyone was nearby. I could hear distant cars, but nothing close at hand, so the moment I was sure no one was eavesdropping I said, "All right, Wolfe, cut the shit and spill it."

There was a long silence, in which I could almost imagine him lurking in the back of my head. *Spill what?* Wolfe finally asked, quieter than I could ever recall hearing him.

"Whatever is up your ass," I said. "Out with it, because we are facing down some serious business here and I need you at peak badass in order to muscle through it."

Wolfe just doesn't like Scotland, he said resentfully, still hiding in the shadows of my mind, more sedate than when I used to drug him.

"Any particular reason for that, or do you just dislike the lack of sunshine?"

Wolfe is a sunny creature, oh yes.

"Screw off with that bullshit, Wolfe. You're clouds and darkness all the way. Why are you stonewalling me now, when I need you most?"

I told you. Don't like Scotland.

I rolled my eyes. "I don't like lots of places. Like California, for instance. That doesn't mean I enter into a state of catatonia destined to cause fatal injury or death when I go there."

You wouldn't understand.

"Probably because you're not bothering to explain it."

That brought on a nice, fat silence. *Maybe expecting him to discuss it rationally is a little too much,* Harmon said, stepping up like he was going to broker a peace.

Shut up, mind reader, Wolfe said, *or you'll learn what your brains taste like.*

"I burned his body months ago, Wolfe. No one's going to be learning what his brains taste like."

Wolfe can do wonders. Push him and see.

I sighed. "This is going nowhere."

Good. Now that you've realized that…leave Wolfe alone.

"I'd like nothing more," I said. "In fact, there were whole years when that was practically my philosophy in life. But unfortunately, I'm looking at an incubus who seems to have followed a very strict all-meta diet, which is worse than steroids for our kind, and unless I get some assistance from someone who's—I dunno, as well versed in hunting prey as I am—I'm kinda afraid I might be at my expiration date, here."

You beat Sovereign. Wolfe withdrew from the conversation, retreating into the shadows of my mind almost reluctantly, but still with that same reserve he'd shown throughout this entire conversation. *You'll beat this one, too. You always do. You even said so.*

"Dick," I said, "this is serious."

It's always serious.

I brought my teeth together and gave them a good grind while I tried to control the wild, angry things that came to mind—slurs against Wolfe's parentage, his life choices, his morality. This was a guy who'd never been shy about showing me the mental film of his slaughters, not bothering to discriminate whether they were men, women or children. Sometimes I forgot, occasionally and very briefly, that Wolfe was probably the most prolific serial killer of all time. He'd been murdering people, viciously and without remorse, for thousands of years. If there was worse than him, I hoped never to meet them without a bazooka firmly in hand.

And yet, for all that (and oh, holy hell, was it a lot)…he'd helped me quite a bit over the years. Without him, I'd be dead eight hundred times over, if not more. Sure, I rarely showed him the gratitude he deserved, because honestly, he was lower than pond scum, but still…whatever was up his ass, it wasn't about that.

So what was it about? I didn't buy the 'I hate Scotland and it makes me super sad' explainer. Places didn't just have that effect on you, at least not enough to take a normally buoyant, playful serial killer and make him all emo or whatever. Especially not since Wolfe had absolutely no emotional depth whatsoever, no attachments to a single person on planet Earth—including his family (now dead)—and featured, exclusively, two modes: *Kill* and *Kill Harder*.

"Okay, well," I said, trying to bounce back from my rejection at the hands of the world's worst man, "I'm open to suggestions from anyone else. Because all the ideas I have right now involve a sniper rifle, and unfortunately, I doubt they sell those in Asda over here." Damn England. Didn't they understand that sometimes you just flat out needed to put a bunch of bullets in someone?

Apparently not, which was more the pity for me.

Draw him back to the USA? Bastian suggested. *Or use your resources to procure a weapon over here.*

"Both valid options," I said. "I'd like to avoid the US if I could though, and we have no guarantee he'll follow. Also, if he can find me over there, it's a safe bet the US government is going to be right up my ass shortly thereafter, which might not turn out that much better for me." They had reached the point in our relationship where they were no longer bothering with being gentle and had decided to kill me. Not that Frankie was exhibiting much more mercy.

Matching him power for power seems improbable, Bjorn said. *Given his bountiful and never-ending list of powers. Though this does raise a point we have often broached with you—*

"Yes, I know. You're always wanting me to add new people to the collection of you seven. But I don't want to. Why can't you understand that? New people get unruly, they have to be managed and convinced to help with their powers—"

We would help you convince them, Eve said, and I imagined I heard her cracking the knuckles she no longer had. *Forcefully.*

"I think that's the way Sovereign did it," I said, "but did I ever do that to any of you?" I waited only a second to answer my own question. "No. Because forcing you to fight on my side through—I dunno, torturing you in my heads or imprisoning you or compelling you via pain—those are wrong." I swallowed heavily. "They're too close to what Mom used to do to me."

But she got results, Gavrikov said.

My eye twitched a little. "So did your dad, but I don't think you'd condone what he d—" My arm lit on fire, and fortunately it was the one that didn't have a sleeve covering it. "See?"

Gavrikov took a second to compose himself before replying. *But I am powerful, am I not? And I might never have fully learned the extent of my powers without his...cruelty.*

"Well, you're all on my side now, so I don't think I needed to get that vicious," I said. "I mean, even Harmon's on the team now." I could almost feel Harmon sigh in my head, like he was too cool to be associated with us. "So...sure, maybe I could have absorbed a few evil metas I've faced along the way, tortured them into adding their powers to us. But...what then?"

Then, Bjorn said, *you would take those new powers and convert this Frankie into free-floating atoms, of course.* Like it was the most natural thing in the world, he said this.

I started to rebut his simplistic analysis, but...other than to be a sniping, sarcastic ass...I really couldn't. Frankie had me overpowered, it was just that easy. It was an arms race I'd lost because it had somehow never occurred to me I was in one. And while it didn't mean I was out of the fight entirely, it certainly made things a lot harder on me.

Not that I was going to give up just because I was outgunned. That had happened to me a lot since I'd left my house the first time, and the only thing it had done was serve to encourage me to get mouthier and meaner.

I started to voice this thought to them, especially the meaner part, when suddenly the Asda behind me exploded, a beam of red the size of a bus blasting a hole through the roof. "Rose," I said, and lurched into flight, zooming into the air and toward the now gaping entry into the roof, intent on finding my new sidekick and hopefully saving her life before whoever was throwing meta powers around in the supermarket killed her.

32.

I dropped through the ceiling of the warehouse-like Asda, descending through smoke that smelled like singed building material, asbestos and who knew what else kind of chemical crap that would have probably given me cancer if I weren't immune to it. The smoke obscured everything, but it wasn't fire-smoke but rather a composite of shelving (I could smell the metal), cardboard, plastic bags, and about a hundred different kinds of cereal (I could smell those, too). Dropping to the ground, I found myself, utterly without surprise, in the cereal aisle.

Rose was stumbling around ahead of me, shoving against the shelf. She locked eyes with me and barely got out, "He's here!" before I saw him, marching out of the haze like the damned Terminator.

Frankie.

I wanted to shout something clever and witty, like, "How'd you find me?" but I was afflicted with a sort of mute, horrified lockjaw, which I did not remedy by throwing a box of Weetabix—whatever the hell those were—at him.

"As though that will—" he started to say, using gravity to send the box flying toward the ceiling—

Revealing the flame shot I'd concealed behind the cardboard box.

He made a motion to dissolve it, and he definitely got most of it, but that last little bit was a real bitch to his face, sparking up as he waved to rid himself of it. He shouted in surprise, hands flying up to cover his wound. I shot another at his center mass, but by now he was dissolving any heat sources that were coming his way, so that game was up.

"Shit," I muttered and grabbed Rose by the arm. With her gripped firmly, I said, "Hold on." I didn't wait for her nod (which came a second later) before leaping into the air with her.

I landed atop the shelf to our right and gave it a touch as I came down on it, a little shove that sent it Frankie's way. It squeaked slightly, but wavered under my meta strength, and then wobbled, tipping over his way.

We didn't stick around to watch it fall. I grabbed Rose and we shot for the exit, blasting out under the triangle entry over the heads of a crowd of stampeding shoppers. Some bargains just weren't worth the cost.

I had to land us to get through the last door, and as I did, Rose staggered a little upon touchdown. "You all right?" I asked as she recovered her balance.

"I just about had a heart attack in there when he showed up," she said, leaning over like she needed to catch her breath. She looked like she'd seen a ghost. "He came out of nowhere!"

I glanced back as some dark-haired dude in a European leather motorcycle jacket almost plowed into me, then apparently thought the better of it at the last second, avoiding the hell out of me. Smart move on his part right now. "Any idea how he found you?"

"None," she said, taking a breath. "Glad you realized what was going on, because my strategy only distracted him long enough to keep me from being completely vaporized by that beam that took the roof off."

I grabbed her by the arm again. I had a little grain of suspicion—what if Rose was the reason Frankie had found us here?

There was no time to debate that, and I was left with two choices—drag Rose along with me, out of here, even if it meant bringing Frankie after us, potentially—again.

Or I could leave her to her fate, which, if this little incident was any guide, would probably be death.

Not much of a choice, I said in my head.

Yeah, you can't leave her behind to be murdered based on a suspicion, Zack said.

I didn't have a chance to answer, but I agreed with that, so I snatched up Rose and zoomed into the sky as one of Frankie's ripper blasts of red cut a wall of red through the triangular entry to the Asda. Rose gasped as I dropped low, hugging the nape of the earth. I dodged between trees, circling around behind the building and then zooming off to the west, figuring I'd use the cover of ground rather than zooming out over the sea, or the Sixth of the Seventh of the Ninth or whatever the hell they called that body of water.

"What do we do now?" Rose asked, raising her voice to compensate for the gusty nature of the world around us. We were flying about ten feet above the rooftops, and I lurched upward to avoid one, then dropped us back down. I wanted to avoid showing up on radar, in case that was how Frankie found us. I kept looking over my shoulder, wondering if he'd come zooming down on us at any moment.

"Escape and evade," I said, feeling like maybe—just maybe—we'd accomplished one of those. But then, I'd felt like we'd accomplished the escape part once before, and now look at us. "We need somewhere to lay low for a while."

"I know a place," she said, "back in Edinburgh. I assume you don't mean my flat."

"Can't take the risk of yours," I said. "I don't know how Frankie's doing what he's doing, but he's seen you enough at this point that if he's got—I dunno, a mole in the Edinburgh PD or something—he's bound to be able to figure out where you live now that he's seen us together repeatedly."

She nodded once. "A friend of mine works in Glasgow during the week and takes the train home on weekends. Her flat's empty right now, and I've got a spare key."

"That'll work," I said after a moment, burying the nervousness I was feeling like butterflies flapping their fat wings in my belly. It was actually perfect, because this was going to be my acid test for Rose, a little something to either congeal or dispense my suspicions of her. Because if Frankie showed up here, in this place we were going to shelter, without any warning…

It'd mean Rose had betrayed me.

Question answered. Then all I'd have to do is evade him again; maybe easier the second time without an anchor that could be reporting my movements back to him…and then develop my plan to kill him, because—yeah, we'd reached that stage of the game. I was decided. There was no way I could let Frankie live. He'd wrecked a decent swath of Edinburgh, and then followed me out to the suburbs to level even more of the town. That was a bad deal, and I felt really responsible.

"Take us on back to the city?" Rose suggested helpfully, and I veered us south, figuring I'd get us there eventually, taking the slow road so as to avoid as much attention as possible. Now we were whipping over empty fields and green forests, keeping close to the treetops and fields.

"I'll get us there," I said, that gnawing worry I was heading into another trap settling in my stomach hopelessly. "Real soon." And then, shortly thereafter, we'd know the truth about Rose, and whether or not she was betraying me to death.

33.

The flat in question was on a quiet side street in north Edinburgh, in what I reckoned was the new town. We landed without incident, and there wasn't anybody around when we came down off the rooftops in a quick drift to the streets. It was quiet, moody. Fog would have set the scene for my purposes a lot better, but it was a clear night and there was almost no noise on the street save for cars in the distance. I looked left and right, waiting for Frankie to come wafting out of the sky followed by a ripper blast that cleaved the building behind us in two, but the quiet hung uninterrupted, a pleasant change from a battleground in the apartment tower or the supermarket.

"Come on," Rose whispered once she'd unlocked the front door to the building. With a last look up and down the street, quiet blocks of residential buildings, I followed and we gently closed the door behind us. Ascending to the third floor, I kept my feet a few millimeters off the ground in order to keep from making noise. Rose, too, seemed to take a cue from me and muffle her footsteps, taking her time and walking like her head was on a swivel. Brilliant play acting if she was betraying me, or possibly just the actions of a young woman who'd tasted danger and knew her life was now thick with it, thanks to her hanging her hopes on me.

Her friend's flat was on the third floor, and sure enough, she unlocked it without issue. I preceded her in the door, listening for trouble. When I didn't hear any, I swept from room to room quickly, hands out and ready. I checked in every closet, under every bed, cringing slightly at the extremely girly pillows and décor, but hey, any old port in a storm.

Once I was satisfied that the only residents of this apartment drawing breath were Rose and me, I came back to the little living room that served as a central hub, a combination living and kitchen with an entry out to the hallway. Rose was peering out the window from behind the curtain, and I walked up behind her and took a look for myself to see what was going on at street level.

Nothing. Nothing was going on at street level. Edinburgh was quiet. Damned quiet, actually.

"How'd he find me at that Asda?" Rose asked, looking somewhat rattled.

"I don't know," I said, a little more cagily than if I'd been certain she wasn't a mole. I mean, really, she flagged me down on day one in the city, saved me from Frankie's thugs when they had me cornered…

Points in her favor—she'd taken a bullet for me, and those can kill metas, probably even empaths. Which prompted the thought, "Let me see your wound."

"Right," she said, and walked me over to the sofa, a white fabric monstrosity that would have looked really good in some granny's living room. It actually fit this room as well, strangely, a sort of concentric circle of style, I supposed, in which that which was old was now in fashion once more. Rose sat down, taking care not to touch the back of the couch, and lifted her shirt so I could see her side.

The bullet hole was still there, angry weal between her ribs. It was mostly crusted over at this point, and the edges had begun to close in with new skin to replace that which had simply been blown away by the hot lead passing through her. She was lacking a giant hole in her side now though, which I considered good for her. Taking a bullet like this in the side might have been a calculated risk to get close to me, but…damn. I mean, that's some serious calculation. Most people considered me crazy for the stuff I'd done, but I couldn't recall a time when I'd wanted to leap into the line of fire for someone else, especially not if that person was on my kill list.

"Looks fine." I rubbed my face as Rose dropped her shirt, my inspection complete. "I think it'll be just about gone by tomorrow."

"I'm going to hit the loo," she said, and got up, disappearing into the hallway. I heard the door close and knew she was in. I debated what to do next, and then got up and crept over to the entry by the hall to listen. I'd probably hear it if she punched the buttons on a phone. I needed to know if she was going to call Frankie, or share her location with him, though if she had a phone on her that was doing that automatically, there was going to be no avoiding the hell coming my way, because he'd already know where we were.

I listened to the sounds of a woman going to the toilet through the door, mind racing all the while. What if she was working for him?

Well... Zack said, *what would be the point?*

To have a spy on the inside with Sienna Nealon, I said. *Duh.*

Yeah, but this Frankie guy is trying to kill you, Zack said. *Why would he need a spy for that?*

He didn't start out trying to kill her, Harmon said. *He started out saying they were made for each other.*

Yeah, if incubuses could stop doing that, it'd be great, I said.

Well, the alternative is for them to seek love with mortals who they'll absorb and kill, Zack said with a thick dose of irony, *so...going after you is probably the least homicidal, most normal they could do, right?*

I pretended he was standing in front of me as I narrowed my eyes in fierce irritation. *You know what? You're awfully annoying, Mr. Knowy McKnowkins. These people are all psychos anyway, so this idea that coming after me as a mating prospect is the sanest thing they can do? No points for that. Why can't I meet a nice incubus boy who doesn't go around murdering people? Because clearly Frankie has absorbed a few souls in his time. Meta souls. And by a few, I mean—*

Tankerloads, Eve supplied. *Fucktons, I think you call it.*

The raw fucktonnage of people he's killed is staggering, I said. *The range of meta powers he's displaying is way beyond anything I've ever seen. I mean, I saw multiple kinds of energy projection in addition to that ripper beam, his mind is unreadable, he's got Gavrikov fire, gravity powers like Jamie, one of the lightsaber ones like Chase…I mean, I don't know how he's accumulated that many powers without someone noticing. The sheer numbers of the mysterious, metahuman dead here in Edinburgh must be staggering. And no one has noticed this until now? How?*

Maybe they've just gone missing heretofore, Bjorn offered. *I lost count of how many I killed that were never found.*

I was torn between saying, "Good insight!" and, "You're a sick bastard, Bjorn. Sit down and shut up!" I ultimately chose neither, however, instead going with, *That's a reasonable point,* because if I was trying to kill one of—if not THE—strongest foes I'd ever fought, alienating the people who were on my side seemed like bad strategy. Even if some of them were hideously evil murderers.

There'd be a rise in the missing persons rate then, you'd think, Bastian said. *These are the sort of things that the police should notice.*

There should be, you're right, I said. *And another thing—those toughs he sent after us in the cafe. How was it that Harmon couldn't read their minds?*

I don't know, Harmon said, and I sensed he was telling the truth. That sort of thing would drive him crazy.

Glancing furtively down toward the hall, I could hear Rose finishing up. *You're sure that whatever they were doing, it wasn't an empath covering their minds?*

Definitely not, Harmon said. *I remember well what an empath feels like, having received a thorough drubbing during the debates from your friend Senator Foreman, one of those very kind.*

I don't think I've ever mentioned this, I said, *but watching him wipe the floor with you there was probably the highlight of that year.*

Ass, he said. *But I suppose I was deserving of some small comeuppance. Arrogance comes as naturally to me as it seems to to…well…you.*

Well, I got some comeuppance today, I said, leaning back on the soft, overstuffed sofa. *Frankie comeuppanced all over me.* I paused. *That sounded way dirtier than I intended it.*

Rose emerged from the hallway as I listened to the sound of guffaws in my head, my lowbrow audience endlessly amused by that sort of double entendre. She leaned against the wall into the main room and stared out at me, folding her arms across her chest. "What do we do now?"

"Well, we have two choices," I said. "Three, really. We can hunker down here for the night and get some rest, get back to a hundred percent. Or we can go out there and get in another fight with Frankie right now."

Rose seemed to hold her breath at the second option. "Or…? That can't be all."

"We can flee," I said. "Run for the damned border, get the hell out of Dodge…pick a cliché that fits, but retreating is option number three."

She let out that breath she'd held. "You don't like number three, do you?"

"I'm fine with a strategic retreat every now and again, when my position gets untenable," I said. "Running away from this fight so I can win the next one? It burns the pride a little, but winning in the end is a good salve for that. Getting killed, on the other hand, because you don't want to show the enemy your back?" I frowned like I'd gotten a whiff of skunk. "That's just dumb. I've run away from a superior enemy or one that's gotten some advantage over me plenty of times, no regrets. But I always get 'em in the end." I let out a long exhale. "And that's what's going to happen with Frankie. I'm going to get him in the end, put the nails in his coffin, put paid to his ticket—"

"I get the point," Rose said, unfolding her arms uncomfortably. "Well, in this event, I must say I vote for resting for the night, and coming back renewed tomorrow, because I don't know about you, but I feel like I'm about to pass out." For the first time, I could see the fatigue etched in hard lines around her eyes, around her mouth. Yeah, she was tired, and I hadn't even noticed. It was possible she'd been running on adrenaline this whole time, and it had just petered out, leaving her low, drained. I knew that feeling well.

"Leaning toward that option myself," I said. The couch was nice and soft behind me. "Why don't you sit down? Take a load off."

"Right," she said, and uneasily walked toward a chair, then

veered to sit next to me on the couch at the last second. She seemed like she'd been warring with herself over what to do, but she plopped down next to me with only a light cringe that I figured was either indicative of her worry over which seating option was socially best or else related to that bullet wound still healing in her side.

I gave her a thin smile. "Bet you're wishing now that you'd just let me pass on by without following."

That got her to smile too, weary but genuine. "No, not exactly, though—well, maybe a little. I mean, I've heard of your adventures, or at least as much as what's reported on the news and blog sites and whatnot." She leaned back with me, pushing some stray red hairs off her pale face. "I know you've had to run before, but—it feels different, being in the middle of it, you know?" She shook her head. "I'm probably doing a rubbish job of explaining it."

"No, I think I know what you mean," I said, drawing another slow breath, trying to relax, trying to keep an eye out for ambush even though I wouldn't see it coming through the walls around us until it came busting through like Kool-Aid Man. "Sometimes the news coverage of me…it's breathless, and leans toward painting me as some sort of…I dunno, invincible harpy or demon that swoops down out of the clear sky and destroys like Armageddon come to town. I'm a force of nature as relentless as the wind—sorry, Reed," I said as though he could hear me. "Unchanging as the bedrock of the earth, unbowed by any challenge sent my way." I sighed. "That's all crap, of course. Sometimes I get my ass kicked. Sometimes really hard. Eden Prairie would be a great example of that. I got whooped into near unconsciousness by a bum rush of metas and only survived because one of my souls triggered a damned bomb of a firestorm. I'm not invincible," I said softly. "Sometimes this happens."

Rose blinked, like she was taking that all in. "I heard something about…in Florida a few months ago…"

"I got shot in the head," I said, using my index finger to mime a bullet hitting me in the skull. "Blew out my connection to my powers, my souls. I almost didn't survive that." She shuddered, and if she was acting, she was Oscar-caliber.

"Yeah, I know, it was nearly the end. So, anyway…it happens. I've been through worse than a seemingly impossible enemy." My face hardened and I glanced at the TV. Part of me wanted to turn it on and see what they were saying about me in relation to this most recent disaster. The other part of me knew that I needed sleep and rest, and knowing that every news channel in the UK and probably the planet was shit-talking me? Not a great sleep aid.

Rose was quiet for a little while, sitting in her own personal puddle of unease, next to someone who was the target of a terribly powerful meta. I'd have been shuffling on the couch if I'd been in her shoes, but she was stock still in what I presumed to be the dawning horror of realizing a truth I'd discovered long ago—that sometimes you got what you want, like, say, meeting a hero, only to have it turn out that you really, really shouldn't have wanted that, because it did not turn out the way you might have hoped.

"I have a question for ye," Rose said, that brogue picking up again now, in this moment of quiet reflection. I stared at the fireplace standing empty in front of us, tempted to light it up with my Gavrikov powers for ambiance, but I vetoed the notion in case the flue was welded shut or something. The last thing I needed was to burn down our safe house. Assuming it was actually safe at all.

"We've been through multiple fights and near deaths today," I said, "and we're waiting to see if a big bad incubus comes kicking down our door. I don't think this is a moment to be shy about asking questions, Rose."

She shifted on the couch next to me. "You seem so… uhm…" She wouldn't look at me, which was a bad sign. "I mean, I haven't heard ye call anyone since I've been hanging out with ye…"

"I'm a fugitive from international justice," I said wryly. "Anyone I call is a target for their own investigation."

"Right, but…" She finally dared to look me in the eye. "Ye've got friends. A brother, I know. D'ye not…I mean, given this, what's going on…wouldn't it make sense to call them, ask for help?"

"I could," I said, leaning back, letting my neck sag so I was looking straight up at the ceiling. It was hell on my spine, but I felt pretty confident I could jerk forward in a half-second or faster if I sensed Rose coming at me in a sudden attack. "And they'd probably come running. But..." I sat forward again, blood rushing back from my head. "Then I'd make them targets for aiding a fugitive, which they've so far escaped, thus ruining their lives just to potentially save mine." I smiled wryly. "I think I'd be better off tucking tail and running rather than involving them in this. I could shoot back over to America in a few short hours, use some of my...connections..." I kept it vague because Rose didn't need to know about my vast Liechtenstein bank accounts, and all the other resources I had access to if I desperately wanted to raise a ruckus, "...to arm up and come back loaded for bear. Or loaded for Frankie, in this case."

Hell, I might not even have to go to America to arm up. Likely as not my bankers had access to resources right here in Europe that could arm me—for a hefty price. I could hire a bunch of mercs from the international market and send them to their deaths against Frankie in endless waves the way my enemies always seemed to send them against me. Get a bunch of guns or maybe a solid sniper rifle and just spill Frankie's brains all over the streets of Edinburgh the way a criminal meta had in a bank in Florida just a couple months ago.

"Given what I saw today," Rose said, doing another little shiver unrelated to the temp in here, which was pleasant enough, "that doesn't sound bad to me at all."

"Yeah," I said under my breath. The only problem with that was the notion that the US might have me under some kind of communications surveillance. Harmon had proven the US government and its agencies to have an awfully long reach, after all, and if they ever caught me talking back and forth with my contacts, that'd be an ace I wouldn't have to play when I might really need it.

And as much of an ass kicker as Frankie had proven himself...I still didn't feel like I was completely overwhelmed. He'd certainly overpowered me, drawing on abilities stockpiled through the sort of mass murder I could scarcely imagine. And he was a definite threat, but…

All I really needed to do was get close to him, and I could use the overwhelming strength of Wolfe and my own unrelenting viciousness to cave his damned head in.

"You're worrying, aren't you?" she asked. "I can see it in yuir eyes."

It probably was in my eyes, given that this Frankie was worrying me from the guts up. I took a breath, trying to cleanse some of the worry. It worked about as well as you might expect given I had an evil, overpowered incubus now trying to kill me. "Worry doesn't really do any good," I said. "Worry's the precursor to fear, and I try not to go through my life fearing people. It's an ugly, unproductive feeling, and Mom taught me to avoid it at all costs."

Rose just stared at me like I'd grown a second head. "Why?"

"Because fear makes you flinch from the punch," I said. She just kept staring at me blankly. "Mom was weird, I guess, compared to—well, probably your mom. She trained me as a fighter, and the thing about fighting is…when you get hit, your instinct is to flinch back, right?" I mimed throwing my hands up and dodging back, hitting the sofa back as I did so, rattling it slightly. "You can't win a fight back on your heels, with your balance all askew. You can't throw a good punch like that, because you have to put your weight into it, and—anyway, the point is, when you flinch, when you're afraid, you can't fight back effectively. You get rocked back on your heels, and the fight's just about over because you have to move forward to attack fully. Fear, worry—none of these things help. They paralyze you, make you lean back instead of charge forward." I took another breath, staring at a point on the wall above the mantel. "I don't like to sit and worry. I like to go on offense."

"Ah, so that's where option two came from," she said. "I thought it a bit of a funny thing to even leave on the table after…well, all we've been through today."

I cracked a smile, grim and half-hearted. "It probably is a little strange for me to be talking about going out and facing him again, given…all this." I glanced at the window and wondered—no, I didn't need to wonder, I knew—if the rescue operations were still going on for the area that had gotten hit by Frankie's blast.

"Sorry to even ask this," Rose said, after another brief lull in the conversation, "but…your name?"

I looked at her, frown lines puckering my brow so deeply that I could feel it. "What about it?"

"Where's it come from?" she asked. "Nealon, I mean. I know your mum was Sierra, and—well, I assume she kinda repurposed her own for your first name—"

"Where does Nealon come from?" I repeated the question back, not really sure what the hell she was asking me. "I have no idea. Why?"

"I was just curious," Rose said. "I mean, uh…I didn't know my da, so—"

"Da?"

"Father," she said. "It's a Scottish thing. But I didn't know him—"

"I didn't really know mine either," I said.

"Oh," she said. "That makes two of us, then. But your name…Nealon…you really don't know where it came from?"

I shrugged. "I don't think most Americans worry that much about name origin. I know it came from my mom's dad, as far as I know. His name was Simon Nealon. He was, uh…well, an Englishman, I think." I tried to summon the only memory I had of him, which was actually a purloined memory given to me by the woman who had killed him. "He died in London in the 1980s."

"How?" Rose asked, with the quiet curiosity of a genuine student.

"He was killed by a group called Omega," I said, feeling a little weird about revisiting this particular piece of my history, which was not something I stirred the coals of very often. I paused, looking within. "A girl named Adelaide, who was a succubus, like me—she was working for them as an—well, an assassin or agent or fixer or something. She killed him in a fight." *Against the express orders of the Omega leadership, because she had been given her orders filtered through Wolfe,* I didn't bother adding, because why would Rose need that little helpful bit of context? *I* didn't even really need it.

"Is that the only member of your family you know of?" she asked. "I'm sorry," she said, getting genuinely apologetic. "This is my thing—like family history? I know my mother's family—my granny and grandpa and all them—back generations. We've lived in the same village for thousands of years, and I can trace that lineage back." She looked down for a second. "I was the first of my family to leave. But, uh…like I said, I didn't know my da, which…kinda drives me a bit nuts, you know?" She looked up at me, squinting. "That this is a—well, it's a passion of mine, to know these things."

"Why didn't you know your father?" I asked.

"He was a drifter," she said. "Passed through, met my ma. Stayed long enough to give her the gift of me," Rose said with a faint smile, "and then he moved on, never to be seen around those parts again. So half my family is a mystery to me. I traced every trail I could of my mother's side—heard all the stories from my grandparents, but…there's this gaping hole in my history. I don't know half myself," she said. "He's who I got my powers from, you see."

"That happens a lot," I said. "Metas drifting and…leaving behind babies. Tends to cause some problems when they manifest and have no guidance." I'd lost track of the number of fatherless metas I'd arrested, ones whose mothers had no idea where their powers came from. Teenagers who suddenly had powers sprung on them without any parent able to stop them? Formula for disaster.

"Well, it's a bit of mystery, obviously, and one I'd like to solve some day," she said. "But it's left me with this endless fascination with…genealogy, I guess. Ancestry. But…I could go on and on." She blushed and looked away.

"It's good to have hobbies," I said, glancing at the window as though Frankie would come battering in any second. "And let's face it…we could use a distraction right now. Or at least I could." I smiled. "Ask away."

"Really?" I nodded, and she leaned in again, earnest expression making me feel surprisingly at ease. "So you knew of your mum's da…did you know about your ma's ma?"

"I never met her, no," I said. "I vaguely recall my mom saying that she spent her final days in the company of an Omega operative named James Fries." Rose cocked her head at that, and I could almost hear the question. "I had a lot of clashes with this Omega group early on. They were kind of a mafia for old gods of the world, dipping their hands into all sorts of criminal and odious stuff. Anyway, I guess they sent one of their agents to keep my grandmother entertained in her last days, an incubus because he could, well…" I shrugged. "Touch her, I guess." I might have shuddered, if I'd ever seen my grandmother and had a visual to associate with that. Not that Fries was a bad-looking guy—evil to the core the way every incubus I'd ever met seemed to be—but not bad-looking at all. As evidenced by the fact that I'd nearly slept with him before I realized what human garbage he was.

"So she died?" Rose asked, still leaning in. It was probably the best distraction I could hope for right now, this round of idle questioning. "Your grandmother?"

"According to my great uncle Raymond, yes," I said. "In Michigan, in 1989, I think." I had a pretty good memory for someone who'd taken as many headshots as I had, both of the battering kind and, more recently, the bullet variety.

"That's fascinating," Rose said, looking at me intently. "What was her name?"

"Hell if I know," I said. "I don't think Mom or Raymond ever said, and I never asked."

Lethe, a whispered voice came from deep within me. The quietest voice, lately. *Her name was Lethe.*

"Well, that's creepy," I said, frowning. "I guess her name was Lethe, according to…well, sources in my mind." *Wolfe, you knew my grandmother?*

Wolfe barely stirred. *I served Hades,* he said. *I knew all his children.*

Of course. Naturally the Cerberus would know his master—and the master's charges.

"Lethe," Rose said quietly. "Hm. Your branch of—well, of metas. Do you know…is it a large family?"

I just stared at her. "I have no idea. Why?"

"I was just wondering," she said, demurring. "If you didn't know your grandmother, but—"

She went on, but I lost the train of thought that was listening to her as something occurred to me that had never occurred before. I was the great-granddaughter of the God of Death. For some reason, I'd never thought about it in those terms before, that the family was…well, that tight. Because if I was the great-granddaughter of Hades, then my great-uncle Raymond and any other of Hades and Persephones's children were only a little removed from me. That meant that Kat was a lot closer in my family tree, in all probability, than I'd ever given her credit for, though I didn't possess the knowledge of how many cousins, once removed, twice removed, great-whatever—to give name to our familial relationship. Suddenly the world seemed a lot smaller, especially when I considered that no matter how you sliced it, if James Fries was fooling around with my grandmother, it meant she was, *at best*, a great aunt removed a few times from him—

"EWWWWWW," I said, doing a full body heebie-jeebie and almost causing Rose to propel herself off the couch in surprise at my sudden reaction. She was wide-eyed, and I'd clearly interrupted her in the middle of some thought she was spelling out, which had caught her with her mouth hanging open. "Sorry," I said once I'd collected myself, "I just…realized a family connection that was…not apparent before."

Shit. If Fries and I had nearly slept together too, that meant…ohhh, yuck. It didn't exactly make us Lannisters, but the family tree was looking a lot more like a family bush the more I thought about it.

Which meant that Frankie…

"Shit," I said, aloud this time. Rose just held her silence, though she'd managed to button her lip closed, which meant she was just giving me the crazy eyes. "I just realized something."

"What is it?" she asked, all attentive, worried.

"Assuming this Frankie is a natural-born meta—" which

was not necessarily a fair assumption, given the way things were going in the world lately, with artificial meta serums flowing lately in America like beer at a high school kegger "—then…he's related to me in some way…and probably not as distant as I'd like."

Which meant that when I killed him…if he wasn't artificial…I was basically killing off one of the few family members I had left.

34.

Wolfe

Norway
175 BC

Winter was hard here in the north, and it made Wolfe shiver, a despised feeling that raised his hackles and made him madder than usual. During these interminable months of all the years since they had come to this place, he had never adjusted to this frigid cold. Huddling in the mead halls at night with the others, hiding his flesh under cloaks and cloths and skins, rankled him. The volume of battle to be had here was plenty, an endless land of clans and clansmen ready to raise sword against these gods. Few raised an eyebrow at Wolfe's desire to feast on flesh, but the people were fattier here, more gristled, and they got stuck in his teeth.

Then there were the long pauses between the battles, the times when the conquest was done and the quiet fell. Wounds were licked, mead was drunk, celebrations went on nigh endlessly, and he sat around all the while wondering when the next fight would come. It always did, but never soon enough for his taste. He wanted it now, wanted the slick blood to be running down his hands now, felt the rankling, twisting feeling burning under his skin, that urge to go out and hunt.

But he couldn't hunt their own people here, no. They were protected. They were the worshippers. Pfeh. This was never a problem back in the Republic. Worshippers were sheep, goats, meant to be eaten as sacrifice. Odin seemed to take a dim view of such things here, which irritated Wolfe to no end.

Save for the sacrifices they gave Lethe. Wolfe thrilled at the thought, when he did get a chance to consider them. Yes…she was thoroughly enjoying herself here. But who wouldn't, being fed…as she was being fed?

Wolfe sat in his perpetual corner of the meadhall, hiding his face under a leathered skin prepared by the tanner. It smelled of the piss used to complete the process, and now Wolfe wore two cloaks of the bound leather of human flesh. It made some of the servants in the hall of Odin look at him askance, worry dotting their fresh little faces. He would have liked to have ripped those off, but then he'd incur the wrath of Lethe, and he didn't dare do that.

Soft footsteps approached from his side, and Wolfe looked to see who dared come to him. None of the powers in this place seemed to fear him, and he respected that—after a fashion. He'd seen them all fight, and had his own opinions of their worth. Odin had certainly earned his place at the top of the heap here. Frigga, Freyja—they were worthy of some respect—which was why Wolfe didn't simply disregard their wishes and tear through the villages around this place with wild abandon. In return they did offer him some pleasant appeasement as opportunities afforded themselves.

And, of course…they seemed to find their way over to him every now and again as well, undeterred by his lone nature and desire to remain apart from their little kingdom.

"You should move closer to the fire," Odin said, looming over Wolfe, his beard still smelling of dinner. "There is no need for you to shiver yourself to sleep at night. We are having the carpenters add chambers, and build some more houses to our expanding holdfast. Soon you will have a room of your own, but until then…there is no reason to deprive yourself of warmth like you were one of Jotun's brood." He almost spat out that name like a curse.

Wolfe would have cursed the name, too. He'd had encounters with Jotun and those kind, and none had been pleasant. All had ended more or less peacefully though, a fact for which Wolfe found himself...unusually thankful. The tall beast of a giant had the coldest, most frightening eyes that Wolfe had seen this side of Lethe before battle.

"Maybe Wolfe is watching out for *your* brood," Wolfe said. "Keeping them safe by keeping his distance. Animal instinct is a hard thing to keep down."

If Odin thought this statement funny or threatening, he did not give any sign save for a partly raised eyebrow. "And we appreciate your sacrifices in this regard. If you seek reward...you need but ask. You have done many great things in the service of your mistress, and through her, for us. If you require an indulgence, it shall be yours. I will lead you to a place where you may exercise all your urges freely, a village only a few days hence which has shown its defiance to us in recent days. I am normally more inclined to patience, but your desire and my need are almost matched horses, in this case, and my patience does not need to be infinite. Freyja thinks their intransigence has lasted too long already, as does your...mistress." Odin smiled. "I expect that if you do not wish to partake, Lethe would gladly take the task of settling our disagreement with them upon herself."

Wolfe suppressed the shudder at hearing her called by her name, her true name, her birth name. Odin never called her that anymore, not since she'd adopted the Norse one that he'd offered her. She'd taken to it like a wolf to the kill, leaving behind Lethe in favor of this...northern perversion.

"You don't like it when I call her Lethe," Odin said with mild surprise. "This is curious, because I know you don't like it when I call her—"

"That's not her name," Wolfe said.

"I begin to believe that your difficulty is with me addressing her at all," Odin said, "and not what name I might use to do so."

"She doesn't belong here," Wolfe hissed, the fire making a distant pop. "She is the daughter of death."

"She plies her trade here with more freedom and fury than

she could in your own country," Odin said. "She has told me of your land. Her father lives in a cave, outcast from those who rule. He survives on the scraps he can gather for his family, not daring to turn loose with the fury of his full power." Odin leaned down. "If he came here, I would have him worshipped as the god he is and not keep him in a cave until time stole all use and life from him. We would rule the world, with a power such as his, and those of his offspring."

Wolfe turned his face away. "Hades has no desire to rule the world." That was a lie; Wolfe had little idea what Hades wanted, save for to avoid the wrath of his brothers Zeus and Poseidon, both of whom had promised in most strident tones a union that existed to annihilate him should he ever slip the last bounds of decency and turn his powers against his brothers and their brethren.

"*I* have a desire to rule the world," Odin said, and he spoke hungrily now. "I would see my eldest son sit atop a throne of bones made of brave warriors, Mjolnir in his hand and his brothers as his regents, ministers across the land. Lethe could rule all the way across the cold steppes to the sea, the places she has told us about. I would see an army march across the wide world, an army of our people, led by her, led by her father, ready to take what is rightfully ours." Odin extended a hand and clenched his fist. "You would be her righteous knight, her good right hand, the one to bring her the sacrifices that keep her…ravening hunger at bay."

Wolfe looked up, staring at Odin's face. There was earnest bloodlust there that Wolfe might once have appreciated were it not wedded to a desire he now found…repugnant.

Eyes met his across the meadhall, hiding behind the fire. Wolfe stared at the urchin of a girl who leered at him, and then looked away abruptly only a moment before he would have risen and offered challenge. His ire began to settle once again, and it was then that Odin spoke.

"You are always watched by others, are you not?" The All-Father stared into his soul with that one eye. "Vivi in particular takes note of you. I see the exchanges."

"She is too young to give challenge, but she treads perilously close to it nonetheless," Wolfe said in a low hiss.

"She is too young to give challenge, aye," Odin said, "but I do not believe that is why she stares at you. She sees beyond these days and into ones far past the reckoning of any of us. I have had the benefit of her sight, this young seer. If she stares at you, it does not mean challenge, for she has all the strength of an enfeebled kitten. It is because she is looking into your soul, and into the days ahead in your fate."

"My fate is my own business," Wolfe said.

"And you share it with none," Odin said, "but she sees it nonetheless. And if you ask, she will tell you what lies ahead for you, for good or ill."

A scream sounded through the meadhall, high, forceful, that of a man in agony. All froze for a moment. The scream cut Wolfe's thoughts about future days to a quick end, continuing for but a few seconds more, and then it cut to its own end, as suddenly as it had begun. Odin held his silence for but seconds, and then, in his resonant voice: "It seems your mistress has taken the first of her evening indulgences."

Wolfe turned away. "So it would seem."

"Her appetite is endless," Odin said, something nearing reverence in his voice. "She goes through lovers faster than I can appropriate them from the ranks of our enemies. It is good that we have no shortage of foes, I suppose, for it keeps her…focused."

Wolfe did not say anything. The scream still echoed in his ears. He did not stay outside her chambers on nights such as these. He did not dare to, having heard the noises that always preceded the screams too many times. It awoke a feeling in him, one that he dared not give voice to. Not to his mistress.

Not to anyone.

"Do you wish to accept my offer?" Odin's voice crackled with power, the temptation obvious to Wolfe, who could almost smell the offered kills through the imagined scent of other things…things going on Lethe's quarters right now. Dark things. Sensual things. "The village is but three days' ride from here," Odin continued, "and there are many succulent conquests waiting therein," Odin said, as if he could scent what Wolfe was thinking. "If none survived our visit…that would be a worthy message to send, I think, should you wish to partake. The manner of their deaths being particularly horrific…well, that would only add to the effect."

"I wish to go, yes," Wolfe said, knocked off his reticence as easily as a bird struck from the roof of a house by a bowman.

"Excellent," Odin said, rising to his feet. "Then we shall leave on the morrow. I will see that a message finds its way to your mistress at the conclusion of her evening…activities." Another scream pierced the quiet of the meadhall, and at the far end of the room, Odin's idiot son laughed and banged his hammer against an anvil, clanging it loudly enough to make Wolfe grimace.

"No," Wolfe said, causing Odin to raise his eyebrow once more, only slightly, the surprise obvious this time. "Just the two of us should go." He cast his eyes toward the hallway where Lethe did her business with the helpless, enfeebled sacrifices, men culled from other armies and given to her as…sacrifices.

Odin nodded once, subtly. "Very well. We shall leave the Valkyrie to her business of choosing the dead. Are you ready?"

Wolfe rose, pulling the skin tight to himself. "I am."

The All-Father smiled. "Very well then, Wolfe. Let us go forth and seek our own satisfaction, in the manner of the conquering." He led the way out of the hall. Another scream sounded as they left, echoing in Wolfe's ear, a low burn in his belly stoking his inner fire to draw some screams of his own, as if in answer to the ones he could hear—but never enjoy—from Lethe's victims.

35.

Sienna

I awoke to light streaming in through the window, unaware that I'd even fallen asleep on the couch. Rose was next to me, her own head tipped sideways where she looked to be resting, eyes open and fixed on me. When she caught me looking she smiled. "Good morning to ye."

"Ouch," I said, feeling a little stiff from my sleeping position. I waited to see if Wolfe would clear it up on his own, but he didn't, so I finally said, *Wolfe,* and a few seconds later the aching sensation in my neck disappeared just like a gunshot wound. Which reminded me: "How's your side?"

Rose lifted her shirt. "Good as new," she said, poking the newly minted flesh where she'd been shot, only a little red spot still lingering to indicate where she'd taken the round.

I stretched and rose, shaking my head as I stumbled to my feet. Cobwebs in the brain seemed to dot my thoughts, an unusual amount even for my usual state of fatigue. I couldn't believe I'd fallen asleep, much less that I'd had the sleep I did, a mostly dreamless affair save for one nightmare that I vaguely recalled—feeling like Frankie was touching me, strangling me, trying to suffocate me.

I took a breath. Well, he definitely hadn't done that, and as much as I might have wished otherwise, I'd never had a shortage of nightmares after getting my ass kicked. Hell, sometimes I even had nightmares after I'd kicked someone else's ass. The brain did like to unpack trauma in whatever way it could.

"Damn," I muttered, thinking of something. Rose looked at me with undisguised querying, and I said, "Gotta hit the toilet." I excused myself from the room and closed the door to the bathroom quietly, as though I might wake Frankie, wherever he was, by slamming it.

That wasn't actually what I was cursing about. I'd meant to reach out to Jamal Coleman the next time I slept, to try and get him digging into what was going on in Edinburgh. He was a savvy character, the kind of guy that could unearth more with a computer than anyone else I'd ever met save one. But I couldn't contact him by conventional means, because he was definitely under FBI surveillance and suspicion, being employed by my brother, a known associate of Sienna Nealon who worked with other known associates of mine. Giving the FBI reason to investigate them would be like throwing fresh meat in the midst of my friends when a hungry lion was prowling nearby.

But I'd wanted to set Jamal to work on some of the burning questions—who was Frankie? How many people had gone missing around Edinburgh—and maybe Scotland in general—that had ended up donating their powers to his cause? How long had this been going on? Where the hell could I find this guy?

Oh, and by the way—any thoughts on how to kill him?

Jamal would probably come up dry on that last one, wearing an embarrassed look. Maybe not, though. He had taken revenge for the death of his last girlfriend, and it hadn't been a super pretty kind of revenge either, poison at long range, pistols at dawn, or something clean and vaguely civilized. He'd looked those men in the face as he'd killed them, cold and angry. That was the kind of death Frankie had coming for indiscriminately ripping apart Edinburgh without concern for who got hurt or killed in the process of his douchebaggery.

I finished in the bathroom and came out, another lost opportunity occurring to me. Even if I hadn't gotten Jamal, I could have contacted Wexford, given him a status update for how things had gone bad up here. I might still have to do that; US intelligence probably knew he and the UK government were nominally shielding me from trouble over here. It was anyone's guess as to how they'd react to that—

Poorly, Harmon said. *Our intelligence and law enforcement agencies don't enjoy being thwarted, not even gently and quietly by our allies.*

Okay, well, it was the ex-president's guess as to how they'd react to that, and his guess was not well. But *will they actively intervene over here, on foreign soil?*

Harmon mulled that over for a moment. *Probably not, unless the UK government asks for their help. To do so openly, or even covertly, and being caught at it? Major diplomatic incident, and not the sort of thing my successor, Richard Gondry—you've never met a dimmer, more cowardly herd animal—will want to risk.*

Good to know, I muttered as I came out of the bathroom.

That said…watch your back, as the proles say, Harmon said. *They may not want to use our operatives on British soil, but they have other resources that aren't nearly as easy to trace back. Catspaws, if you will.*

Mercenaries, I said.

Or worse. You'll need to be careful.

"Great," I said as I came around the corner back into the living room, and stopped talking because Rose was already looking at me funny. Like I needed more problems right now.

"What's great?" Rose asked.

"The reaction to everything that's happened, I'm sure." I strolled over to the coffee table in front of the couch and picked up the TV remote, clicking it on. "Why don't you see what your friend has for breakfast while I take a minute to digest the goings-on as reported by the ever-reliable crusaders in the news media?"

Rose nodded as the TV came on and took a minute to adjust to the signal it was getting. BBC News popped up a few seconds later, one of those impeccably British news readers inflappably speaking to the audience about goings-on around here.

I'd avoided British news for the most part since I'd been here. It didn't bear thinking about, most of the time, worrying what others were saying about me. I'd found it to be a trap of sorts, the kind I could easily wander into but not so easily get out of. Public opinion was a tricky thing for a control freak, because it was utterly out of my control.

"...fracas in Edinburgh," the news caster was saying. He was a middle-aged guy, looked like he probably wore glasses off camera, but he had the sort of gravitas that I tended to find easier in Englishmen than anywhere else. Wexford had it in spades. "Reports are now consistently firm—59 dead, 123 injured. Sienna Nealon has been sighted fleeing the scene, as well as overflying Edinburgh yesterday—"

"Welcome to the obvious conclusion," I said, and flipped the channel. To my surprise, one of the American news channels popped on, and I wondered if this was some sort of international satellite package or what, because I hadn't seen this in any of the hotels I'd stayed at since arriving.

"...some reactions online," the host of the show was saying, "I think we can safely say that Sienna Nealon has been, to use the current phrase, 'destroyed' on the internet last night." The guy wore a smirk. "It's become obvious that whatever good we thought she was doing was all misrepresentation, that this whole time she wasn't the hero we believed in; she was a criminal busy covering up her own crimes. And the fact that they were such loathsome crimes— there should be an investigation into why the previous administration covered up for her, and why they—not just tolerated but actively supported her for years, keeping her in a governmental role to oversee metahuman criminal affairs—"

I clicked the TV off and dropped the control, not gently. It clacked hard on the coffee table.

"What?" Rose asked, still banging about in the kitchen. "What is it?"

"It would appear I've been 'destroyed' on the internet again overnight," I said, feeling the acidic taste of disgust. "So what else is new." I said it really jaded, but the truth was, even after all this time of people finding ways to assume the absolute worst of me, regardless of what I was doing or trying to do...it still hurt to be so thoroughly misunderstood.

"People who talk about someone being 'destroyed' on the

internet?" Rose shook her head. "They seem like the kind of coddled little weasels that would fold like a bitch with one good punch."

I cocked an eyebrow at Rose's devastating assessment. "You're not wrong."

"You've still got fans out there," Rose said sincerely. "People who believe in you, who don't automatically leap to the worst possible conclusion when things go awry."

I glanced back at the dark TV. "There can't be many of them left after these last few months."

"Ahh, they're out there," she said. She glanced around the kitchen. "Sooo…there's not much in here, unfortunately. I found a little English breakfast tea…and that's about it. Apparently my friend hasn't hit the shop in a while. Needs a little M&S run."

"So we have to go out if we want to eat," I said, coming to that very reluctant conclusion.

"So it would seem," Rose said, making away from the counter. "I mean, we could resort to cannibalism, if you'd prefer, and I think you have a very strong chance of besting me in any such contest—"

I snorted. "I can't eat a ginger." She cocked her head in surprise as I delivered the punchline. "I feel like I'd be able to taste your lack of soul in the meat."

Her eyes widened, and she stood there for a second, mouth slightly agape, and then she started to laugh. "Ahahaha! That's—that's genuinely funny! Hahahah!"

"And I didn't even think it was one of my best," I said, and a few seconds later we settled back into a glum silence. "Out we go, I guess." I looked at the door with grim reluctance, like something was going to come crashing in at any second. Because that was the kind of state we were in.

36.

When we reached the street, it was clear Edinburgh was in a funk. It was were quiet, the sounds of cars in the distance but only occasionally nearby. It was like a grim blanket had settled over the city, pushing down on it, suppressing the life out of it.

Now a fog had crept in, albeit a thin one, and where I might have expected a normal, steady flow of human traffic down a street like this on a regular morning, here I was seeing people out in ones and twos, heads down, their utter silence a strange tableau to behold.

Rose and I looked left and right, and ultimately she nodded to the left, so I followed her. She seemed to know where she was going, and as we walked I heard her stomach rumble. She touched it self-consciously and said, "Sorry." As though she had to apologize for being hungry because I'd had her hunker down last night.

A guy walked past in a soccer shirt, head down, shuffling his feet. The cool morning air was causing my skin to prickle, and I said, after he'd passed, "I don't *get* soccer. I mean, I don't get many sports, actually, but especially not soccer."

"It's football," Rose said, a trace of crankiness oozing its way out.

"Soccer."

"Football."

"You saying it over and over doesn't make it something different."

191

"The rest of the world calls it football," she said, "and you Americans call it soccer. Why the hell do you think you get to name it?"

"When you're back to back World War champs," I said lightly, "you get to name things." I didn't give enough of a shit to provide anything other than the snarkiest of answers, bereft of any sincerity. "It's a fringe benefit of having enough nuclear firepower to destroy the planet ten times over."

Rose's shoulders shook slightly with mirth, then she got serious. "Might makes right, is that it?"

I got a little quieter in my answer, because now we'd left snark behind and crossed over into a serious point. "Sadly, it always has, and I don't see that fundamental truth of human nature changing anytime soon."

A couple of guys walked past, looking at Rose and me, taking a keen interest in us. They didn't stop as they passed, but I saw one pull out a phone as he went by, and he had it up to his ear a moment later.

"Shit," I said, and tried to decide whether it would be a good idea to zap it out of his hand with a light net. I went back and forth a few times, but he turned into an alley behind me before I could land on a decision. If he'd been definitely guilty…no problem, right? But who knew whether he was just calling his mother or dropping a dime on me to Frankie?

"That guy was suspicious, right?" Rose asked, leaning in to whisper to me.

"He was." I twitched as I walked, looking around like my head was on a swivel. I really missed my blonde wig right now, because as lame as it looked, it really did change my appearance enough that when coupled with an accent, people didn't suspect I was Sienna Nealon.

Now…? Especially given that I'd already been sighted in Edinburgh? That guy was probably just calling the cops. And who could blame him for it?

Another guy was standing across the street on a phone, watching our progress like he was a motion-activated security camera. I caught a glimpse of another guy sending furtive glances at us from one of those glass bus stands that was

192

bracketed by ads.

"This is going to turn bad, quickly," I said, leaning toward Rose. I was thinking I should snatch her up and fly before things got hot here. "Too many people looking at us here." I mean, on a New York street, you could expect most people to just be doing their own thing, but here? Everybody seemed to be in full, 'If you see something, say something,' mode, and damned sure looking to see some shit. "We need to skedaddle."

"Okay," Rose said, and she got closer. "How do ye want to—"

We were only about fifty feet from a T intersection at the end of a block, and I was planning the best escape. Flying out right in the middle of the street seemed like a bad idea, but worse would be just standing around waiting for cops to show up or…

Damn.

That familiar bald head came bobbing around the corner, looking at us as he turned it and strode, unchallenged, into the street. Rose and I stopped where we were, in her case because she was struck dumb, in mine because he was close enough that if I grabbed Rose and zoomed right, he could probably throw up one of those ripper blasts with the wall of red that rose above it like a force field that'd cut me off before I made it twenty feet.

"Sweet merciful Zeus," Rose said under her breath.

"By all accounts," I said, "he was not that merciful."

You can say that again, Wolfe said.

"Hello, Sienna," Frankie said, and he cocked his head, grinning. "Have a good night?"

37.

"I did," I said, figuring I'd crack wise with him while I was trying to decide on my course of action. "I'm surprised you didn't come visit me in my dreams, since you seemed to think I was your density, George McFly without the charm. Or the hair."

He ran a hand over the slick top of his head and still grinned. "I was rather busy doing other things, lass." Being called 'lass' by a handsome Scotsman was on my list of melty-excitey turn-ons. Being called 'lass' by Frankie kinda killed the dream, though. "That's a good look for you," he said, apparently noticing I was still clad in the ripped-up clothes he'd destroyed when last we'd met. "Like roadkill."

I stepped off the curb. "Well, I am on the road. And we both know you're going to try and kill me. But a lot of people have tried, including yourself, and hey, I'm still here. In your case, I think we can chalk it up to performance anxiety. I'd say it's natural, but really, most guys who try and kill me don't have the kind of power you do and then choke at it, so...I think it's just you."

Intentionally pissing him off was perhaps not the wisest use of my time, but every second I did it delayed the battle, and—I hoped—piled a little more excess emotion on the fire for him. If I made him mad enough, maybe he'd get sloppy. Flimsy as it was, that was kinda my only hope at the moment.

"All right, well, let's not muck about," Frankie said, and

then he fired off two blasts of those ripper beams. They went churning down the street, one of them aimed to go straight through Rose, who squealed as I yanked her out of the way. She'd already been in motion, but not quite fast enough for my taste. The blast ripped through the asphalt and concrete as it shot past, showering me with concrete shards as it tore apart the ground on either side of me and left trenches a foot deep in their wake.

"Ride my back," I said to Rose as I flung her over my shoulder and let her sort out how she wanted to carry out my command. I started to zip off straight up, but Frankie anticipated this and sent out two more blasts, one that walled things off to my right for a second, which was the direction I had been intending to flee, and another that cut things off to my left—well, behind me now that I'd turned. Out of the corner of my eye, I could see that he'd leapt off the curb and closed the distance between us to thirty feet or so.

Penned in on both sides by his blasts for the moment, I tried to decide my best course of action. If I tried to run right, he had me blocked until that wall faded behind his ripper blast. Same thing to the left. His hands were glowing, and he was clearly gearing up to send another one at me and Rose, who'd adjusted her grip so as not to touch my skin, but she still had me clutched around the shoulders and was hanging on for dear life.

Couldn't go left, couldn't go right, and he was about to fire another round up the center. The red walls that rose out of the blasts as they ran across the ground were just starting to fade—back by him, not next to me, like a tinting of crimson on the world.

That presented an interesting tactical possibility.

"Hang on," I said to Rose, and she squeezed me tighter around the shoulders.

I put my head down and launched right up the middle at Frankie.

He saw me coming and his eyes widened. He was charging up a blast that was going to come straight for us, designed to hit me and probably turn me into several bite-sized pieces of Sienna rather than the inimitable whole. Having seen what those attacks did to concrete and drywall, I didn't have any desire to watch one work on the human body. I figured it'd be a lot like dropping into a giant blender, and yuuuuck.

I shot at Frankie, raising my speed to the point where Rose barely had time to squawk out an "Eeeeep!" before I was coming at him at warp freaking speed.

He dodged to the side at the last minute, apparently deciding saving his own ass was smarter than trying to deliver that blast he'd been charging. It went sideways, wrecking a building to the side, but I shot past him and didn't stop. He'd damned near trapped me just now and as exciting as it would be to attack his ass with Rose on my back, she was like a literal millstone around my neck at the moment, and that was not a disadvantage I could carry into battle with a threat as dire as Frankie and expect to walk out the other side.

We passed Frankie wide, and were heading for the buildings that lined the end of the T intersection ahead. I looked right for just a blink and saw something funny—that same guy in the European biker jacket that I'd seen outside the Asda yesterday when Frankie and I had clashed out in Dunfermline. He was staring at me openmouthed as I pulled up, avoiding collision with the building in front of me.

I zoomed into the air and over the skyline of Edinburgh. I didn't want to stick around in case Frankie was going to come after me, but I mentally filed away the biker guy to try and figure out what was going on with him later. Serial killers and incubi (but I repeat myself) were notorious loners. Was he carting this guy around with him?

And if so…why?

38.

"What the hell do we do now?" Rose asked, yelling into my ear over the wind.

I stayed silent a little longer than I probably needed to. "Well," I said, "probably not get that breakfast unless you want to fly to Glasgow or something to get it, because—I mean, damn, Frankie was on us within minutes of walking out the front door. And it felt like the whole street was watching us." That was an eerie feeling, and one that I wanted to avoid in the future by getting another wig, posthaste. I'd left my bag behind on a rooftop yesterday, and I thought I remembered it being somewhat close to the police station. There was another wig in there, a redhead one, which would obviously make Rose and me look somewhat silly walking side by side, but what were you gonna do?

"I'm finding myself curiously not so hungry at the moment," she said, though her stomach rumbled again.

"Hrm," I said, seriously debating the idea of flying somewhere else in Scotland or even down to England. What was the likelihood that Frankie had a network outside Edinburgh? Because based on what I'd seen on that street, he had one in place here. Another curious thing for an incubus. Something was rotten up in this place.

"'Hrm' what?" Rose asked. She had an edge of worry in her voice, the kind that was perfectly understandable after watching your heroine and girl crush (clearly) get pummeled all around your hometown for a couple days. Her dreams were turning to ash before her eyes, and my goddess feet were turning to clay.

"There's a lot of things happening here," I said. "This isn't just a serial killer mystery anymore. Frankie's got a headquarters, he's got people working for him; I think he's even got a network, like a real, legit network of spies that just ratted us out to him. He's carrying some dude with him that wears a leather motorcycle jacket and looks like he just dropped out of a *Fast and Furious* movie—"

"That guy from Asda!" Rose said, getting it. "He does look a little like a skinny Vin Diesel, dressed like that."

"So, anyway, there's something else going on here," I said. "Much as Frankie's trying to kill me—and by extension you, sorry—there's something deeper at play here. He's got way too many powers to have just coincidentally accumulated them over the course of a few years if he's a new meta." I bit my lower lip. "On the other hand, if he was a five-star badass waiting in the wings these last few...why choose to debut now? He could have made a real splash anytime after Sovereign left the playing field." I chewed that over for a minute. "Unless...he was around during the Sovereign fight, and decided...no, learned about how to unleash his incubus powers after that...yikes." I took a hard breath.

"What...what are you talking about?" Rose asked. "Did I miss something?"

"Just me running in logical circles," I said. "Basically, I'm thinking—see, succubi and incubi are the outcasts of the meta world. In traditional terms. Metas used to live in cloisters, like a village where they'd all group together for the sake of convenience, safety, heritage—"

"How delightfully provincial," Rose deadpanned. "Sounds a little like home."

"—but incubi and succubi were outcasts from these 'polite' societies," I went on, hoping that in telling her this, I'd be able to find the connection sitting in plain sight. "I never knew why until I discovered that I could use the powers of the metas I absorbed. Because if you think about it, that kind of power in the hands of a guy like Frankie? Total incentive to go and eat as many metas as you can—"

"And we're back to cannibalism," Rose said.

"—and who wants to make nice with someone who's eyeing you like a filet?" I took another deep breath. "The secret of what incubi and succubi could do with the powers of others—it became a carefully guarded secret over time. Elders didn't pass it along. My mom had no clue, even though her mother was a full-blood succubus who had to have known, since she was a daughter of Hades." I steered us in a lower orbit over Edinburgh while I thought, trying to untie this mental knot. "So Frankie…maybe he figured out by watching me and Sovereign what was possible for him." I took one more sharp breath. "Which means…he's been building his power this whole time, probably, in order to get this many meta souls under his belt."

Something about that didn't sound right, though. Rose must have noticed it. "Ye're making a face. Why are ye making a face?"

"There aren't that many metas left in the world," I said, chewing my lip, ignoring the sensation of it drying out because of all the cool wind blowing into my mouth while it was flapping. "To end up with this many powers…" I got a cold feeling inside as another idea presented itself. "Right. Well. We've got to go back to Police Scotland." I banked us around and started heading for the point in the distance that was the station house I'd already visited.

Rose let out a small yelp. "But why?"

I turned up the speed and darted low, hoping to get us there unseen. I crested the rooftops and flew low over them, prompting Rose to let out another cry of worry. She clamped on tight, and I steered us carefully. "Because I need a question answered, and I don't think I can find it anywhere but there."

39.

Being a redhead didn't feel particularly different than being a blond, or my usual shade of darker brown. I was usually vengeful, so it didn't feel like a huge transition for me to have my flame-red tress wig on as I walked into the Edinburgh PD and saw that Maiden Aunt was, once again, behind the front desk.

She caught sight of me immediately, and her mouth came slightly agape as she probably caught the change immediately. I mean, it's not every day you see someone completely change hair shades overnight, and I could see the questions forming in her mind, which was…worrying, given the current climate of everyone hating Sienna Nealon around here. And everywhere.

"Weren't you a—" Maiden Aunt started to say, but her face changed in a second, from absolute curiosity to something more like numb contentment, and she burbled out, pleasantly enough, "Why was it you're here then, dear?"

I glanced at Rose, who was staring intently at Maiden Aunt. She flashed me a smile and I knew that she'd changed the woman's emotionally state radically, from deep curiosity to…I dunno, afterglow, maybe. She seemed happy.

"Need to see DI…Whatshisname," I finished rather lamely. What the hell was his name?

"You mean Detective Inspector Clements," she said, correcting me with a leisurely sort of enjoyment and a song in her heart. Not snotty, just nice.

"Yeah, that guy," I said. "Mr. It's-Not-On-My-Desk."

She started to reach for the phone and then said, instead, like she'd just had the most magnificent idea, "You can just go on back, dear. You've been here before."

I gave Rose the sidelong and she flashed me a thumbs-up. "Sounds good," I said. And it did sound good, especially after dealing with nothing but jerks and people who wanted to kill me over the last day or so. "You really are the bright spot in all this, Rose," I said to her as we headed off down that hallway to the right once Maiden Aunt had buzzed us in.

"How's that?"

"I mean this last couple days has been hell," I said as we walked side by side, "and—" I cut myself off, thinking maybe I should just shut it, because let's face it. People who hang around in my close proximity have a target painted on them, as had been proven over and over again. Zack, my first love. Breandan, the Irishman with a heart of gold. Hell, even my mom had been killed because she was standing too close to me when bad guys came a-calling.

There were others too, whose names I remembered but that I didn't want to think about too often. Rose must have sensed my emotional state by the look on my face, because she took my thanks in stride. "Well, you know, I'm just doing what I can. Wish I could be of more help."

"There is one thing you can do for me," I said as we turned the corner into the bullpen.

"Name it and it'll be done." She looked serious as hell, like she would have bowed and offered me the hilt of her sword if she had one.

"When the time comes that I tell you to run, you bail the hell out, head for the hills, and hide like your life depends upon it," I said. "Because I don't want you around for the final fight with Frankie. It's going to be brutal, and he'll use any card he can play against me, including holding you hostage, and I don't want to give him that leverage. Okay?"

She sucked in a hard breath as we moved through the bustle of the bullpen. "Why do I feel like I'm saying goodbye to the great champion before she heads off into her final battle?"

"I don't know," I said ruefully, "because I don't intend for this to be my final battle." Of course, most people didn't intend for their last battle to be their last—it ended up being so because they got outmatched.

And I was so, so outmatched.

We walked up to the desk of DI Clements and he looked up at us in surprise, and especially at my hair. "We're playing twins today," I said, nodding at Rose and cutting him off before he could even say it. He relaxed a titch, like I'd stolen his thunder along with his question. "Do you keep a file of all mysterious deaths? Unexplained? The ones the coroners can't quite pin to any specific cause of death?"

He blinked at me. "It's a database, I suppose."

"And missing persons?"

"Similarly in a database."

"Great," I said, "I need that info."

He looked like he wanted to argue, but suddenly found himself looking so much more compliant. "You know, I could do you a favor, I suppose," he said, his practiced reluctance to do a damned thing melting away as I caught a wink from Rose. "How far back do you want to go?"

"Summer of 2014," I said, running through it in my brain.

"Four years?" he asked in mild surprise. "All right." He bent over the keyboard, pulling a hunt and peck that made me want to shove him out of the way and do it myself. If I'd known what I was doing.

Rose watched with similar disbelief. "It'd be quicker for a turtle to cross Edinburgh," she said. "In winter. While they're hibernating or whatever it is they do to survive the cold."

"Oh, ha ha," Clements said, taking it all very jovially. "You guys are so funny." He sounded like he meant it sincerely. "Here you go, I've got the figures." He squinted at them. "Huh," he said, blissful, "that seems kinda high."

I bent over his shoulder and looked, and…uhmm…yeah, it seemed high. "How the hell did—what the—you're losing *five thousand people a year* in Edinburgh to unclassifiable death and you didn't even notice?"

"Well, in fairness, in 2013 it was…" He squinted at the screen again. "Five hundred. Huh. Yeah, okay, five thousand is high. But you're not even counting the missing persons data, which is…hummm…twelve thousand?"

I didn't even know how to respond to that. "How in the f—what the hell—how does no one in London know that this is a problem—"

"Well that's easy enough to answer," came a voice from across the room, and I turned, rising in time to see a familiar bald head bobbing over the bullpen walls. Frankie strutted his way through the aisles and police officers moved out of his way, nodding and speaking quietly in acknowledgment of him as he came, like he was some sort of duke or lord. "It's because London hasn't gotten accurate figures from us in years." He smiled. "Why, they didn't even know we had a problem worthy of solving until I left them a trail of breadcrumbs…for you."

"Shit shit shit," I said under my breath and started to grab Rose, but she was already grabbed by someone else. Eyes wide, Detective Inspector Clements had an arm around her neck, clutching her tight like a hostage situation was unfolding before my eyes. He even had a gun to her head.

"Ladies and gentlemen of the Edinburgh police department," Frankie announced, "you have the dangerous fugitive Sienna Nealon in your midst." He turned dead serious, teeth clenching, amusement and loathing all mixing together. "Would ye kindly…show her how we deal with murderers in Scotland?"

40.

Wolfe

Greece
31 B.C.

The news that had come north had been dire, and Lethe's reaction even more so. Never a joyful soul outside of battle to start with, her anger had been swift and fierce and loud, the denunciations ringing from her lips all the more scorching and strenuous for the fact that they flowed all through their journey across the short sea through the land of the Danes and down the bulk of Europa to Greece.

Wolfe stayed silent as he could by her side, seldom sleeping at night. The news had caught him unawares, and was blurred, the last words of a messenger slave who had nearly rode himself and his horse to death to reach them, carrying the words of Raymond, the son of Wolfe's master, telling them to harken back for war, that Hades had gone mad on the march in fury over the death of his grandchild.

"I firmly believe this was one of Acheron's children," Lethe seethed as they crossed the sunny plain, the Aegean Sea to their left, cliff faces giving them an excellent view of what lay before them. The cavernous realm of Hades was minutes away, and they had yet to meet so much as a single guardian. "Surely she has led my father into this calamity." She spoke in the language of the Nords, as she did always now.

Wolfe guided her back into their original tongue. "What does it matter, if the fires of war are now lit? We will carry the torch forward, bring claw and blood to the friends of Olympus in this land as we did for the Nords."

Lethe's eyes flashed. "You know I have long resisted Odin's calls to expand their frontier, to increase their borders. Conquest invites forceful response from the threatened, and our kind—metahumans—exist in every land from here to the sea in the east. You know this, having fought more than our share on that journey."

"And we beat any that opposed us," Wolfe answered her. "You should have let your Nord friends come. Odin wished to."

"Odin wanted to bring his grand design for a union from sea to sea to my father's lands," Lethe said in silence, focused on the ragged path that led along the sloping cliffside. It meandered toward the sea as the land lost its rocky rise ahead. "And my father would likely answer him eagerly. I saw no cause to bring their ambitions closer than strictly necessary."

"Because you fear the world they would make," Wolfe said.

"Because I fear the world they would leave," Lethe said in quiet. "How long have we walked and ridden across these lands, Wolfe? How many times have we seen tribe and man fight back against those who would seek to cow them? We have watched wars over matters trivial and serious, petty insults and grievous wrongs. We have perpetrated many, because we could."

Wolfe stayed quiet for a moment. "You have taken more than your share of the conquest sacrifices."

Her eyes flashed. "I have. I like the feel of a man as he burns upon my flesh. Aye, and women, too. I sacrifice them for pleasure, but in numbers small. This thing that Odin would bring? The numbers of sacrifice would be too great and shocking for even the two of us to imagine. It would be nothing less than a scourging of the world, the death of all in the path of his ambition."

"And why shy away from that?" Wolfe asked, voice a hiss.

"It is your destiny, the destiny of your house to bring death to the world, to show them the truth they deny all their lives to the end. You should be the dark fury that lingers over them all their days, reminding them of their fleeting mortality, making their lives all the sweeter by virtue of reminder that they have so few and that they can be nulled at any time. You should be the one who rises above these lands, doling out your whims. Not Odin. Not Zeus. Not Hades...you."

Lethe stirred atop her horse. "You let your feelings color your judgment, Wolfe." She looked at him, and he felt a sting—she knew. "You may not find death, brought by me to so many others, quite so alluring should it come for you."

"And I may just embrace it," Wolfe said. "You don't know. Death makes prey of the lessers, and I am no lesser, at least not to any but you and your father. Why deny this truth? Why subsume yourself to Odin, to anyone?"

"I am hardly invincible, however great my anger may ring," she said quietly. "And neither are any of my family, not even my father."

"But together," Wolfe said, his heart leaping as he spoke the words he had longed to say all these years, "together we could be—"

He stopped because he sensed someone ahead, and snapped his head around to see a man standing in the path. He was bronzed, dark-haired, and was calm in manner, plainly unaware of what rode his way at a canter.

"Lethe, daughter of Hades," he said pleasantly. "Wolfe of the Cerberi." Perhaps he did know, then, announcing them by name. "My name is Janus. I believe you met my mother, Artemis, and my sister, Diana, when last you passed through these lands."

Lethe drew up short upon her horse. "Why do you block our passage, Janus, son of Apollo?" She knew him then. Wolfe recalled the mother and sister, the huntresses, but this creature standing before them...was a different matter entirely.

"I come to you now as family," Janus said. His eyes were brown as wet dirt, deep shadows beneath them. "In your absence, I courted and married your sister, Cocytus."

Lethe stared at him, unrelenting. "I congratulate you on a superior match. But I still await your explanation for why you impede my passage. I come to see my father. Speak your words, make them plain, and then remove yourself from my path—or I shall remove you."

Janus stared back at her calmly, and then moved himself, without comment, out of the road so that they might pass. Once he had done so, Lethe urged her horse forward, and Janus spoke once more. "You will not find him there. In the underworld with your kin."

Lethe took the reins of her horse and jerked them, prompting a great whinnying outrage from the horse, so abused. Wolfe stayed on his steed, unmoving. He was still debating whether to fillet this Janus. "Where might I find him, then?" Lethe asked, eyes narrowed, her patience waning.

"In the company of death," Janus said calmly. "There was…an incident…involving one of my children and a local market." He bowed his head. "There was death. Lord Hades…lost control of himself, regrettably."

"Who cares?" Wolfe said, taking a seething breath.

"Zeus cared," Janus said. "The others cared. Hades lost his mind with grief, and was inconsolable. In his actions, his mad stride through the nearby towns, he found no relief, even as the deaths added up to far outweigh what was taken. Something needed to be done."

"And you did it?" Lethe asked, quietly seething. She dismounted with ease, crossing the distance between them to stand before Janus, hand perched above his head like a sword ready to fall. She had one of those too, but it was at her side.

"I did not," Janus said, and Wolfe could almost hear Lethe's breath hiss out. "Your mother, Persephone, did this thing."

"You lie!" Lethe recoiled from him as though struck, putting the tip of her blade at the base of his throat. "I will cut out your lying throat, and then you will spread this filth no more."

"You may kill me, if that softens the blow," Janus said, making no move, a placid look on his face. "But it will not change the truth of what has happened—Lord Hades went mad with grief, and in an effort to save his brood from war and annihilation at the hands of Zeus and the others, your mother struck your father down, settling matters for all involved."

"Impossible," Lethe gasped. "She could no more hurt him against his desire than she could turn a rock against someone as a weapon of war. He could have taken her very soul from her before she reached him."

"But do you think he would have?" Janus asked, the voice of reason. It should have infuriated Wolfe, but for some strange reason, he felt utterly calmed at this news, at this chain of events, even though it heralded of destruction in his life that he could scarcely conceive of. "Struck down his wife as she approached him, no obvious ill intent? She took him by surprise, Lethe, the only way that anyone could, save for perhaps one of your own siblings."

"These lies that flow from you," Lethe said, voice rising, "they pollute my ears and stain them with your—your deceits. He is not dead, for death is undying."

"And yet…" Janus said simply. "He is gone. If you do not wish to believe, I cannot blame you. I would not care to lose my father, and would certainly not trust the simple words of a stranger, even though they might be family unknown to me."

"Where did this calumny happen?" She put her blade back to his throat, and a tiny dot of red appeared where the tip of the sword poked through his skin.

"To the north, the market town," Janus said. "He fell before destroying another village. Persephone…struck true just in time to save the lives of every man, woman and child in—"

"I care not for the men and women and children of this world," Lethe said, seething. She yanked the blade from Janus, and left that tiny wound opened upon his neck. If it troubled him, he showed no sign. "I will seek the truth of what you have said. And know this—if you have lied to me—"

"You will strike my head from my shoulders, I am assured," Janus said. "But if you choose to do so, it will be out of pique, not because I have lied to you in this. Hades is dead at the hand of Persephone. All in these lands know the truth of this, but if you must see for yourself—feel free to do so."

"You do not have the power to give me leave to do anything," Lethe said, seizing her horse by the reins and mounting it with a leap. "You are not the head of this house."

"There is no more house," Janus said quietly. "With your father gone, Zeus has called for your brood to be… separated. His servant, Alastor, is even now in the caves of Hades, overseeing this task. Your brothers and sisters and all their chattel are being brought to the base of Olympus. There they will dwell near the rest of our kind—"

"I will be thrice damned before I consign myself to the house of Zeus," Lethe said, spitting her displeasure upon the ground in a great glob. "My uncle may consider himself the king of us all, but I am a daughter of death and will not be ruled by a cad such as he, a man who can keep no lust under his robe for even a moment."

"He is an intemperate man, to be sure," Janus said, unblinking, "but if you will not submit to his rule—if you will not follow your mother back into the protection of Demeter—then—"

"You need not say it," Lethe said, seething, between gritted teeth. "I sense keenly what you mean, and I shall not long linger in these lands once the truth of what you have said has been proven to me beyond any doubt. I will see this place where you claim my father fell, and I will pass onward from these borders, and your accursed thunder-farting-shit-brain will not need trouble himself any longer with a thought of where I go, for I have friends the lands over who would see me live in their domains. Uncle Zeus can direct his cock toward a steady stream of goats in the fields sooner than he would bring me under his dominion, the old—"

"Yes, I get the gist of your insults," Janus said. "Forgive me for not conveying them to Zeus in their original form, but I wish to leave you, my unwitting sister by marriage, an out should you ever wish to return."

"Do whatever you see fit," Lethe said, sitting tall on her horse, "but for my part—I shall never return to these lands." And with that, she turned upon her horse and galloped off, without waiting to see if Wolfe would go with her.

Wolfe, for his part, stared at Janus. His mind pulled at him, urging him to take the reins of his own steed and follow, toward north, where Hades died and after Lethe.

But another part tugged at him, twisting in his gut. *She doesn't want you. Doesn't want your…worship.*

"And what of you, Wolfe?" Janus asked, staring at him cannily. "Already your brothers have moved their allegiance, swearing to the house of Zeus and taking the lead of Alastor, his wrathful right hand."

"I…" Wolfe said, like a force had acted upon him from atop his horse. The desire to tug the reins one way was strong, crying out at him, to be after Lethe before she grew too far from him.

"You know that following her is a dead end, do you not?" Janus asked. "She rides to a rendezvous with a hard truth— that her father is dead. She may not have seen him in centuries, but it remains that he was a protector, a voice in her head during her formative years, and a presence in her thoughts and life that…she may never replace."

"She is her own person," Wolfe said, but it was a struggle with his own warring emotions to get even this out. Something had clamped down upon him, twisting his feelings inside. His love, his lust, his craven desire for Lethe was striking hard against an immovable truth—*If you touch her, you will die as the rest did*—and finding it…immovable.

"Of course she is," Janus said. "She could not have survived on her own and made such inroads in the north without being so. But her days at home are waning now. She will go and see the truth of what I have said, and then she will ride beyond the borders of this land, for good. Maybe she will go north, back to the Nords. Perhaps east once more, following the path you set out upon last time. Who can say?"

Janus took a few steps forward, looking up at Wolfe on his horse. "But what will happen to you, Wolfe? Will you follow at her heels forever, continuing to eat the scraps that she and Odin throw to you? Because your master is dead."

"Hades...has not been my master for a long time," Wolfe said, but it was so difficult, the loyalty breaking like a brittle blade upon an anvil. What had Hades done for him other than present him with strength enough to be feared? Odin had offered him more, and Wolfe still loathed the one-eyed bastard.

"You have followed a master and then a mistress," Janus said, brushing the neck of Wolfe's horse with a stray hand. In normal circumstances, Wolfe would have killed any man who dared do such a thing. Here, he let it pass for...some reason. "Always, things were promised. Ephemeral rewards for tangible loyalty. And how has that worked out for you, Wolfe? How long has it been since the bond between you and your brothers has been renewed?" Janus's eyes were knowing, and still that did not raise Wolfe's ire as it should have. "Centuries away from home. Away from kin, from blood. They are different people than when you last knew them."

"What...do you want from me?" Wolfe asked, hands shaking as that little part of him screamed, yearned to take the reins and ride after Lethe, to follow her to Hades, to oblivion, to whatever end she commanded—

But he did not move. All he did was listen.

"I do not want anything from you," Janus said softly, still stroking the horse's mane. The beast was not calm for anyone, yet here he stood, as soothed as Wolfe himself. "But Zeus would have your loyalty as he has that of your brothers. Theirs was willingly, easily given. Yours...I sense...is harder to come by. But we all have our orders, and mine are clear— the children of Hades that will not submit will by no means be allowed to gather loyalty of our other brethren, for that would be...dangerous."

Wolfe clenched his teeth, feeling a sudden urge to strike Janus's head from his shoulders. "If you mean to kill her..."

Janus made a tsking noise, either at the horse or Wolfe.

"Not at all. She will be permitted to pass the borders of these lands one last time, but...she will not be allowed to return. Spies will follow her, from the House of Zeus, of Poseidon, of all of us. For safety's sake, you understand. Lethe...she carries a seed of danger, one that threatens all of us." He stared up at Wolfe. "It is fortunate that this...love I feel in your heart for her...that she did not...consummate such a desire with you, bring you into her, for that would make her...a nightmare. Fearsome beyond belief. But your journey with her needs end, for your sake as well as hers, for how long could she be trusted not to sup upon a draught of invincibility that sits right before her?" He laughed, but it was bitter. "No. She must be alone, and definitely kept away from you, to keep the full breadth of her powers well under control, because to do otherwise would be...fatally dangerous. Yes? You know what I mean?"

"I do," Wolfe said, that last urge to scream, to slit Janus's throat, to follow after Lethe with fury to any end...it seemed to die, a thread torn out of the tapestry of his feelings right there.

"Good," Janus said, and patted the horse's neck one last time. "You should come with me. I will introduce you to your new master."

"Zeus?" Wolfe sat there atop the horse, the pull gone, now pliant, as ready to be led—for now—as the horse he was upon. Something dark and angry sprang up within him, but faintly, and he marked Janus with it, a fury that he felt buried deep like a mark in his skin.

"Zeus is a busy man, with much to do," Janus said, turning his back. "No, you will answer to Alastor, as I do. He is a faithful friend to those who serve, you will see. And a powerful enemy to those who cross him." Janus looked back, a glint of triumph in his eyes. "Something I think you will respect."

Wolfe found himself nodding, though he did not know why, and taking the reins of the horse and jarring it forward. It moved, following Janus as the man slowly walked him down the path toward the caves below, where the house of Hades had finally, after all these centuries, reached its end.

41.

Well, this was a shit sandwich of a tactical situation, I reflected as the entire Edinburgh police department came charging in at me. Rose had a gun to her head, and the implication was pretty clear—move and she was going to be learning to think again without a hell of a lot of her brain tissue. If she survived.

The place, which had seemed so open and inviting before now, seemed claustrophobic as fifty cops fell upon me with batons and nightsticks and fists and feet and everything else they had at their disposal. I swear to God one of them hit me with a red Swingline stapler, like a feral version of Milton from Office Space.

"Geez, guys," I said, kicking a female detective so hard she sailed into a partition between desks, "was it something I said or something I did?"

There wasn't a lot of conversation here; they just charged and grunted and generally made themselves a vicious pain in my ass by raining down all sorts of physical abuse upon my person. I'd seen something similar once before, the night I lit a commerce park in Eden Prairie, Minnesota on fire because a bunch of metas I'd stuck in jail, quite deservedly, teamed up for revenge on yours truly. This was a little different, though. It was still Horde Mode, as Reed would have called it, but this mob was coming after me of their own free will, or so it seemed.

I was pulling my punches big time, too. One guy came at

me and I backhanded him such that his head snapped back and he lost his footing. He was promptly trampled by three other cops trying to club me senseless, the milk of human kindness for their fellow lost in the mad rush to tear me limb from limb at Frankie's order.

Frankie was still at the other end of the room, and I caught glimpses of him now and again as he stood up on a desk, watching the fun. He was grinning, and wouldn't have looked at all out of place if he'd had a popcorn bucket and was stuffing his face while watching. Somehow he'd turned the entirety of this station against me and my red-wigged self at the drop of a hat, and if it had happened a little more organically and a little less frothing-at-the-mouth-ingly I would have easily believed that they were just aiming to kick my ass because I was Interpol's Most Wanted right now.

But they'd gone nuts in a way that sane people seldom did, and the fact that it happened the way it had suspended my ability to believe these were law enforcement officers doing their duty. They may not have been as rabid as those reporters in Eden Prairie, but there was an element of human response missing from the way they bum-rushed me, that dash of uncertainty that any human would feel when charging at a superhuman weapon who'd killed literally hundreds of people, and you're armed with nothing but batons and staplers and—shit, was that a monogrammed paperweight that clipped my ear? I think it was.

Of course, that moment, when I was being overrun by a room full of angry cops, wasn't the moment to draw a lot of conclusions, which is why most of my brainpower was dedicated to kicking and punching and occasionally biting, maybe with a dash of clawing thrown in, given my somewhat limited fingernails; anything to get these people to not whack me with batons in an effort to club me to death. The fact that there wasn't a lot of strategizing going on—not one call of, "Hey, you go left, I'll go right, and we'll pincer the hell out of her by beating her skull in from all sides!" was another strong indicator that things had seriously jumped the track here.

"Okay, well," I said, whacking a lady cop and knocking her

clean out, "this is about enough of this." I leapt up and over one of the cubicles, kicking someone as I went past. I landed in another cube and then jumped again, coming down two rows over, using my levitational abilities to extend my jump.

A couple gunshots rang out behind me, and I froze. Rose had a gun to her head when last I saw her—did that mean…?

Someone grunted and took a punch to the face a row back, a sound as familiar to my ears as a toaster dinging was to most. There was a thud and then another, and someone landed on the desk above me and then skidded down, a big red mark on her cheek and a pistol in her hand.

"Rose," I said in surprise, looking from her to the cubicle entry in surprise. "How'd you—"

"Lulled him," she said, rubbing her face. "One of the others lashed out though, and it didn't feel too grand when he connected. Like a mob, they are."

"Yeah," I said with a fair amount of chagrin. "Come on, let's get the hell out of here before they figure out which cube we've ducked down into." And I yanked her by the arm and shot out the door of the cubicle, suspended a few inches above the carpet.

Yelps of surprise greeted us as we emerged and dodged down another row, then up and over the next, low to the ground. Cops were streaming through the bullpen now, and quiet ground was going to be harder and harder to come by the longer we drew this out. Of course, I could fight my way through them, but if this was mind control, these people could get hurt or killed (because as controlled as I was, it was a fight involving life or death, and even throwing a punch could be lethal, if it came from me), and I didn't want that.

I paused for a second, gathering my thoughts. Frankie barked sharp orders, his Scottish accent more prominent than ever before. "Block the doors! Don't let them scarper!"

"Ideas?" Rose asked as she sat there next to me in the quiet cube, our momentary cover just that—momentary. The sound of footfalls all around us made it impossible to tell where the nearest threat was, because they were everywhere and stampeding closer to us all the time.

"A few," I said, and stuck out my hand, beckoning for her to hand me the gun she'd purloined from her captor. "No offense, but I know you UK folks don't much truck with those."

She handed it over instantly. "I suppose, what with you being an American and all…"

"Yeah, I know what I'm doing," I said, and slipped the pistol into my waistband. It was a little bitty popgun, maybe .380 at best, compact and properly European. I got the desire to do everything subtly and with maximum economy, whether it was the smaller houses that came standard over here or the rally cars they seemed to prefer over big SUVs. My understanding of that ethos, though, stopped at ammo, because .380 was a caliber for people just weren't serious about getting killing done. Still, work with the tools you had…

"So…what are ye doing?" Rose asked after I'd put the gun away. She was looking at me really questioningly, probably because she'd expected me to just put a bullet in Frankie's head from across the bullpen and be done with this whole thing. And I wished I could have done that, but with a .380, I wasn't going to throw away the limited shots I had across a crowded room.

"Deciding that this is not the field of battle I'd prefer for this confrontation," I said, and then generated a blast of fire that I sent shooting skyward. It ripped out of the ceiling, consuming everything in a ten-foot radius above us that could be burned and weakening the rest. That done, I scooped up Rose with a hand around the waist and shot into the air. Again, she kept from making any squeaking noises as we launched out of the roof of the station and streaked across the city sky, leaving the ambush behind us.

"Mercy," Rose said, and I couldn't tell whether it was a comment on my handling of the situation or some sort of plea. "That was…"

"Intense, yeah," I said, looping north and hitting the deck again, flying low over the city.

"So…are we leaving town now?" she asked. "Now that we know that everyone's against us, including the police?"

"No," I said, feeling a solemn resolve settle over me. "No, we are not."

"Ummm, okay," she said. "Then…where are we going?"

"To the last place he'd expect," I said, as our destination came in sight, a tower rising high over the north of the city. I grinned at Rose, admiring the wide-eyed look she gave me in return. "How long do you think it'll be before he comes looking for us in his own headquarters?"

42.

As I changed my attitude to bring us up the side of the tower, the shift in direction, legs down, head up, from where we'd been a moment earlier necessitated Rose moving herself as well. She was pretty good at keeping up with the shifts of my body as we flew. I imagined she was getting used to it by now, something that couldn't be said of most of my other flying companions, save for maybe my uncle, Friday, and his adaptation was less about moving with me and more about letting me carry him like a giant lump of weight.

Still, when I changed direction to shoot up the side of the tower, Rose had to adjust herself accordingly, her hands snugged just south of my neck. She'd been pretty careful not to touch my skin thus far, but now, as she shifted, her exposed wrist touched directly against the side of my neck, something it took me a few seconds—and a hint of a burning feeling as my powers started to work—to notice.

"Rose!" I said and shook her slightly to jar her wrists loose of where they were touching me. That faint sensation was enough to wake me up, not that I'd been in danger of sleeping as I flew into potentially very hostile territory.

"Sorry! Sorry!" she said, and then, "Whew. I felt that."

"Yeah, me too," I said, though I'd only caught it briefly. I shuddered through the length of my body. It had burned a little, under my skin, even from so brief a contact. Though it was unlikely I would have absorbed her completely without knowing it was happening, I counted myself lucky that I hadn't zoned out, because the idea of Rose becoming another passenger in my head was…

Well, actually, it was probably more appealing than dealing with the bunch I had in there already.

So little appreciation, Harmon said. *After all we do for you.*

It's not that I don't appreciate you, I said, *it's more that every once in a while, I think it might be nice to be left quietly alone with my own thoughts.*

I've felt the same my whole life, Harmon said. *Unfortunately, that never happened, even to this day.*

One sympathizes, I said, truly sincere. He didn't seem to take it in the spirit in which it was intended.

I flew in through the gaping hole in the side of the building, trying to ignore the giant swath of wreckage that extended out from this point across the city. I landed on the slab, which still had a massive hole down its center, scouting the room to see if Frankie had left behind any guards. There wasn't anyone in this room, but there were couple doors off the sides of the apartment's living room, and I started toward one of them right away after I dropped Rose off my back.

She kept quiet and shadowed me as I kicked in the door. A brief cry of alarm got cut off when the door I'd kicked collided with the crier. It knocked him flat, bounced him into a wall, and once I pulled it off of him I was confronted with quite the spectacle.

Not only was there a man with a breathtaking head wound before me, but I was in a room that was…well…just…holy shit.

"Sweet merciful Zeus," Rose breathed behind me.

I knew what she meant. There were corpses piled in this room, about ten of them, and none of them smelled like roses, but neither did they show signs of advanced decomposition. I looked at the one on top of the pile, then stooped to look at one beneath, and judged that they couldn't be more than a day or so old. "Damnation," I muttered, because that was not the last thing in the room.

Prioritizing before I dealt with the other thing that had caught my attention, I headed for the man who'd caught the door with his forehead when I kicked it in. The injury was probably non-fatal—not that I cared at this stage of the game, but I needed something from him. I stuck a hand on his forehead, and waited as that sweet, tingling feeling started beneath my fingertips where my skin met his.

A few seconds later, I was in his mind, skimming for a very specific piece of information. I found it, then breathed a sigh of relief. "He hasn't seen Frankie since yesterday, after we left," I said, feeling like this leant some credence to my scheme of hiding in plain sight. But it also suggested that this was not Frankie's only base or place of residence or staging ground—whatever you wanted to call it.

Which was really, really scary when taken with the other thing that was here in the room.

"That's good…right?" Rose asked, studiously trying to avoid eye contact with the pile of corpses. She also looked a little green, like she was trying to keep that breakfast we'd yet to have down.

"Probably," I said, finally turning my attention to the thing that was lining the shelves on the walls at the far end of this narrow room. "It's certainly better news than what we're dealing with here."

"What…are we dealing with here?" Rose asked, following my gaze to the racks of shelving that were filled to brimming with a green chemical solution in vials ready-made for injection.

"What we're dealing with here," I said, making my way over to those racks and running a hand over the vials until I pulled one off, at random, "is something that shouldn't be here at all." My eyes flitted down the labeling, and I closed them, cursing this discovery, cursing what it meant. I couldn't read the language on the vial, so I let someone else do it for me.

'Standard enhancement serum,' Gavrikov said. *It's written in an obscure dialect used in only one place I've been…Revelen.*

"This is the stuff that takes an ordinary human…and turns them into a meta," I said, fingers running over the vial's smooth glass. "This is how Frankie's so powerful." I looked up at the pile of bodies, and it felt like a weight was settling on my shoulders. "He's unlocking the latent powers in normal humans…and then stealing them, and with them… their souls."

43.

Hours passed in the dreadfully dull silence. The sun crept high overhead behind the clouds, not showing me a hint of sky, the same shit I'd seen every day since coming to Scotland. I kept expecting the main door to the apartment to open at any minute, Frankie to stroll in like he owned the place—which he totally didn't; the lease wasn't even in his name, we discovered while prowling—and start throwing down again. I hadn't decided much in my hours of stewing, but I knew that if we heard him coming we had to go out the nearest window, because unless I could sneak up behind him and put a bullet in his brain, this was not the right ground for a final encounter with him. This apartment building was still occupied, in spite of the gaping holes in the floor and ceiling and side of the building, and even if not, there were countless people in the city around that would get hurt if he kept throwing those damned ripper beams around.

It was a curiously dark, unsatisfying feeling, the lurch of uncertainty about knowing what to do next. Usually, I could make a decision to orient things my way, and either head into a final rendezvous with the meta criminals I faced on my terms, or theirs, but usually not in the midst of a field of crowded civilians. The powers at Frankie's disposal, though, were so massively destructive, and his ability to keep me at bay so significant, that I agonized about my choice of battlegrounds. I needed to fight him somewhere that a minimal amount of damage would be caused.

To that end, I looked out the giant hole in the wall to get a sense of how far his beam had traveled after he'd attacked us here. I stared through the hole in the side of the tower and squinted out, trying to see the end of the crack the trailing ripper beam had left. It had certainly created a craterous divide in the buildings below, but it extended only a couple hundred yards before coming to an end, I realized. I had feared it went on for miles, but I could see it in the distance, the place where it seemed to narrow down to nothing and disappear, buried squarely in the middle of a brick apartment block.

At least that gave me something to work with. I needed a space of distance that didn't include housing nearby, somewhere abandoned that would include a wide gulf of space where the beams couldn't do any harm to anybody...I thought of that massive park I overflew, the one that sat in the shadow of Edinburgh castle. That might be a good choice, if I could find a way to get Frankie to come to me.

Oh, who was I kidding? I was priority number one for him right now.

"Ye've got a look on your face," Rose said, breaking our long mutual silence. The shadows were getting long down below, and I came back into the room with the serum because I didn't want to chance some minion of Frankie's sighting me from a rooftop or something.

"I usually do," I said lightly. "Most of the time it's a general anger. Occasionally, I'm just hungry. Right now, it's contemplation of murder. Dark, dark murder. Or murder in the dark, I guess." When that didn't get her to stop looking at me intently, I said, "I'm trying to figure out how to structure this next fight, Rose. Because this...I can't let it go on. Frankie's got to die next time we meet."

Rose pursed her lips. "I feel like there's a subtext beneath those words, like a part of the sentence you left off...'Or I do.'"

"That's always a hazard in my line of work," I said, curiously resigned about it. Then again, I usually was.

"Death doesn't bother you?" She was staring at me with a faint trace of horror.

I thought carefully before answering. "It's not that it doesn't bother me. I don't...want to die. But I can't let Frankie keep doing what he's doing."

"I don't get it," Rose said. "We talked before about retreating. But this time...you won't retreat. You could go find help—"

"I could get people involved in this who have less chance of survival than I do."

"—or arming up and coming at him with...I dunno, stronger weapons...a rifle—"

"Look at the bodies in there, Rose. Frankie is killing thousands of people in order to grow his power, harvesting them like designer meta genes. And other than assaulting a police station, I don't know a definite place around here that would yield me a rifle."

"There are people you could call, surely? I mean...ye didn't come here by just picking this country out of a hat, I assume."

The idea of Wexford occurred to me again. He hadn't given me a phone number, probably because he wanted to maintain some level of plausible deniability. Also, he probably hadn't foreseen bizarre circumstances where somehow our serial killer would turn the Scotland police against me. Hell, who had foreseen that?

"Those police officers," Rose said, "they went after you like dogs on command. How did he even do that?"

"If I had to guess," I said, feeling pretty worn down by speculation, each time I had to stop and answer a question like a pin poked into the balloon of my enthusiasm, letting a little more out with each prick, "I'd say he absorbed a male and female siren." When she frowned, I said, "Sirens can control the opposite sex merely by speaking to them." Or so I'd heard. I'd never actually faced one, but my old friend Breandan, the late Irish lad who'd fought by my side during the war, had told me about his deceased girlfriend, who could wrap men around her little finger with nothing but the sound of her voice.

She took that in stoically, and finally said, "There has to be another way than rushing into a fight with him right now."

"Of course there are other ways," I said. "There are always other ways. I could fly to Mongolia tonight and hang out in Ulan Bator for the rest of my days, secure in the knowledge that Frankie probably wouldn't find me. I could go seek out a third world country that's in shambles, and declare myself a goddess to them, killing their dictator and taking over, making them worship me as the travel-sized dose of awesome that I've always known I am at heart. I could fly across the Atlantic and hit up a National Guard armory, possibly kill a dozen or more guys in the process, and come back loaded for bear. I could knock over a police station in Birmingham, maybe, and have the same effect—come back with rifles and pull a *Hot Fuzz* on this town, a shootout in the streets that leaves Frankie and a dozen more dead, I don't know—"

I put my head in my hand. "For some reason, none of those options appeal to me too much. Most of the time when I go into a fight with someone, I know a lot more about why they're fighting."

She sounded puzzled. "But he's an incubus and you're a succubus and he wants—"

"That's what he *says* he wants." I took a breath of the dusk air that had filtered into the room, and looked out through the cracked door. The sun was setting out there, the sky on fire as the clouds looked like they were lighting up at day's end. "But he's coming after me hard now, and maybe it's because he's feeling scorned…or maybe it's because what he said wanted all along isn't the thing he actually wanted." I shook my head. "There's so much about this that doesn't feel right."

"Like you're walking into a trap?" she asked, and sounded… terrified.

"Frankie is ungodly overpowered," I said, taking my hand away from my face. "Anytime I fight him I'm walking into a trap. He can dissolve my attacks with a wave of his hand, throw ones back at me that are not only cataclysmically destructive but also can't be waved aside. Any fight I get into with him has an element of danger for me and everyone around that a lot of my previous battles haven't carried. I mean—"

An electronic squeal in the distance shut me up. Someone was accessing the emergency warning system for Edinburgh, and it sounded like a PA at a sporting event, but with less clarity.

"Sienna Nealon." Frankie's low voice carried across the city, and I stepped out of the room we had been sheltering in, not because I needed to in order to hear him, but because my feet carried me by instinct. "It's time to come out, Sienna. Ye cannae keep doing this any longer."

"Shit," I said, hanging my head.

"What?" Rose asked, voice rising. "What?"

I had a feeling I knew what was coming before it came.

"I'm going to give you one hour," Frankie said. "One hour to come out and face me…and after that…well…if you think the citizens of Edinburgh were dying fast before…" His voice held a tinge of madness, sadistic glee running through every word, and I knew he meant it. "…I'll start killing them by the hundreds…until you do come out…"

44.

"My God," Rose breathed. "That's…that's inhuman. Surely he can't—"

"Of course he can," I said, strangely calm. I turned, looking over the wreckage of the abandoned apartment. It smelled of dust from where the walls and ceiling had been ripped apart, motes of it caught in the last rays of sunset streaming in from outside. "He's got the power to do almost anything he wants now. Killing thousands? Well within the scope of his abilities."

Rose looked right at me, her eyes anchoring on mine with a plea. "You can't be serious. You can't go out there and dance to his tune—"

"I should just let those people die?" I asked, mentally readying myself. Of course I was going to go out there and face him.

"Yes," she said, like it was the most obvious thing in the world. "Ye can't beat him. Why throw yourself into this when the odds are—well, they're bloody impossible!" Her Scottish accent got thicker in the moments when she was heated.

"I do impossible things all the time," I said coolly. "It's a just another Tuesday."

"He knows you'll come out," she said. "That's why he's doing this." I stopped and froze. "He knows that when Wolfe held your city hostage, you came out and faced him when it was suicide. He's pressing your buttons, playing to—

to your flaws. And you're letting him!"

I sat there in silence for a moment. *She's right,* Harmon said. *He's borrowing a page right out of the Wolfe strategy book.*

Clever, Bastian said.

That was the annoying thing about being famous; even when you didn't talk about these things, word about them tended to get out. I'd read one of my unauthorized bios. They got a lot wrong, but the gut-churning hours and days I spent imprisoned "for my own protection," in the basement of the Directorate while Wolfe was ripping his way through Minneapolis to draw me out? Vividly painted, probably by any number of former agents of the Directorate who'd fed me and watched the door while I stewed within. Kurt Hannegan himself had been quoted in the pages of the one I'd read, talking about my misery at knowing what was going on outside and feeling powerless to do anything but throw my body into the gaping maw of Wolfe to make it stop.

"Why do you have to do this?" Rose asked quietly. "Every time, you play the hero, even when it's stupid, even when it's against your interest, even when you're—well you're bloody overmatched here, Sienna. You've got nothing but a gun, and he's got thousands of dead at his disposal. Why would you even…bother…when it's this nigh impossible? When he's already killed this many…" She gestured at the cracked door to the room where we'd found the serum and the bodies. "What are a few more when you can't stop him?" She paced a little closer. "Why do you always have to play hero? Is it a territorial thing? Is it ego?" She shook her head, breaking away from staring at me, tears in her eyes. "Because I don't get it. I just don't get it."

"Picture someone dying in quiet desperation," I said in a whisper. "They can feel it coming. Pain. Agony, really. They can't see…hope." My voice cracked a little. "The world is getting dark around them, and there's a moment when they realize…no one is coming to save them. Death is going to take them, slow and steady and unstoppable. Impossible to avoid. They can scream and wail and cry out and beg…their last hope is this fleeting, impossible chance…that someone is going to hear them. That someone—someone who can help, who has the power to help—will come."

She waited in silence as I fell into one of my own. "Those people in that room…they died like that." I nodded toward the cracked door. "Crying out. Screaming at the end, probably. Can you imagine how scared they must have been? He just…drained them. Took their lives like they were nothing, like a soda can to drink dry and then discard. They must have been…so afraid…to be dragged here, screaming, crying, knowing that an end was coming and that they were powerless to do anything about it." I lapsed into a pensive silence. "Do you think he left them in there, in the dark?" I sniffled a little. "I think he probably did. It's how I imagine it in these situations. Some poor soul, in the dark, alone, crying out…wishing someone would hear them…someone would come along…someone with the power to save them…" My voice broke. "Like I did every time my mom locked me in the box."

Rose just stood there in the desperate silence. "My God."

"I thought I was going to die, hopeless, helpless and alone," I said, wiping my nose with my sleeve. "Every time. It didn't matter that she let me out every time but the last…I still imagined I was going to die in there, trapped, afraid. No one ever came to save me." I squeezed my fist in the memory. "But I got powerful enough to save myself. So, yes, people have died. Frankie's done a really organized job of killing here. Thousands are dead, and they've died…probably exactly that way." I cast a long look over my shoulder at the cracked door, at the shadow of the bodies I could still see within. "But I can't stand back and let it happen…again."

"I'll…I'll go with ye," Rose said, wiping her own eyes. "I don't know what help I'll be, but—"

"No," I said softly. "Rose…you can't. You should go home. Back to your home, I mean. Out of here. I'll drop you off at the edge of town before I leave and you—you should just get out of here. Go back to your family."

"I dinnae have a family anymore, Sienna," she said quietly. "My grandparents are dead. And my ma…she passed on, too. That's why I left my home. There was nothing left for me there."

"I can understand that," I said.

"So I'll come with ye," she said, taking a step forward. "And one way or another, we'll make an end of this Frankie bastard."

"You can't come with me, Rose," I said. "This is something you won't understand—" No one could understand it until they'd been pursued halfway around the world and found that…no matter where they go, they'll never really be safe. "You need to go live your life."

"I dinnae have one," she said. "Did you not hear me? I have no family left. I want to fight. With you—"

"You'll be a hostage for him," I said, taking a step back.

"Then—then kill me," she said, sputtering up to righteous indignation. "Absorb me like one of yuir souls, and use me that way, if you think I'll get killed on the field of battle." She thrust out a hand—

I dodged back. "Rose…you won't get this now…but hopefully you'll understand someday—"

"Wait," she said, lunging forward again as I dodged back, heading for the hole in the building, "don't—"

I flew out without her, and heard her shout my name into the wind as I dodged around the building and out of sight, flying toward Calton Heights…and hopefully my final rendezvous with Frankie.

45.

Wolfe

**Edinburgh, Scotland
1986**

He knew it was her when he saw her get out of the car. She walked slowly around it, the steady walk of a warrior who had left her battlefields confidently behind, who had nothing to fear here, on this street in the middle of civilization. Her hair was dark, her skin was not, and she stayed focused on looking sideways for motion on the street even as she gathered her groceries from the trunk.

Wolfe crossed the ground to the open garage door slowly, announcing his presence by not cushioning his footsteps, by not muffling his breath. The subtle way her posture changed when she heard him coming told him that she was alerted to his presence, but she moved coolly to turn around, not the quick spin of a woman who had been the first Valkyrie, coming around to face an opponent.

Her blue eyes did not betray a hint of surprise at his approach. Her hands were free, groceries left in the trunk behind her, available to fight in case he was a foe. She kept her fists unclenched, the better to thrust a stray finger or two into the weakest points of his body, an impromptu knife if she needed it. Her instincts were still intact, then, which did not surprise him. Perhaps it would have surprised his employer, but then…Omega didn't know Lethe the way that Wolfe did.

"I must confess my surprise at seeing you here," she said in the language of her birth, then switched to modern, accented Scottish English without missing a beat. "It's been a long time, Wolfe."

"You've been hiding," Wolfe said, stopping on the driveway, the full, waving yew trees above swishing gently in the summer breeze.

"I haven't been hiding that hard," she said, gazing at him smokily, watching him for sudden movement. "Ye killed my husband, Simon."

Wolfe bristled. "I had nothing to do with that. It was a rookie agent that did it. One of your kin."

She didn't stop gazing at him with suspicion. "I'm sure ye had no influence over it at all. I bet yuir boss, that shite-for-brains Alastor, he passed the death sentence all on his own. Maybe ye want to blame it on that lad Janus? Try and convince me that he had some hand in it?"

"Believe what you want," Wolfe said, a little sulkily. He bared his teeth slightly. He hadn't expected her to know.

"I don't really care, you understand," Lethe said. She folded her arms in front of her, but not so tightly they couldn't be unwound for a fight in less than a second. "Simon and I, we were closer to enemies than friends these last years. I told him not to go work for yuir fair-haired friends, but did he listen to me? No."

"He had other lovers," Wolfe said, vomiting out this bit of information unintentionally. He'd meant to keep it in reserve, save it for when he needed it, not throw it out meaninglessly in hopes she'd sink her teeth in it, but he'd done it nonetheless.

Her reaction was cool. "Well, of course he did. I'm a succubus and we've lived apart for years, you daft prick. I've had other lovers, too. Don't reckon there's as much evidence of mine as there is of his." She looked at her feet, but only briefly. "Babies and whatnot." She shifted, then glanced at the door to her house. "Reckon I might as well invite ye in."

"Most don't," Wolfe said.

She flicked her cool gaze over him. "Most don't know you as I do. If you mean to try and kill me, you'll do it out here just as easily as inside, and I'd like to get my groceries in the refrigerator." She leaned down and picked them up lightly. "Come on then," she said, "be a dear and get the trunk as ye pass, will ye?" And she went inside.

Wolfe stood on the driveway a moment, then slowly made his way over to the trunk and shut it, then walked over to the door and went in after her.

She was already bustling in the kitchen, the refrigerator door thumping closed as he let the one to the garage swing shut behind him. "Would you like something to drink?" she called to him through the pass over a counter into the kitchen. He was standing in an open living room, furnished with shag carpeting in colors that resembled vomit.

"No," he said, and glanced at the wood-paneled wall. Pictures hung of two girls, their progression from babies to adulthood. The eldest had a lean, hungry look in her eyes, serious in her teenage pictures. The younger wore a smile that grew more malicious as she aged, culminating in a smug shot that looked as though she might spit in the eye of the photographer—after first sleeping with him.

"You admiring the pictures of my children?" Lethe worked her way over to the counter and leaned down, looking through the pass-through at him. "My girls?"

"No," Wolfe said, averting his eyes. He felt nothing but revulsion looking at them, a flash of anger that someone had managed to give her children and survive the process. "I doubt they're worthy of note. I saw you on battlefields, blood running down your naked body. You can't tell me either of your coddled girls would be able to do anything of that sort."

"Charlie, no," Lethe said, turning her head down toward the drink she had in hand. "Sierra, though…she might surprise ye."

Wolfe snorted. "I've seen your other children. Do any of them yet live? I would be shocked if they did. Sovereign killed the last of that tribe with some gusto."

"One's still alive," Lethe said, steely reserve flashing in her eyes.

Wolfe almost growled. "Which daughter was this?"

Lethe watched him carefully. "If you don't know, I decline to tell Omega. Let's just call her Juliett, and say she's out there."

"The last of the valkyries," Wolfe murmured. "Does she carry your blade? The one forged by the same man who made Mjolnir?"

Again Lethe grew quiet. "No. That was meant for me."

"That was meant for a warrior," Wolfe said, bleeding his disgust over the overstuffed furniture, his eyes sweeping over all he beheld and finding a revolting end for a woman who had slaughtered legions—thousands—maybe hundreds of thousands—in her time.

She favored him with a very calm look, eyebrow raised just a tick. "You don't think I'm a warrior?"

"Does this look like the domain of a warrior to you?" Wolfe raised his hands, taking it all in with a sweeping motion. "I followed the daughter of death, the chooser of death, the first of the—"

"Ye followed me, ye daft idiot. From Greece to China to southeast Asia and across the Middle East to Norway." Her eyes burned. "Whatever you're seeing here is what you're expecting to see."

"I didn't expect to see the greatest warrior I've ever known turned into a meek Scottish housewife," Wolfe spat.

She put her hands on her hips. "And I didn't expect to see the fiercest third of the Cerberus brothers turned into an Omega housepet, but here we are. Ye let Janus into your head all those years ago, and off ye went yuir way while I went mine."

"I kept doing what I was best at—"

"Oh, I've heard tell."

"—and you," he seethed, spitting, "you settled yourself, resigned yourself, pissed away your legacy—"

"Ye have no idea what I've done, boyo."

"—no sword in your hand, no weapon in easy reach—"

"I am a weapon—my best weapon—or have ye forgot it?"

"I think you are the one who has forgotten," Wolfe said,

dripping his anger. It was like ten lifetimes of fury had built up and was pouring out now. "Forgotten who you were."

"I may be a couple thousand years old," Lethe said dryly, "but I remember who I was just as clearly now as ever I did. I serve no master, and control my own destiny, which is more than I can say for ye—"

Wolfe crossed the distance between them and slapped the glass she'd left on the pass-through counter, sending it shattering against the wall. Lethe watched it sail coolly, unmoving, as Wolfe hissed, sticking his face into hers.

"Ye want to give me a kiss now, Wolfe?" she asked, whispering. "Ye always did; ye were always just too much of a gelding to make the move."

He opened his mouth and breathed hot, stinking breath right at her. "I should eat your face in tribute to him, to mitigate the insult to his memory of what you've become. I have become more death than you have, and whatever pathetic shadows you've spawned in the years since we parted are nothing but lesser branches of a dying tree. I have never been more glad than I am today that Hades died at the height of his power. For to see this as the result of all his efforts would disgrace him beyond measure. Some cosseted housefrau sitting on a seat of cloth comfort, with pictures of runty children on the walls and her pathetic husband dead and unavenged. Death would not have let this or any such insult pass, but you are not death, you are not Lethe—"

"I go by Lisa now, thanks," she said, even as ever.

"—and you are not even a thin shadow of the woman I knew," he said, ripping himself away from her by only the thinnest measure of control. "You have become as pathetic and soft as everyone else."

"Think whatever you like, Wolfe," she said as he stood, refusing to look at her. "You don't know me, and you haven't for a long time."

Wolfe just stood, seething. "True words." He turned his head, slowly, to look at her. "Alastor and Janus are curious about you. About your offspring. Thus far I've said nothing."

"Because you know nothing," Lethe said. "You didn't even

know about—"

"I don't care," he said. "Our old loyalties are dissolved as of today. The bond I swore to your master, to you—it is broken. If Omega sends me after your pitiful children or their spawn, I will no longer honor any of our prior history. If they come in my path—I will kill them."

"You will try," Lethe said.

"I—will—kill them," he said. "I will wear their skins like I would any other."

"You may end up regretting that," she said. "Do you forget what I am?"

"*You* forget what you are," he hissed. "And I know—I know—that whatever your daughters are, they are not kin to death, do not carry even your thread of his power, because if they did, they wouldn't be sick, tired, weak prey like you. They'd be hunters." He pounded his chest. "Like me. Not weak." He stalked to the door. "Not cowering, hiding in the tall grass of opulent society as though it were some sort of genuine cover from predators." He looked back and found her standing there, small behind the counter, nothing like the woman he had known, the warrior of days past. She truly was…prey. "Go and live your life as one of them but know that someday, someone stronger and with less compunction than me will appear on your street. You will not know them. You will not be ready, for you are no longer a person who is ready—and they will take you that day, as you took so many back when you were a warrior. They will take you for death, a thing you no longer even know—and I wonder if you ever did." And he left, tearing the door from the hinges in his fury, knocking the car aside in his flight to escape this woman that he no longer even recognized.

46.

Sienna

I flew hard for Calton Heights, lifting myself high above the city so that all could see me, and adding a little light from Gavrikov as well, burning my hands like candles as I crossed the sky. I figured there was no way they could miss me, streaking like a comet over Edinburgh, all majestic and glorious.

And they didn't miss me. At all.

The rifle impact caught me in the shoulder and caused me to ditch the fire immediately, going dark as I tumbled. It wasn't a small rifle, either, probably something in the 7.62x51mm NATO, or what we in the US knew as .308 Winchester. I'd been shot by one of these bullets not that terribly long ago, and I remembered it hurting about as much as it actually hurt now.

I wasn't going to make Calton Heights, I realized perhaps a little belatedly as I plummeted toward the old burial grounds below, a dark shadow lacking light sources in the growing twilight. My consolation was that the graveyard was uninhabited, a consolation that was not particularly comforting as I slammed into the earth, my fall mitigated only at the last second by Gavrikov.

Any landing you can walk away from... Gavrikov said in my mind.

"Do I look like I'm walking anywhere?" I muttered. My

right arm was busted, my left leg had slammed into the earth and rebounded, breaking as it did so. Oh, and I had a not-trivial hole in my right shoulder. "Wolfe…?" I asked in what had become something of a standard invocation to me, like some sort of prayer to a deity I couldn't see, or maybe a curse to a devil I knew all too well.

Why do I even bother? Wolfe asked. *You keep waltzing into these situations, asking to be killed.*

"Jaghole," I said, "I was not asking to be shot any more than you were asking to be born with your ass-ugly face. I was just trying to get to Calton Heights so I can whip this guy's ass without exposing an unnecessary number of civilians to death and maiming and possible mind slavery to a turdwad like Frankie."

Noble cause, Harmon said. *Really, if someone's going to enslave you to their mind, I think most people would like to be assured they've got a greater good in mind.*

"I think most people would rather just not be enslaved at all," I said, "but I can see how you might have come to that dumbass conclusion given your history." I started to pick myself up, my knee having realigned and my arm having knitted itself back together. My shoulder was still pushing out the bullet, an ungainly little piece of metal that was poking out of my skin like a lead mole. It landed on a piece of gravestone a moment later as I levered myself up to my feet. "Can I say…ouch?"

I could almost hear Wolfe shaking his rattling head in my own. *This is foolhardy.*

"Well…yeah," I said. "And way to come off the bench with the advice now, team player."

Wolfe is not a team player.

"So said every one of your performance reviews for Omega, I'm guessing." I looked around the darkening graveyard, trying to keep my head somewhat low. "Anyone get a bearing on where that sniper was positioned?"

Pretty far back, Bastian said. *Almost like they'd positioned them to keep you from leaving town.*

"Clever," I said. "Box me in."

It's like old times, then, Eve said.

238

"Har har," I said. "Funny. Listen, you guys…Frankie here? He's got a wealth of info and power at his fingertips." I switched to speaking inside my head, listening for movement outside the graveyard. *I could really use your combined experience here, okay?*

I'm with you, Harmon said. *I'm not much of a strategist…and it doesn't seem like my telepathic powers are much working at the moment on these enemies…actually, this has been a terrible day for me in general…I'm finally starting to understand how inadequate most people must feel as they go about their daily lives—*

Let's focus on me here, okay? I said. *I'm the one taking bullets and about to have to dodge ripper blasts and God knows what else when Frankie shows up here.*

Yes, well, I suppose I'm with you, Harmon said a bit archly. *Since my alternatives are to die and…oh, yes, to die.*

Yes, yes, Eve said, and I could almost see her rolling her eyes. *You have my support.*

Ditto, Bastian said.

I have nothing better to do, Gavrikov said dryly.

Let us drive our enemies before us and hear the lamentations of their women, Bjorn said.

Pretty sure that was Conan the Barbarian's line, Zack said.

It was a good line, Bjorn said. *It spoke to me. I am with you.*

Do you even have to ask? Zack asked.

"Good," I said, and then realized that once again, there was one lone, silent holdout. "Wolfe?"

He stirred within me. *What?*

I rolled my eyes. "Heading into death here. It'd be nice to know you're on board for what's about to happen, maybe thinking about how we can make ol' Frankie die."

Rip off his head, Wolfe said. *That will kill him.*

"Not quite what I was looking for."

Tear out his entrails and strangle him with them.

"Not sure that's—"

Break every bone in his body and then shake him hard enough that the shattered pieces turn the rest of his tissues into liquid jelly.

"Wow," I said. "That sounds like a real crowd-pleaser. I'm just not sure it's applicable to the moment."

Turning a foe's internal organs into Jello with their own fragmented bones is always applicable, in every situation.

"Look," I said, trying to keep patience rather than alienating the surly maniac in my head right before I'd probably need him to heal me. A lot. "I know how to kill him once I'm close. It's getting close that's proving to be a problem thus far."

He was surprisingly quiet. *I wouldn't worry about it.*

"Uhmm, I kinda am worried about it," I said. "And if you want to live, you should be, too." Not that he was living, but these guys were strangely attached to the kind of half life they'd been experiencing in my head for these last few years, it seemed.

I'll give it some thought, he grunted, and then disappeared back into the recesses of my mind. I started to yell at him to get his head out of his furry hindparts, but something stopped me.

Movement down the hill. The graveyard was on a natural slope, and I'd come down in the middle, between a patch of lines of tombstone. I'd stood out there having my little conversation, figuring trouble would be along shortly.

And here it came.

Frankie emerged from the darkness, stalking up the hill, a grin on his face, and the last light of day shining down on his bald head. He was headed right for me, had apparently seen me from a ways off.

"No more running away," I said, putting a hand on a grave, acting like I was steadying myself.

This ended now.

47.

"What do you want?" I called out to him as he came up the hill, taking his sweet damned time, boots squishing in the wet grass.

He paused, his pinched features smooshing even further together. "Whatever do you mean? I want to smite you down, of course. It's why I called you out."

I stared at him over the darkening cemetery. He stood in the middle of the lines of graves, looking a little like one of them in the dusky, darkening twilight. The clouds overhead were lit a dark purple, the last light of day fading rapidly. "Bullshit." He stood there, about thirty feet away, eyebrow raised, just a little too far for me to charge in and break his neck. "If you'd wanted to kill me, you could have done that at any time. You could have snuck up on me and struck me down when my back was turned. Hit me with one of those ripper blasts, zap my head off my shoulders. Hell, even have your sniper friends aim for my head instead of my shoulder. You could have killed me any time. So…what do you want, Frankie?"

Frankie just smiled.

The same thing any hunter wants, Wolfe said. *Prey. A worthy hunt.*

I froze, my hand still clutching the cool tombstone, and I looked at Frankie. There was a certain animalistic cast to his face, his teeth looking a little pointed.

"I already told you what I want," Frankie said. "I want you

smited." He paused, uncertain. "Smote?"

"I get the point either way," I said, and heaved the tombstone at him.

I didn't hesitate or wait for it to hit its target, either. I followed behind it as it was struck by a blasting red ripper that sprayed stone at me. I dodged sideways and rolled to my feet, crossing the path Frankie stood on, ahead on my way to another tombstone. I bound this one in light as I uprooted it and then flung it at him. It shattered as he rent the rising night with another ripper, the path and the very air splitting as he employed his power.

"Is that the only trick you've got?" I shouted, whirling like a dervish and firing flame and light nets. I fully intended to blitz him with everything at my disposal, working to get close so I could beat his ass and…well, in the spirit of Wolfe, maybe rip out his spine and show it dangling in front of him. Assuming he hadn't absorbed a Wolfe in his travails, because if so…whew, this fight was going to be a lot harder.

"It works, doesn't it?" I caught a glimpse of him waving his hands as the fire dispelled and the light nets vanished under the influence of gravity powers. He unleashed a searing beam of red that zinged past my head and I slid low. It passed over me, near missing a tall tombstone in the process.

I kicked another stone in his direction, cringing at the pain in my toe as it sailed. I went low and laterally, grabbing a smaller one and sticking it under my arm. Lucky thing he chose to have his minions bring me down in a graveyard. I was only about ten feet away now, but he was firing a spectacular number of multi-colored beams at me. I saw a chunk of ice go shooting by and almost admired his kitchen sink approach. It mirrored mine.

Sliding down under temporary cover of another tombstone, I kicked it at him (ow) and watched it sail into its own destruction only a few feet away. This one had dissolved, almost like Frankie had Augustus's power over rock, which kinda screwed with my contingency plan. I threw the one I had under my arm right at his face and gave it a second to fly before—

He dissolved it too, but I wasn't planning on having it

impact. He had a hand up, probably planning to dissolve the fire blast or light net he seemed sure I was going to send after it. Like I had in Asda yesterday.

I didn't send either of those things in the wake of the tombstone.

I sent myself flying at him, fist first.

Rocketing at a human being at high speed is always an uncertain thing, especially when dealing with a seasoned fighter. My biggest hope was that absorbing all these powers had made Frankie complacent, like so many of my other foes, and that he was leaning so hard on his ripper blasts because they were super powerful and could keep me at a distance.

As my fist made contact with his already open-in-shock jaw…I took it as confirmation I might just be right.

Frankie went flying back, partially dodging my attack. I came in with a hard sweep of his feet and caught one. He deftly lifted the other and spun, adjusting like a gymnast in midair to come in for a perfect landing. It was a cool move, but one that almost any high-powered meta could pull off.

It was also really, really dumb, because he was just sitting there, twirling. Right in front of me.

I grabbed him by the collar and brought him down, smashing him into the ground. He took a sharp landing across the asphalt path, head slamming as I waterwheeled his face into the hard aggregate. It made a sharp crack, sweet music to my ears, and he cried out.

"That's right, punkass," I said, lifting my arm up. I was going to bring down a punch on the back of his head, one good blow to finish him off and end this. "You shouldn't have messed with the—"

A blazing red blast seared past me, catching me mid-thigh on the left side. I hadn't even noticed him sticking a hand up in the air, hadn't noticed him twisting his broken wrist to let loose a ripper blast.

I damned sure felt it, though, as I teetered and fell over. The ground came rushing up and I landed beside Frankie, crashing into the earth, no arm or leg left on that side of my body to stop my fall.

48.

Losing an arm and a leg in this fight hurt a hell of a lot more than landing on my face, but without any sort of limb to break my fall, that was no peachy walk in the park, either. My nose broke, my face screamed from my cheekbone and orbital bone above my eye, the agony radiating out across my face like someone had lit the nerves on fire as though they were fuses that hissed and cracked across my face.

Sienna, Harmon said roughly, *I know you're in pain, but*—

YOU KNOW NOTHING OF PAIN, I thought, really loudly, at Harmon. Was the sky blood red? It sure felt like it was.

Tactically speaking, Bastian said—

STFU, DRAGONBOY, I said. *My freaking LEG*—

You— Eve started.

Sienna— Zack said.

I FUCKING KNOW MY ENEMY IS LYING NEXT TO ME, I said, writhing. Ever try to roll over with one arm and one leg missing while your body is screaming pain at you? It's not easy.

I did it anyway, my face scratching against the hard asphalt surface of the graveyard path, and I lanced out, slamming the side of my hand into Frankie's throat. I could see him through squinted, teared-up eyes, and he was rolling toward me, fury in his.

His hand started to glow as he brought it around. If he managed to get it in line with me, I knew I was toast, so I snaked my fingers around his neck and crushed his throat.

That sent a shockwave of surprise through him that bought me a few seconds. I didn't dare let go, figuring he'd probably heal quickly, and that this wouldn't kill him. *Wolfe,* I said.

Do you not feel your bones already regrowing? he practically yelled in my ear—quite an accomplishment when my nerve endings were already howling through my body.

"I'm feeling kind of a lot right now," I said. "Sensory overload." I dragged Frankie closer to me and headbutted him, but since it was one-armed and I was fairly immobile, it didn't do a lot but misshape his nose further. He was already bleeding profusely from it, and his eyes were blacked, one swelling rapidly. I guess he didn't have an inner Wolfe.

Lucky me.

I kept my hand anchored on his throat, dragging him closer, and headbutted him again. Blood ran in my nose, thick and heavy, the smell of rich iron still coming through in spite of the screaming pain, giving an immediacy to my actions. I couldn't let up. The world was getting hot around me, cool night receding in the heat of the moment, my fingertips tingling from all the trauma and blood loss I'd—

Wait.

No.

My fingers were searing, screaming where they touched his skin, my powers working to drag his soul out of his body. His mouth was open but no sound came out, his windpipe crushed beneath my fingers. He choked, gagged, desperate for breath. He jerked on the concrete, so roughly it tore his skin, leaving bloody streaks across the pebbled walkway.

But…a succubus's powers couldn't work on an incubus…?

Frankie made a horrible, gurgling, screaming noise as air forced its way out of his crushed throat, and the crescendo of pleasure and tingling and fire rushed through my hand as my powers reached their crescendo. It was like a symphony of joy played through my phantom, painful limbs. His soul left his body with a great rush, burrowing into my head and knocking me over, my newly regrown left leg and arm keeping me from rolling completely over.

I stared up at the dark sky, my brain unable to fully analyze what had just happened. Little details rushed in like a flood—

Frankie…wasn't an incubus at all.

But…the bodies…the dead…?

My head was whirling, swimming with the newfound soul that was lurking within me, floating in my mind along with the others.

Well…what have we here? Bjorn said.

Fresh meat, Eve said with a wide grin.

"Wait," I said, pain lancing through my newly regrown limbs. I pushed over and got to my knees. "He's not an incubus."

Well duh, Zack said, *which is why he's in your head now.*

"But he threw all those powers at me," I said, staggering over to a tombstone. My pants were shredded, like I was wearing shorts from mid-thigh on my left leg, and short sleeves on my left arm. It was some seriously schizophrenic clothing, and I say that as someone who regularly burned off all her clothing. "How…?"

I heard soft footsteps behind me, and I whirled to see the guy in the Euro biker jacket standing back a ways, toward the entrance to the cemetery down the hill, peering up at me.

"You!" I shouted and he flinched back toward the massive wall surrounding the burial grounds, cordoning it off from the streets around it. "You did this!"

"No, he didn't," someone said behind me, and I turned just in time to get clocked in the nose by a woman descending out of the sky, a flash of her red hair the only clue that told me who she was before she knocked me to the ground.

Rose.

"I did it," she said, eyes gleaming in the dark, and her hands glowing, one with fire, the other with the distorted air from the manipulation of gravity…powers that no empath…no normal meta…would have…

Powers that only a succubus could.

49.

Rose didn't give me any recovery or breathing room; she came at me with speed unlike anything Frankie had, pounding me along the ribs and chest with a flurry of punches that seemed to be enhanced with meta strength and maybe even gravity, because they hit like a planet landing on me.

I flew back through six tombstones, and then something seemed to grab me from behind, yanking me back like a rubber band around my waist. I crashed into one of the crypts at the back wall of the graveyard, bringing down the lintel archway with my back as I went through it. I realized, dazedly and a little belatedly, that it was the exact feeling of a gravity tether yanking me. Yeouch.

Pieces of stone came down with me and one of them broke my arm. I didn't really feel it, because it was already numb from going through the tombstones and the lintel.

Rose hovered overhead, sailing through the spot where a perfectly reasonable crypt arch had been just a moment before, when my back hadn't interrupted its continued existence in the same spot it had occupied for hundreds of years. "Did ye figure it out yet?" She wore a very un-Rose-like grin, which was disquieting, and her hand glowed with a blue superheated plasma now, which was probably worse.

"That you put the 'suck' in succubus?" I asked, mouth thick with blood from where I'd bitten my tongue on landing, and shifting painfully as I felt Wolfe rushing to piece me back together. "Yeah, I got that. I'm a little fuzzy as to

247

why you've been playing my faithful ladyservant these last few days when you could have just crushed me while I was sleeping."

Rose cocked her head at me, then smiled again, enough to make me shiver. All that human kindness she'd shown me the last few days? The warmth that had come to define her for me? All gone, leaving nothing but cold disdain that leaked through in her answer. "Well…because I didn't know ye, of course. I mean, I knew you as well as everyone else did, which was…not at all, really. I knew the TV you." She leaned closer, but not close enough I could put a fist through her smirking face. "I wanted to know the *real* you."

"Why?" I looked around; there was nothing but stone fragments to throw at her. What else could I toss at her but rocks? A really well placed one, if it got past her gravity powers, might bust her skull, but that was pretty iffy. She was damned fast, faster than me, and that was cause for worry when taken in combo with everything else. "Were you looking to write the next unauthorized biography?"

"My dear…" Rose said, smirking almost sadly, "have you seen what I've done to this town? Bending people to my will? If I wanted to, it wouldn't be unauthorized at all." She leaned in a little closer. "And I'm debating on that. But the truth is…I wanted to make you suffer like you've never suffered before."

I stared up at her. "Just because? Or did you have a non-psychotic reason?"

Her jaw tightened. "Oh, I've got a very good reason indeed. You ruined my life…and you never even noticed." Her eyes were crazy wide, and also…just crazy.

"Care to shar—" I started to say, but she rained down pain on me like a Scotland sky letting loose with rain on a summer day.

She hit me in a hundred places, the strikes coming seconds apart. Each one felt like a touch at first, and then my nerves caught up with how hard she'd hit me. Internal organs ruptured. Bones broke, shattering into pieces. I spat blood in a mist, and gave up any thought of getting up, now or ever.

"Now, take a deep breath and sit there, Sienna, my love,"

she said as I nearly choked on my blood. "You see yourself as a righteous hero, don't you? I caught a few whiffs of that in our conversation. But you're not that righteous, really—just between us girls?" She leaned in, face hovering over mine. "You're a scared little twat, frightened of her mommy still after all this time. Yeah, now I know you, don't I?"

She stepped back, and here I saw the Euro biker over her shoulder. "This is Eugene. Ye've seen him, haven't ye? He's the flyer who's been taking poor Frankie around town." She grabbed him by the neck and brought him close, and he just stood there, eyes wide open, letting her take hold of him. He jerked a few times, spasming, and then his eyes flickered closed, and he dropped, dead, the puppet's strings cut. "I guess I didn't really need his power, but…"

"You know," she said, eyes boring into mine. She took a deep breath through her nose, savoring the feeling of a newly absorbed soul, I was sure. I'd felt it before myself.

"Did ye enjoy the taste of Frankie? He's a rare one, that fellow. I'd never seen that kind of power before we unlocked that lad." She was smiling impishly, and my brain started to work again. If I could get a hand up, use Frankie's superblastingripperbadass power against her… "Of course, I had to make it look like he had others…you've met a Rakshasa before, haven't ye? Illusionist? Any one of Frankie's powers that I couldn't use for him at a distance, like the fire dispersion or gravity? I had to make out of an illusion. Him flinging chunks of ice? Chopping up the couch with a lightsaber when he really just punched it in half? All my Rakshasa abilities, pulling the wool over yuir eyes. Dead useful, that power…"

My hand shook, moving at my side. *Wolfe…how's that healing coming along…?*

How's not being murdered coming along? he threw back.

Uhhh…poorly?

Same, he growled. *I've never seen a body this damaged, ever. Not even my victims, in some cases.*

That's…bad, I thought.

"I picked this spot for us," Rose said, "when I laid out that first body here, the one I knew would draw you to town.

This graveyard has a rich history, of course. But that's not why I chose it…any graveyard would have done." Her eyes swam in front of me. "Can ye guess why?"

I blinked at her, and readied my ripper blast, steadying my hand. If I could just catch her in this… "Because you're fucking dead?"

I went to trigger it, stepping into my head, and Frankie reared up within, an angry specter in my mind, furious howl of rage catching me by surprise. *NO,* he said.

It landed like a slap on the side of my head, his refusal, and then, a moment later, Rose seized me by the face. I shot fire at her and it disappeared like it had never existed, the memory of the heat flicking like a sunny day across my flesh and then gone as though there'd never been anything but the cold. I fired a net at her face and it was gone a second later, shredded by gravity. I tried to rise with flight, but she pressed down on me, both hands on me, and crushing me into the ground. I tried to reach for my last power…the last gambit…

Bastian, I said, *make me a dragon…*

And for a moment, there was nothing but silence.

Then…I heard the screaming.

It was in my head, in my skin, all across my body. Nerve endings jangling, a fire in my very flesh, cries of pain in my ears. It was the sound of Wolfe and Gavrikov and Bjorn and Zack and Eve and Bastian and Harmon and even that bastard Frankie, and one other voice in the chorus of agony…

Mine.

My skin was burning, on fire with pain, and Rose was doing it to me, her fingers digging into my flesh, burning me to death with some kind of power—

Succubus power.

The sound in my head was a cacophony of pain, and suddenly one voice after another went still and quiet, the screaming quelled, until there was only one voice remaining where there had been so many before—

Mine, alone.

Rose pulled from me, letting go of my face, withdrawing

with a breathless gasp, something dark and sated showing on her face, peeking out of her dead eyes. I toppled back, landing roughly on the soft earth in the middle of the crypt, smell of dirt and blood mingling together in my nostrils. Rose breathed, just breathed, leaning down over me, inches away from my face so I could see every pore and smell her faint, sweet, sickly perfume, and I said:

Wolfe.

There was no answer.

Gavrikov!

Nothing.

Bjorn! Zack! Eve!

Nada.

BASTIAN! HARMON!

The only sound was the wind blowing through the graveyard, broken at last by Rose's quiet laughter as she lurked above me.

"Did ye figure it out yet?" she asked. "Where your little head friends went?" I had a sickening suspicion, but I could not seem to give voice to it. My head lolled, against the soft earth, the pain still coursing through my skin like it had been peeled from me, layer by layer.

Something settled in my gut as the realization burrowed into my head, something I'd never had to come to grips with before, never even considered. My belly boiled, nausea sweeping it, threatening to empty the contents of a stomach I had yet to fill today. Even still...I wanted to throw up emptiness.

Because emptiness...was all I had left inside.

"You're...the stronger succubus," I said at last, the wave of nausea sweeping and rising at the thought of what she'd just done.

She raised a finger and pointed at the side of her head, grinning, fingers twisting in her red hair. "That's right... they're in here. Now...now yuir little souls? They're *mine*."

50.

Rose let out a long, bloodcurdling cackle, and it echoed across the empty graveyard. I couldn't see straight, something felt so off in my head. The skies stretched black above me, the last light now faded and darkness swept in, held at bay only by street lamps somewhere beyond my sight, beyond the curtaining wall that wrapped the burial grounds.

She leaned in over me, red hair falling over her face like a tunnel between us. "Now what are you going to do, my lonely little dove? Ye've lost your power, your little souls—no fire, no flight, no healing, no dragon—only you, ye poor little thing." She laughed, and it carried a deep malice that I hadn't even caught a hint of when I'd been traveling with her like a partner over the last few days. "Now, my dear…you're powerless. You're not even the stronger succubus. So—"

I didn't wait for her to finish her explanation, because in spite of the ringing silence in my ears, I'd come to the conclusion it was going somewhere I didn't want to go—probably toward my death, now that she'd drained me of all the souls in my body save one—the one that came factory installed.

Swinging a piece of broken gravestone, I managed to catch her in the blind side, suddenly thankful that she hadn't gotten her hands on a Cassandra-type in her mad rush to suck up any meta power she could.

It cracked her solidly in the head, and Rose let out a grunt of pain. I rose and punched her in the jaw twice, catching her completely off-guard. I didn't chance it any more right then, either. My next blow was my index finger and middle jammed full force, directly into her eyes.

I could tell I popped them both, hitting them with meta force like that. She did something, though, that I wasn't expecting, some power unleashed that I hadn't felt before. My body was propelled through the air like Gavrikov had launched me, sending me flying over the top of the crypt wall and sailing through tree branches. I took a few hard hits as I crashed through stone walls, including one to the back of the head that scrambled my brain even more than it already had been before I came down in the middle of a street with a solid crack.

"SIENNA!" Rose screamed, half mad. A geyser of flame and energy blew out into the sky like a tower of light, a beacon that even my flagging brain couldn't miss. "I will find you, you little shit! You think this is it?" A blast of blue lit up the night. "I'm yuir worst enemy! I'm going to hurt you worse than anyone ever has, including yer ma! You hear me? This isn't over!"

I believed her, and felt the cracking pain of a few broken ribs along my front and side. I didn't know whether they'd happened in the landing or when she'd hit me with that blast that launched me, but they'd happened…

And with Wolfe…they weren't going away anytime soon.

"Find her!" Rose screamed in the darkness behind the wall, and somehow I knew she had allies with her now, like that Euro biker dude she'd drained. Maybe the Edinburgh cops that "Frankie" had turned against me.

All along, it had been Rose, running the longest con I'd run across since…well, since Sovereign had revealed himself for who he really was.

The rumble of a car in the distance woke me to the approach of a vehicle, and I realized I was lying on a road. I picked myself up, staggering, the hardest time I'd had fighting back against gravity since before I'd gained Gavrikov's powers. Stumbling feet warring with my warped sense of balance, I put one foot in front of the other and dodged out of the lane as the headlights approached.

Rose had a guy who could fly, and the cops on her side,

and heaven only knew how many other people.

I was just one girl, alone in a foreign country, the whole damned world against me…

And I was no longer the most powerful metahuman in the world.

I was just an ordinary succubus now.

…Being hunted by the most powerful meta in the world.

All the pains, the broken bones that I couldn't immediately heal, the chill of the night air…I started to shake, but I needed to keep my head. I left the road, out of the headlights, dragging myself into the bushes on the other side. I kept myself from collapse by the barest margins, grabbing solid boughs within the bush and using them to prop me up. I ignored the stinging feeling of nubs and small branches pushing into my palms. Among the cacophony of other pains, I barely noticed them.

"She went that way!" Rose called, and I heard voices acknowledge her. Flashlights clicked on, more beacons in the night, beyond the graveyard wall, and I could hear the steps of a search party leaving the graveyard.

I rustled the bushes, peering out at the approaching car. It was a bigger one, a truck of some kind, built for transporting goods and high off the ground. As soon as it got close, I loped into a hobbling run, slid underneath, the pavement tearing at my bare skin on my shoulders. Ignoring the pain, I seized a solid hold under the truck and felt it grip me, dragging my skin along the road until I could lift my weary body up under the frame.

My entire body ached, screamed at me, but I didn't dare let go. I would hold in this position for hours, all night if I had to, for miles and miles, until hopefully Scotland gave way to some other place, like England, or maybe eventually France, if I was lucky. I would go until I couldn't go anymore.

There was a desperate danger out there in Rose, who wanted to hunt me. To hurt me.

To kill me.

And against that…I saw only one option.

I was going to run away.

Again.

51.

Wolfe

Now

Flat houses of stone and brick lay under a grey sky. A wind swayed the tree nearby, a tall pine that reached high above him, his skin prickling in the grim air. Something about this felt wrong, strange and artificial, and Wolfe felt...cold.

"Where the hell are we?" Zack Davis asked, looking around, his blond hair rustling in the wind.

"Scotland," Gerry Harmon said, impeccably dressed in one of his frivolous suits. They would be so useless for hunting.

A house with a stone wall stood to their left, a paved street running right down the middle. They stood arrayed on the pavement, right in the middle of it, no cars in sight, nor audible, nothing but the wind to cover them. To one side, a round-topped mountain stood high in the distance, rising high and bare of even a single tree.

"We know we're in Scotland, idiot," Eve Kappler said, lurking next to the massive Bjorn. "But the question is...for the purposes of this delusion...where in Scotland?"

"We're in that girl's head, are we not?" Aleksandr Gavrikov, pale, shaking, lacking his familiar fire, stood looking around as though something might come for him from any direction, at any moment. They all looked like that, in one way or another.

Prey.

Wolfe did not slouch, did not look around, waiting for the annunciation. It would come, surely, but until then…

He could feel presence out there, in the air itself, a crackle, a hum, like living things lurking just beyond his sight.

He knew something was coming. This Rose…she was a child of death, a hunter. She wouldn't keep them waiting l—

"Well, what have we here?" Her voice was calm and melodic, her hair an even brighter, blazing color in this place, against the grey, Scottish skies. She drifted toward Harmon, electric gaze meeting that of the former president, whose own appearance was so much more dowdy and dull than this fiery goddess who had appeared before them, a playful smile perched on her lips. "A telepath. I dinnae have one of you…I'd been feeling a bit covetous, but…" She floated down, dressed all in white, and touched Harmon on the face. "And so distinguished a guest, no less, the former president. Sienna did truly get into all manner of trouble, didn't she?"

"Up until now she hadn't run across anyone who could stop her," Harmon said, a little stiffly. He was trying to keep her at a wary distance, but one could not defy a god in her own realm.

"Times change," Rose said with a sweet smile, and then turned her attention to Bjorn and Eve in turn. "An Odin and a fae. How boring." And she moved past them, as though they didn't even exist.

"How rude," Eve said.

"I am the son of Odin," Bjorn said, bristling. "You cannot speak to me this way."

Rose turned, still smiling sweetly. "This is my head, darling…I'll talk to ye however I choose."

Bjorn bared his teeth. "You can't—"

He let out a scream a moment later, and Rose did not pause, did not come back to him; just stood there, sweet smile as sincere as it had ever been. "Yes," she said as he dropped to his knees. "I can. I will. I own you now, you hear?" She leaned toward him and put her hands on her knees as if she were talking to a child. "And I have no use for you, so…shut up and be silent, will ye? That's a good

256

lad…"

She moved on, brushing against Zack, who stood, looking as though ready to run from her. "And you…you were her first love, weren't ye?"

"Maybe," Zack said.

Rose laughed. "A normal human, then…but you may have your uses."

"You can't use me—" he started to say.

She grabbed him by the face and pulled him close, planting her lips on his. He reacted with shock, eyes rolling back in his head as she swept him off his feet and he spasmed, once. She broke from him a moment later and he, too, slumped to his knees, but for the opposite reason of Bjorn. "I told ye…I can do anything I want here." She extended a hand to indicate the world, and everything as far as the eye could see, the green fields and treeless mountains. "This is my world. Here…I'm yuir bluidy goddess…so…if you don't want to worship me…" Her voice hardened. "Get ready for hell."

Rose paused at Gavrikov. "You're a duplicate as well. Stay quiet and ye'll get along fine." Passing him, she brushed into Bastian. "But you…you're a unique one." She looked him over appraisingly. "I don't know if I'll ever need to become a giant dragon, but if so…I suppose I'll give you a whistle."

Leaving the last of them behind, she threaded her way to Wolfe, standing apart from them all. In a throaty voice she said, "And then there's you, love…the crown jewel of them all."

Wolfe just stared back at her.

"I've been coveting ye all along," Rose said. "Near instantaneous healing. And when you couple that with the hardened skeleton of, say, a vampire, or the invulnerability of an Achilles…well, I think you'd have a body that could… fight just about anybody, don't you?" Her smile was alive, eyes alight with possibility that, in another time…Wolfe might have found…

Frightening.

Wolfe gazed at her, smokily. "I never needed that. Wolfe's skin was hard enough."

"Oh, I'm sure," she said silkily. "You're a big, brute man,

aren't you? A legend among metas. I've heard the tales of you from way back when. Slaughter was always your forte, wasn't it?" She leaned in and breathed on him. It smelled like blood. "Well, it's mine, too."

He looked her over, small frame that reminded him vaguely of…but no. She was too tall, her hair too red. "You…are a granddaughter or great-grandaughter of Hades," he finally said.

She smiled. "You're damned right I am. And my question to you is…will ye serve me as ye served him? Protect me… the way you protected him all those years ago?" Her eyes seemed to glow with madness. "Make me…invulnerable… to her?"

"Don't do it, Wolfe," Zack said, still upon his knees, like all the life had been wrung out of him and the pavement clung to him.

"This bitch just stole us out of her head," Eve Kappler said, voice harder than Wolfe had heard it in years.

"And…she is a bitch," Bjorn said. He spoke between gasps, agony still bleeding out from what Rose had done to him.

"Enough," Wolfe said, breaking his quiet as he gazed into Rose's eyes. He could see the hunger there, waiting for his answer. There was strength, she'd already shown, so much…and a cold, a cunning…she was predatory, always seeking the next prey… "You are a true inheritor of death…" he said, his own a low rasp.

"No," Bastian said quietly.

"This is not right," Gavrikov said.

"…and I am with you…" Wolfe said, as Rose smiled sweetly at him, "Inheritor of Death."

Sienna Nealon Will Return in

BADDER

Out of the Box
Book 16

Coming September 12, 2017!

Author's Note

What do I say about that? I've been planning this moment, that ending, since before the original Girl in the Box series ended. In fact, I had a concept for how I wanted to do this entire Scotland trilogy – that's right, Sienna will be in Scotland for three books – and I can say, as I write this, I'm well into work on book 2 – it's going marvelously so far. I'd originally planned for it to happen around book 7 or so of Out of the Box, but…I kept having ideas. And I kept having to put off my research trip to Scotland. So those two factors conspired to land us here, now, at book 15 and…yeah, that just happened.

I don't want to belabor the point, but there are obviously a lot of unanswered questions at this juncture. The answers are withheld intentionally, for dramatic effect. Wait, dear reader, for the truth is out there. By the time the Scotland trilogy ends, it will be almost like an epic fantasy played out, an enormous, sprawling arc of a story that will get to the root of exactly why Rose is the way she is…and, of course, why she hates Sienna enough to do what she's done here.

To wrap things up, let me say thanks for reading! If you want to know immediately when future books become available, take sixty seconds and sign up for my NEW RELEASE EMAIL ALERTS by visiting my website. I don't sell your information and I only send out emails when I have a new book out. The reason you should sign up for this is because I don't always set release dates, and even if you're following me on Facebook (robertJcrane (Author)) or Twitter (@robertJcrane), it's easy to miss my book announcements because…well, because social media is an imprecise thing.

Come join the discussion on my website:
http://www.robertjcrane.com!

Cheers,
Robert J. Crane

ACKNOWLEDGMENTS

Editorial/Literary Janitorial duties performed by Nick Bowman and Jeffrey Bryan. Final proofing was once more handled by the illustrious Jo Evans. Any errors you see in the text, however, are the result of me rejecting changes.

Linda Short, Adam Perry and John Clifford lent their Scottish expertise to this book, helping me to make it sound a little more authentic (hopefully). Any errors or inaccuracies are the fault of the author, because I'm kind of a screwup sometimes.

The cover was once more designed with exceeding skill by Karri Klawiter of Artbykarri.com.

The formatting was provided by nickbowmanediting.com.

Once more, thanks to my parents, my in-laws, my kids and my wife, for helping me keep things together.

Other Works by Robert J. Crane

World of Sanctuary
Epic Fantasy

Defender: The Sanctuary Series, Volume One
Avenger: The Sanctuary Series, Volume Two
Champion: The Sanctuary Series, Volume Three
Crusader: The Sanctuary Series, Volume Four
Sanctuary Tales, Volume One - A Short Story Collection
Thy Father's Shadow: The Sanctuary Series, Volume 4.5
Master: The Sanctuary Series, Volume Five
Fated in Darkness: The Sanctuary Series, Volume 5.5
Warlord: The Sanctuary Series, Volume Six
Heretic: The Sanctuary Series, Volume Seven
Legend: The Sanctuary Series, Volume Eight
Ghosts of Sanctuary: The Sanctuary Series, Volume Nine*
(Coming 2018, at earliest.)

A Haven in Ash: Ashes of Luukessia, Volume One* *(Coming Fall 2017!)*

The Girl in the Box
and
Out of the Box
Contemporary Urban Fantasy

Alone: The Girl in the Box, Book 1
Untouched: The Girl in the Box, Book 2
Soulless: The Girl in the Box, Book 3
Family: The Girl in the Box, Book 4
Omega: The Girl in the Box, Book 5
Broken: The Girl in the Box, Book 6
Enemies: The Girl in the Box, Book 7

Southern Watch

Contemporary Urban Fantasy

The Shattered Dome Series
(with Nicholas J. Ambrose)
Sci-Fi

Voiceless: The Shattered Dome, Book 1
Unspeakable: The Shattered Dome, Book 2* *(Coming 2017 – Tentatively)*

The Mira Brand Adventures
Contemporary Urban Fantasy

The World Beneath: The Mira Brand Adventures, Book 1* *(Coming August 2017!)*
The Tide of Ages: The Mira Brand Adventures, Book 2* *(Coming August 2017!)*
The City of Lies: The Mira Brand Adventures, Book 3* *(Coming August 2017!)*

*Forthcoming, Subject to Change

Made in the USA
Columbia, SC
15 May 2019